Straight Ways

and

Crooked Paths

Straight Ways

and

Crooked Paths

Ella's Story

Terri Lynn

XULON PRESS

Xulon Press
2301 Lucien Way #415
Maitland, FL 32751
407.339.4217
www.xulonpress.com

Unless otherwise indicated, Scripture quotations taken from the
King James Version (KJV) – *public domain.*

Paperback ISBN-13: 978-1-66285-286-2
Ebook ISBN-13: 978-1-66285-287-9

Dedication

To Haylee

Acknowledgments

Many thanks to: My family for your love and support, especially Haylee for sharing your love of a good story and sweet spirit of encouragement with me.

Illustration Credits:

The front cover and all sketches are the creative work of Katie Lawver.

Epigraph

"Consider the work of God: for who can make that straight, which he hath made crooked?"

Ecclesiastes 7:13 KJV

Table of Contents

Introduction

She awoke to a beam of sunlight shining between the curtains of the bedroom window. The warmth of the sunlight on her cheek contrasted the cool of this October, Missouri morning. Ella lay awake while her husband, Jackson, was still lost in peaceful sleep. It had been months since he had been really at rest, and she was thankful.

She wanted to hold on to the quiet and stillness of this morning for as long as she could. She knew that it was a stolen moment in time. It was a time within another time. Ella and Jackson were at peace. They were at peace with each other and at peace with God. Here on their tiny little farm, nature, God's creation, was at peace with its Creator. But men were not at peace. They were at war.

Yes, war, and too often over the past months it found its way right here to her doorstep. As Ella lay there, looking for the courage to face the day, she knew that she couldn't do it alone. She quietly prayed, "Lord, please give me strength and faith to trust this day and the days ahead to You. Help me to remember that everything is in Your hands and part of Your plan and whatever part that You have for us in that plan, we would obediently follow for Your glory and honor. Amen."

She reached over to the side table and picked up the leather Bible that Jackson always kept close by. She opened it to a passage in Psalms and soaked in every word. Psalm 56 had been a great comfort to them both over the past months.

She remembered the stories that her Papa and her Mama had told her from the Bible when she was a little girl. They told her of a King named David and how the Lord delivered Him so many times from his enemies. She knew that God's Word was not just a book of stories, but instead a living, breathing Word. She got lost in the pages.

Jackson began to stir, so she gently slid out from under the warm blankets so as not to disturb him. She whispered to him, "Sleep, Jackson. Sleep and dream sweet dreams". In this moment all was well.

She reached for the shawl hanging by the front door, wrapped it around her, and stepped out onto the front porch. There was a doe and two fawns at the edge of the tree line helping themselves to a morning feast of apples that had fallen from a tree. Not only were the apples starting to fall, but the leaves on the trees had started to fall, too. The beautiful colors were a sight to behold. There was evidence all around her of the majesty of God and His handiwork in just this tiny little corner of His Creation. She never tired of taking in the beauty of what He has made. "His presence is everywhere, in everything," she thought to herself.

She couldn't remember a Sunday, when she was growing up, that her family ever missed church. Even when there was no minister, or the weather didn't allow them to travel, Papa made sure that they gathered as a family for the study of the Word, prayer, and family worship.

She remembered the very first time that she personally felt the presence of God and what an impression it left on her. It was a one warm, sunny day while she was playing out in the meadow. As she closed her eyes and lifted her head up to the sky, she felt the sun on her face and the presence of God near her in a special way. She didn't understand exactly what that would mean to her at the time, but she would never forget that day.

Precious memories started to flood her mind, the sweet days of innocence. "Oh, if only I could go back", she thought to herself. She knew that things could never be the same. Men and war had made sure of it, but she wouldn't think about that now. She found a memory of her Papa and a smile for her face.

Chapter 1

Memories of Papa

E lla closed her eyes. She was a little girl again. She could almost feel her Papa's arms around her whisking her up in the air and setting her on his shoulders. From there, she felt like she was on top of the world, that nothing could touch her.

Daniel O'Connor was strong and tall. In little Ella's eyes there was nothing that he couldn't do. There was nothing that he wouldn't do for his wife and children. The time would come when he would prove that, but right now, she just wanted to remember the gleam in his eye and how he was often so full of mischief. She wanted to remember how he made Mama laugh. She wanted to remember how he made his children laugh. She felt a longing in her heart to see him smile again.

Papa told her stories about how he came to America from Ireland when he was "just a wee lad". She could almost hear him say those words with his thick Irish accent. He told her that his father had been a farmer in their homeland. "Life was hard for me Dad and Mother. I remember the journey to America was long and we grew weary of seeing nothing but the sea."

"Once we arrived, we made our home in the city. There was no farm for me father to work. He had no money to buy land. He worked hard, but only had enough money for us to rent two rooms to live in. Twas better for our family there than it was in Ireland, but we still struggled to survive. And, I," Papa would pause, "I missed my homeland. I missed the green hills of Ireland and the beauty of its sea."

As soon as her Papa was old enough, he worked to help support the family. "Me dad wanted me and me brother to do better for ourselves," Papa told us. "He told us to save some of the money that we earned so that we could leave the city some day and have a chance to make a good life for ourselves."

"Is that how you came to Missoura, Papa?", Ella remembered asking him. A big smile came over his face and with a gleam in his Irish eyes, he scooped her up on his lap and started to tickle her. She giggled as he put her back down. "Yes, lass, that is how I found my way here to your dear mother and eventually to all of you."

Papa left home, with his parents' blessing, when he was seventeen years old and made his way to Kentucky. He continued west until he finally came to Missouri. It was in Missouri that he met Caroline Shaw better known to Ella as Mama.

"It was love at first sight for me, but it took me awhile to convince yer mother that I was the man of her dreams." She remembered him flashing a smile at Mama who grinned at him with a roll of her eyes. "I don't understand it", he said, "but, she didn't take a liking to me at first."

"Oh, Mama," cried little Lila, "How come you didn't like Papa?"

"Daniel O'Connor," scolded Mama, "Quit filling these children with such rubbish." Papa laughed.

"Didn't you think Papa was handsome?" asked George with a snicker.

"Oh, I thought he was handsome enough," she told him.

Papa had piercing green eyes, dark hair, and a smile that was contagious.

"He was just a little too proud and a little too sure of himself, that's all," she explained.

Papa went anywhere he thought that he might run into Caroline Shaw, including church. He had been to church a few times as a child. He had seen his mother pray, but his religious experience ended there. Then, one night a traveling preacher passing through was invited to speak at the next gathering of the congregation. He preached a sermon out of Romans and shared the truth that "For all have sinned and come short of the glory of God" (Romans 3:23).

Papa told his children the story many times. He said, "That night, for the first time, I understood that I was a sinner and that I needed a Savior. The preacher told me that Jesus Christ shed His blood on the Cross of Calvary to pay the debt that I owed for each sin that I had ever committed. I was grieved in my heart that innocent blood was shed for my sins."

"What did you do Papa?" Ella asked him.

"I begged the Lord to forgive me," he told them. "I changed. Children, your father became a new man that night, a new creation."

Mama saw the change in him. He had a humble heart. She fell in love with the "new" Daniel O'Connor. They married that year. Ella was born, then, Thomas, Lucy, Georgie, and Lila.

"We had good parents," Ella thought to herself, "and a good life."

Papa bought a piece of land and worked hard to build Mama the home of her dreams. They started out in a little cabin at the edge of the meadow, facing the west, so that they could sit together and watch the sun go down in the evenings. Papa put the big house together, little by little, with his own hands and the help of good neighbors. They weren't just the people who lived down the lane or up the hill or on the other side of the creek. They were our friends and we counted on each other. The Caldwells, the Whiteakers, the Randalls, we were like family.

They worked together, prayed together, played together, fought together and now.... some were even fighting against each other, neighbor against neighbor, family member against family member. She couldn't think about that now. She was determined to stay lost in days gone by.

Papa didn't have much farm experience when he first came to Missouri. He had helped his father on their home farm in Ireland as a small boy. He also did some farm work as a hired man on his journey west, but that was the extent of it. It didn't matter. Papa was smart, determined, and he was a good listener.

His father knew a great deal about farming and talked about it often with his sons. Papa remembered all of it. When he came to Missouri, he learned everything he could about local crops. Some things he learned by trial and error. Nevertheless, he put all the pieces together and became a very good farmer.

4

Papa never had opportunity for formal education. He learned to read some on his own and got better at it with the help of Mama. He could write his name and was a natural at deciphering numbers. He believed that education was important and wanted his children to have a good one.

The O'Connor children learned to read and write and do arithmetic. Sister Lila was such a little book worm. She loved to get lost in stories about people and places far away. They didn't have many books of their own, but a good neighbor, Mrs. Whiteaker, who had come to Missouri from back East had brought a collection of books with her. She was very generous to share them with anyone who had a passion for reading.

Papa loved music. He had a beautiful tenor voice and could sing Irish tunes that made Ella long for a homeland that she would never know. And, oh, how he could play the fiddle. What lively gatherings they had off their front porch in the summertime: moonlight, music, dancing, and laughter. Their home was the place where people liked to gather. Papa knew how to enjoy every minute. He taught his children to do the same.

Papa didn't like liquor. That was unusual for an Irishman. He was far too practical. He had seen liquor destroy many good men and their families. He watched the love of liquor even affect his own father. But, most importantly, he viewed drunkenness as displeasing to the Lord. Papa lived his life and made his decisions based on what was right according to Scripture.

Papa believed that we should "love thy neighbor as thyself". He would take his children along to deliver some of their extra milk, eggs, and vegetables and sometimes a fresh baked loaf of bread that Mama had made to someone he had heard about in need. Most people appreciated and loved him.

He was respected for what he had accomplished. His family worked eighty acres, raised cattle, hogs, chickens and milked cows without the use of slave labor. They depended on each other and hired men from time to time. Papa knew what it was like to fight his way up from the bottom. He believed that every man had a right to be paid for his labor and be free to make a better life for himself.

In matters pertaining to the community or politics, his opinion was held in high regard, but even though he didn't believe in slavery, he didn't take a stand against those who did. He didn't see it as his fight. He viewed the topic of slavery as more of a personal conviction. This would deeply impact his family later. It would eventually become almost impossible for anyone in the South to not take a side regarding the issue of slavery.

Ella found herself on her knees, "Thank you, dear God, for the gift of my Papa and Mama." She knew that it was by God's Sovereign Hand that she was blessed with the family that she had been given. "And, please, dear Lord, watch over the rest of my family: Tom, Georgie, Lila, Lucy, and Jackson. Keep them safe and protect them."

She was reminded of her loving mother and remembered how her mama would pray by her bed each night for her husband and each of her children. She would ask God to protect them and keep them safe. Ella felt so safe in her mother's arms. How she longed to feel those loving arms around her again.

Chapter 2

Memories of Mama

E lla's mother's raising was quite different from her
Papa's. Her mama's ancestors came from England
before the Revolution. They worked hard to build their
new life in the new land. They were proud patriots who did
not hesitate to take up arms when the Revolution began.
Her grandfather joined the Continental Army and fought
courageously with them throughout the course of the war.

When Mama was about twelve years old, her family
moved from Tennessee to Missouri. Her father had heard
about the territory west of the Mississippi. Taming a new
frontier intrigued him. He wanted to be a part of something bigger than himself just as his father before him had
been. He bought a choice piece of land, built a cabin for
his family, and they started making a new life.

At first Mama missed Tennessee, but, eventually,
Missouri started to feel like her home. She knew that she
belonged there. For ten years, her family worked hard and
built their homestead together. It was a good life until her
Pa took sick.

He started having headaches. He was tired all the time
and couldn't keep up with the farm chores. Mama and

Papa tried to help, but they were busy with their own place and taking care of Ella and Tom.

Ella's grandparents decided to sell the farm and go back to Tennessee. Her mama's older brother, Henry, had stayed there and kept the old homestead going. So did her mama's older sister, Malinda, and her husband. They were all supposed to eventually join the rest of the family in Missouri, but God had a different plan.

The journey back to Tennessee took quite a toll on her Grandpa. He never really recovered. He grew weaker and weaker and passed away that winter.

Mama never saw her Ma and Pa again. She was the only Shaw that made a permanent home in Missouri. Even though she missed them all very much, she knew her place was in Missouri with her husband. She wrote to them often and cherished her memories.

Lila asked her once, "Does it make you sad, Mama, that your family is so far away and that you don't have your Pa anymore?"

Ella never forgot what her Mama told Lila that day.

"No, child, the Lord has taught me to be thankful for the time that He gave us to be together. My life is here with your Pa and with you children. Besides, time and distance can never cut the ties that we have to our family. They are always with us in our hearts. There have been so many times that I have felt their love all the way from Tennessee. Usually, it's just when I need it the most. I hope that when the day comes that I go to meet Jesus, you will feel my love like I still feel my Pa's."

Ella closed her eyes and thought to herself, "Oh Mama, I wish you were here to put your arms around me and tell me that everything is going to be alright. I miss you so much, but I do still feel your love just like you said I would. I haven't forgotten, Mama. I never will."

Her Mama had always been there for her with a warm hug and a smile, eager to wipe away her tears. Caroline Shaw was raised to be very proper and ladylike. English influence was strong in the Shaw home. She was taught that a lady did not show her emotions openly. Displays of affection, while not forbidden, were not especially encouraged in their family. That didn't matter. Mama and her brother and sister knew how much they were loved. There was no doubt. Mama passed that love onto her own children.

Mama was smart. She had a good bit of education for a lady of her time, and she was a good teacher. She could do anything. She could cook and sew, keep a good house, raise a garden, raise her children, take care of her husband, and still find time to serve her neighbors and love the Lord with her whole heart. "Like the Proverbs 31 woman," Ella was reminded.

Mama would raise up early in the morning to read the Word and pray for her husband and her children. Then, she started breakfast. She assigned chores every day for each of her offspring, so they always knew what was expected of them

The boys helped milk the cows and feed the rest of the animals. When they got older, they helped Papa during planting season and harvest time. Lucy, Lila, and Ella helped Mama with the cooking, the housekeeping, and the washing. They gathered eggs and fed the chickens.

Ella always helped Mama in her garden. Sometimes, it would be just the two of them, planting, weeding, picking, and tasting. They would talk and sing hymns while they worked. Those were special times for just the two of them.

Schooling was saved for the winter months with lessons planned for right after the morning chores. But, even with all the work and schooling that had to be done, Mama and Papa always made sure that there was time to just be a family, to play, and to have fun.

In the summer, the children would go swimming in the creek that ran through their homestead. The whole family would have Sunday afternoon picnics together. Sometimes they would go fishing, or riding, or walking in the countryside.

On cold winter evenings, the boys would lie or sit on the floor and play with their toy soldiers as Mama would read stories by firelight or Papa would play music and sing. The girls would play with their dolls or sometimes work on a sewing project. They were a family. The children were loved, and they loved each other.

Papa and Mama loved each other, too, and the children knew it. There was something special about the two of them together. The Lord brought them together. They were truly two hearts who had become one. One was not complete without the other and the two of them together made one life that was beautiful and full. That is what Ella hoped her marriage to Jackson would become.

Jackson. Not only was he her husband, but her best friend. She recalled the warm, summer afternoons when, as children, they would spend time together down by the creek. They would sit alongside it and skip rocks, their feet bobbing up and down in the cool, clear water. There were many afternoons spent fishing and evenings spent collecting dew worms and catching fireflies.

It seemed that no matter what the activity, Jackson, was always sure to be full of tall tales. He would entertain Ella with stories of pirates and sunken treasure and tales about pioneers along the pioneer trails. He loved and longed for adventure back then. She missed that about him.

War has a way of changing a man. Jackson no longer yearned for adventure. He just longed to be at home with her on their little homestead. His desire was a quiet, simple life, a life with peace and contentment.

Ella had gotten so lost in her memories that she forgot that Jackson was fast asleep in the cabin. Ella made her way to the kitchen stove and started a pot of coffee. Then, she went to see if Jackson was stirring.

Chapter 3

Leaving Home

J ackson awoke to the smell of coffee and Ella leaning over him with a sweet smile on her face. He smiled back at her and said, "Good Morning, Ma'am. That coffee sure smells good. Could you spare a cup for your favorite soldier?" Ella frowned and said, "I can spare a cup for my husband, but don't remind me about soldierin', the army, the North, the South, or the war. Don't joke about any of that, Jackson." Jackson sat up and wrapped his arms around her, "Hey now, I was just playin'. I'm sorry, El. Forgive me."

The war had cost so many people so much. It had taken its toll and it was only by the grace of God that they had made it this far. Yes, they were both alive and they were together, but they both had deep wounds and scars that would change them forever. Sometimes Ella just couldn't hide from it.

Jackson got up, got dressed, and sipped on the cup of coffee that Ella had poured for him. He looked at her as if he were trying to find words, but she already knew what he was going to say. She looked away and tried to change the subject. "Sure is a beautiful morning, isn't it?" She didn't wait for an answer. "I saw a doe and two fawns out by the apple trees while you were sleepin'. They sure were pretty. You should have seen 'em." she said.

Jackson silently walked over to her, put his hand on her shoulder, and slowly turned her around to face him. He put his hand under her chin and lifted her head up to look into her eyes. "Ella, I know that you don't want to talk about it or even think about it, but you know that I gotta go back." She closed her eyes and nodded as he kissed her on the forehead. She knew he couldn't stay. He was only home on furlough.

It had been hard for him to leave his regiment in the first place. It wasn't that he didn't miss her or that he didn't want to be home. It was because Jackson was so loyal. His loyalty was one of the things about him that she loved so much. He was loyal to her. He was loyal to his family. He was loyal to his neighbors. He was loyal to the men that he fought beside. He was loyal to his country.

However, he and Ella had paid a high price for his sense of loyalty. He believed in preserving the Union. Like her Papa, he believed that all men should be free, but Jackson wouldn't take up arms against his family and his neighbors for any cause.

His sense of loyalty left him divided too often throughout the course of the war. For him, there was no choice. He would join the Missouri State Guard.

"Are you leavin' today?" she asked him. "Yes," Jackson replied. "Since the Yankees chased the Confederates south after the skirmish at Booneville, they're gonna be lookin' for the Guard and for Confederate soldiers. It won't be safe for any of us at home again until the war is over."

Jackson paused for a moment. "I may not be back home for a while."

Ella was fighting back the tears, "Yes, Jackson, I know," she said. "Don't do anything foolish. I will be waiting right here for you to come back to me, but only when it is safe again. Just, please, promise that you will come back, please!"

Jackson hugged her tightly and made her the promise that she asked for. "I promise, Ella," he said. "Now, we best be getting ready to get you back to your family."

She pulled herself together enough to put some bread, dried meat, apples, and some vegetables in a sack. She wanted to make sure that Jackson had enough to eat. He was wearing the new shirt and trousers that she had sewn for him. She fetched his coat and boots.

"I put new buttons on this to replace the lost ones", she said as she held up the coat. "Tom sent a new pair of boots for you. This family won't have you traipsin' around Missoura' unprepared." She managed a half-hearted smile.

Jackson admired the shiny new buttons. "Why, no one in my outfit will have a finer set of buttons than these." He smiled back at her. "You'll understand, though, if I don't wear it until I get back to the regiment?" he asked, as he packed his coat in his knapsack along with his Bible. "I don't want to make it too easy for the Yankees to know which side I'm fightin' for." She nodded.

The men in the Guard had to supply their own uniforms, usually made by their wives or mothers. It was the only thing that she could really do for him, and it gave her a small sort of comfort. She did her best to make sure that she made him something that he would feel proud to wear. She knew he appreciated it.

Ella had a small suitcase that belonged to her Mama. She filled it with her things and headed for the front door. Jackson had hitched up a horse to the wagon while she was packing. His horse was tied to the back. He helped her into the wagon, and they left their home not knowing if or when they would be there together again. They began the journey to the O'Connor farm in silence.

Jackson and Ella's homestead bordered the edge of her Papa and Mama's farm. Her Papa had given them a small piece of acreage for a wedding gift. When Jackson left with his regiment the first time, he insisted that they move Ella and their livestock up to her parent's farm. He wouldn't worry so much knowing that Thomas and George were looking out for her.

Neither Tom nor George had joined up. Even when the order was instituted to draft the men ages eighteen to forty-five, a man could pay a tax and be exempted from joining up if need be. Tom and George paid the tax and chose to stay out of the war. It wasn't that they were afraid to fight. It was out of respect for their Pa. They just preferred to fight their own fights and stay out of other people's business.

Missouri had become a hotbed of anger and violence. Jackson knew that his wife and his property would not be safe there without him, especially now with more and more raids happening by bushwackers and jayhawkers. Neighbors had begun turning against each other. Even families were turning on each other. War does something to people. It changes them. Forever!

As they journeyed down the road, they passed by Caldwell Plantation. Jackson didn't turn his head. He kept his focus on the road, but Ella turned and peered on the majestic plantation that Jackson once called home. She remembered back to when she was a little girl. The house was so full of grandeur and so full of life then.

Chapter 4

Remembering Caldwell Plantation

R ichard Caldwell had the finest plantation house in the county. It was on a large piece of land that any man would be proud to call his own. The plantation was across the road on the north side from the O'Connor farmland.

The property included a large meadow bordered by clusters of mature trees. Right in the middle of the meadow, there was another cluster. The shade from these trees was the perfect place to protect a grand house from the heat of a hot Missouri summer day. That is where Jackson's Uncle Richard built the house, in the center of that cluster of trees. The house was not as large or grand as some of the plantation homes in the deep south, but it was beautiful. Caldwell Plantation was the only one of its kind in this part of the country.

His Uncle Richard and Aunt Jane started out in a log home. It didn't take long, however, for his uncle to find a way to get the milled timber that he needed to build a proper plantation house. The river made it possible to transport the timber from a sawmill east of it and slave labor made it possible to get the wood to the homestead.

Uncle Richard had been an apprentice when he was young and learned some about building a house. What he didn't know, he got advice about from a builder in New Orleans. The builder even came to Missouri for a while to help get the house started. Then, Uncle Richard finished it.

Folks speculated about how much it cost him to build it, but he didn't talk about those kinds of things. He didn't care about what folks thought of him. He was a man that once he set his mind on something, he would see it through, and he made Caldwell Plantation a reality.

Inside the house, there was a grand entryway with a large, ornate oak staircase on the left side of the room. It was wide at the bottom and narrowed as it reached the second floor. The foyer was larger than any of the rooms on the main floor even though it wasn't really a room. Ella called it the ballroom because it was there that Uncle Richard and Aunt Jane would host a party or gathering.

There was a modest parlor to the left that was Aunt Jane's favorite place and another room to the right where Uncle Richard would enjoy his cigars and conduct his business. He called it the library even though there were only a few books in it. Behind the parlor was the dining room. The fireplace with its polished stone and shining chandelier made it the finest room in the house. Behind the dining room and staircase was a hallway that connected the dining room to a small room behind Uncle Richard's library where Cassie and Obadiah stayed. The hallway concealed another narrow staircase and the back entrance to the house. It was used mostly by the house servants to access the summer kitchen. The main kitchen was off the back of the house behind the dining room.

Ella was remembering the first time that she came to Caldwell plantation. It was one summer when her family was invited to a picnic that they were having for the neighbors. She remembered how delighted she was as Papa drove their wagon up the lane that led to the house.

At the end of the lane in front of the house was a small, circular garden of flowers. There was a path around it where the guests could turn their carriages and wagons around. Little Ella was enchanted by the small marble statue in the middle of the garden. It was the figure of a woman holding a basket of flowers. The perfectly trimmed bushes and the array of flowers made the whole place look like something out of a dream. She was in awe of the tall white pillars on each side of the stairs leading up to the house, the grand front porch, and the large oak door that, to her, seemed big enough for even a giant to walk through.

Uncle Richard and Aunt Jane stood at the bottom of the front porch, greeting their guests as they arrived. Uncle Richard shook Papa's hand, while Aunt Jane hugged Mama. "Oh, Caroline," she said, "it is so good to see you. Look at these children. My, how they are growing up to be such fine young ladies and gentlemen." She turned to Papa and said, "Daniel, you must be so proud of this handsome family." Papa smiled and gave us all a look of approval.

"Thank you, Jane. You are so kind," Mama replied. She leaned over the wagon and pulled out the two pies that she had made for the gathering. "The girls and I did a little baking and thought these might be a welcome addition to your table."

Aunt Jane graciously accepted the pies and directed Ella's Papa to take the family and join the party.

"Thank you, Jane, Richard, for your gracious hospitality," Papa said as he tipped his hat. "Come along now children," he said to us. We obediently followed and joined the festivities.

The gathering that day was wonderful. Everyone was wearing their Sunday best. Papa was dressed in his good trousers and suspenders and the new shirt that Mama had made for him. Mama looked beautiful in her green dress and the new bonnet that Papa had bought her for her birthday. "It was yellow, I think," Ella thought to herself, "yes, and it had a cream satin ribbon."

Mama had made new dresses for each of the girls that summer. The dresses were made from the same pattern, but each was a different color. They were cotton, of course, with a ribbon added to the waist. The ribbons were an extra special detail, making a statement without bragging.

Lila's dress was lavender. Lucy's dress was pink. Ella's dress was a soft blue. Each dress had puffed sleeves embellished with lace around the edges, another statement, subtle, yet not too bold. Mama wanted Papa to be proud of his children, but she would never do anything to intentionally put on an air.

Thomas and Georgie wore their best trousers and new handmade shirts. Papa had shined up their shoes. They wore their suspenders and their hats and looked like little men. Ella remembered Georgie complaining, "Mama, why do I have to wear my Sunday clothes when it ain't even Sunday." Mama said, "You hush now, Georgie, you children are going to make a good impression today and you will wear your Sunday best." Georgie conceded with a simple, "Yes, Ma'am."

Thomas was always more compliant. He was a good boy with good manners who knew what was expected of him. He didn't seem to mind wearing his Sunday clothes.

Georgie, on the other hand, tended to be restless. He was respectful and obedient. He wasn't reckless, but he was mischievous like Papa. He was always busy and if he wasn't, it meant trouble. He was so curious and wanted to explore everything. As a "wee lad" he was ready to take on the world. Good manners and proper etiquette just seemed so silly to him.

When Mama would remind him of his manners, he would reply, "That is no fun. It makes me feel like I can't breathe." Mama would scold him and tell him to stop exaggerating. "I think," Ella thought, "that he was trying to tell us, in a child's way, that it was suffocating to him. I think that it is still suffocating for George."

As she stared at the plantation, she could picture all the little details of that day. There was a long table set up on the green grass with a tablecloth and silver platters filled, almost overflowing, with food. The food was delicious: roasted pork, fresh bread, apple pie, sweet potatoes and all the fixin's that you could dream of. It was a feast that rivaled Mama's Thanksgiving dinners. They played yard games and visited with the neighbors. They drank punch and sat in the shade admiring the splendor of their surroundings.

It was a wonderful day, but what she remembered most was that it was the first day that she laid eyes on Jackson Caldwell. Jackson and Nathaniel were sitting alone next to a shed. Ella saw them from a distance and was curious, of course, so she wandered closer. Nathaniel ignored her, but Jackson looked up, as if he were waiting for her to say something.

"Hello," said little Ella. There was a pause.

"Hello," replied Jackson. Then, there was a longer pause.

Ella noticed something in Jackson's hand.

"What's that?" she asked him.

Jackson held up a wooden horse without saying anything.

"That's real nice," she said, "Where did you get it?"

Jackson replied, "My Pa, he whittled it for me." Ella nodded. There was more silence.

"Is your Pa here?" asked Ella.

Jackson looked down at the ground as Nathaniel jumped up, storming off like he was mad at the whole wide world.

"Did I say somethin' wrong?" Ella asked, a little surprised.

"No. It ain't you that's botherin' him," said Jackson.

"What is it then?" Ella was always a little too curious for her own good.

Jackson hesitated at first, but for some reason he thought she would understand, "Our Ma and Pa died a while back."

"Is that how you came to live here with Mr. and Mrs. Caldwell?" she asked him.

"Yeah. We were on our way here from Tennessee when it happened. Uncle Richard and Aunt Jane are takin' care of us. Nathaniel ain't been right ever since. He just misses our folks so much that he don't know what to do with himself sometimes," Jackson explained.

Ella was sad for Jackson and Nathaniel. She didn't know what to say. So, she just sat down against the shed next to Jackson. They didn't speak. They just sat for a while. Then, Ella asked a question only a child would ask in a moment like that, "Do you wanna play a game?"

At first, Jackson didn't know if he should go after his brother or follow Ella. He decided that he would follow Ella. "Nathaniel seems to like being by himself these days anyway," Jackson thought to himself. Little did Ella know that she had made a friend for life that day, her best friend. Little did she know how she would grow to love this little orphan boy. Little did she know how much Caldwell Plantation and the people who lived there would impact her life one day.

Chapter 5

Nathaniel and Jackson's Journey to Missouri

The Caldwell and the Dooley families were neighbors in Tennessee. The Caldwell brothers married Dooley sisters. James Caldwell and Molly Dooley were Jackson and Nathaniel's Ma and Pa. Richard Caldwell and Jane Dooley were their uncle and aunt. Richard and Jane were the first to leave Tennessee. James and Molly soon followed.

James and Molly had a homestead in Tennessee where Jackson and Nathaniel were born. Letters from Uncle Richard and Aunt Jane about Missouri and their life there tempted James to uproot the family and go farther west. There was a small group leaving for Missouri that spring. James, Molly, and the boys packed up their wagon and joined the small wagon train. It was one tragic day along that wagon trail that brought Jackson and his brother to Caldwell Plantation.

Jackson told Ella about it once. It was back when they were still children. He and Ella had been playing a game with Nathaniel and some other children. Nathaniel got mad, over what seemed like nothing and stormed off as usual.

"Why is he always doin' that?" Ella asked Jackson.

At first, Jackson hesitated. Then, he said, "It's because of what happened to our Ma and Pa. He just stays mad all the time." Then, Jackson told her about the day his parents died.

The journey for his family to Missouri was mostly uneventful. Everyone got along fine. The route wasn't overly difficult. Crossing the river went much smoother than they expected. The weather was mostly agreeable.

"It won't be long now boys," James told his sons. "Another couple of days and we'll be puttin' down roots for a new home."

"What's it gonna be like Pa?" Nathaniel asked.

"It's gonna be a lot of hard work, but it will be worth it," Pa answered.

"We'll help ya', Pa," Nathaniel told him. "I'm nine now, almost growed up. I'm stronger now, so I can help you build our new cabin."

Mama smiled and said, "My, that sounds ambitious."

"I can do it, Ma," promised Nathaniel.

"Of course, you can, son," said Pa.

"Nathaniel would do anything to please Pa," Jackson told Ella as he continued to recall the events of the day. "He wanted to be just like him."

"You boys can do anything that you put your mind to," their Pa told them. "You have been strong and brave on our journey west, and you are growin' up to be fine young men." It was a proud moment for Nathaniel.

"Some nice folks had taken a likin' to me and Nathaniel on the trip," Jackson told Ella. "Gramps (as the boys affectionately called him) and his Mrs. asked Pa if me and Nathaniel could ride up in the wagon with them. We liked hearin' his stories, so Pa said we could. Gramps had been a soldier once. He told us all about it. He told us stories about his first journey west and what it would be like when we got settled in Missouri.

Jackson had never talked about this before. Ella kept her eyes fixed on him as she hung on his every word.

"We didn't know it, but we were bein' followed by indians. I don't really know why, maybe horses or supplies. Gramps was drivin' the wagon. Nathaniel and me were sittin' up in the seat next to him. His Mrs. was riding in the back of the wagon tryin' to stay out of the sun. We were talkin' and laughin' and then we heard a shot and a lot of hollerin'."

Jackson paused. Ella could see that he was fighting back tears, but he didn't stop talking.

"The horses panicked, mama's and children were screamin'. Then, there were more shots. Gramps hollered at his Mrs. to get down. I looked back to find Ma and Pa, but Gramps pushed us down into the wagon. I saw Pa for just a second. He was holding his rifle in one hand and holding onto Ma with his other hand. They were runnin' towards us. Gramps' Mrs. was trying to cover us up with her feather pillows and quilts behind a sack of flour. Nathaniel was trying to get to the back of the wagon, lookin' for Ma and Pa."

"What happened to them?" Ella asked.

Jackson replied, "I didn't see what happened. The Mrs. grabbed a hold of me and held me tight, but Nathaniel saw everything. I never asked him. All's I know is, Pa and Ma didn't make it to the wagon. We became orphans that day and Nathaniel has never been the same since."

"How did you get here?" Ella asked him.

"Gramps and his Mrs. brought us to Uncle Richard and Aunt Jane. At first, we were both so scared, and then Nathaniel just started actin' mad all the time," he told her.

The two young boys found themselves in a new home without their Ma and Pa and in a new family that they hardly knew. They were welcomed into the family, but it was still hard for them. Uncle Richard and Aunt Jane treated them as if they were their own sons and gave them all the privileges that their children had. Jackson grew to love them all, but Nathaniel wouldn't let his guard down. He was older and understood better what had been lost to them when their parents died. Deep down Nathaniel was angry. His anger grew with each passing year.

Uncle Richard and Aunt Jane were patient with him, but Nathaniel often made it difficult. He would act like he didn't care about them or that he wasn't grateful for all that they had done. Uncle Richard and Aunt Jane's children didn't always appreciate the way that Nathaniel behaved. They thought that he should show Uncle Richard and Aunt Jane more respect. This caused problems between Nathaniel and some of their boys.

Uncle Richard and Aunt Jane had a large family. William was the oldest. It was his job to keep an eye out for Nathaniel and Jackson. In a way, you could say he was the peacekeeper. It was hard for William, but you would never know it. He never let anyone know how he felt about things. He seemed to take everything in stride. His father was a lot like that when he was a young man.

Uncle Richard knew hardship. He and his brothers had been given up by their parents to be apprentices when they were young. The journey from Virginia to Kentucky and building a new life there was more of a challenge than their father was prepared for. He found himself in debt and needed his sons to help pay off the debt. They were separated from the rest of their family when Uncle Richard was only twelve years old. Probably the reason why family was so important to him and why he didn't hesitate to take Jackson and Nathaniel in when they were orphaned.

When their father's debts were paid, and the boys were free, the Caldwell brothers left Kentucky and went to Tennessee. They worked as hired men for a time. Then, they each received a land grant. The Caldwell men met the Dooley sisters. They each married and started their own families.

Uncle Richard's farm prospered more quickly than his brother's farm. James did not like the idea of slave labor. The time that he spent as an apprentice made him aware of how important a man's freedom was. Uncle Richard, on the other hand, took advantage of it. He was able to make the most of his land, and with the help of his slaves, buy more land and acquire his wealth.

He heard about opportunities west of the Mississippi River in Missouri. He sold everything, the land and anything that the family couldn't take with them. He received a large sum for his property and was able to purchase the land that would become Caldwell Plantation. Then, he bought more slaves to help him work it.

This never made much sense to Jackson. Uncle Richard knew what it was like to not have his freedom. Why would he choose to "own" other men? Did he feel entitled to be a master because he had done his time as a servant?

He was a fair and responsible master. He was not as generous as some, but he insisted that the slaves were treated well. Still, they were no more than property to him. There was no connection between Uncle Richard and the men and women that he owned. He didn't converse with them. Rarely did he even look at them.

Oddly enough, slavery was not a topic that Uncle Richard ever talked about with the rest of the family. It was almost as if the slaves were invisible. There was evidence of their presence because of the amount of work that was done daily on the plantation, but they went about the work almost unnoticed by the rest of the family.

Aunt Jane ran the household with only two servants. There was a house servant, Cassie, and a man servant, Obadiah. Most people called him Obie. The rest of the slaves maintained the gardens, cared for the livestock, and worked the fields. They stayed in small cabins on the other side of the creek down by the edge of one of the fields. They were out of sight and out of mind. There was an overseer and a watchman who stayed down there with them. For many years, Uncle Richard didn't have much trouble with any of his slaves running off.

His overseer instilled fear to a certain degree. However, Uncle Richard mostly maintained control of his slaves by making sure that they stayed ignorant of what was happening outside of the plantation. They were never allowed to leave for any reason or interact with anyone on the outside. The only exceptions were Cassie and Obie. He thought that if the slaves believed there was no place to run, that they had no other options, they wouldn't run.

Uncle Richard rewarded his slaves for being loyal and productive. Sometimes, he would provide them with extra portions of meat and fresh vegetables on special occasions. He would give them shorter workdays on the holidays that the family observed. Rarely was there any trouble or problems in his slave community. It was the deep friendship that Nathaniel and Obie had with each other that would become the spark that would turn slave life on the plantation upside down.

Uncle Richard and Aunt Jane's children were still expected to do their fair share of work, even with all the slave labor on Caldwell Plantation. William, Sterling, and Nathaniel managed the field work and interacted with the slaves the most. James and Robert cared for the livestock. Jackson fixed things. Petey, being the youngest, got whatever jobs no one else wanted. The girls: Elizabeth, Mary, Joanna, and Sarah all helped their mother with the running of the household. Canning, spinning, knitting, and sewing were all on their lists. Everyone doing their part made Caldwell Plantation magnificent, the envy of so many in the county.

No wonder Jackson didn't look as they drove by. It was hard enough for Ella to see it the way that it was now. It had to be even harder for him. It looked abandoned, unkept. The garden that had once been beautiful and trimmed was overgrown. She could barely see the statue that stood in the center. It almost looked as if no one had lived there for years. "There had been no family unaffected by the war," Ella thought to herself. It truly had taken its toll on the Caldwell family, too.

Chapter 6

The O'Connor Family

They were almost at her childhood home when Ella felt Jackson reach for her hand. "We're almost there, Ella. Do you want to tell me what you've been thinking about?" She held his hand tightly, but looked away as she said, "Just rememberin', I guess."

Jackson stopped the wagon, squeezed her hand, and let go. He turned to her to say, "You know, El, I was thinking. Maybe I should go see Uncle Richard one more time. I want to make sure things are right between us. I can't bear the thought of something happenin' and him not knowin' that nothing has changed how I feel about him or the rest of the family."

Ella replied sharply, "Nothing is going to happen! Do you hear me? Nothing is going to happen! You are going to come home in one piece and then things will go back to the way they used to be." By now, she was crying. Jackson pulled her close to him and held her tightly until she could get a hold of herself.

"I'm sorry, El. Don't you worry about anything. I'll be back, and everything will be alright," Jackson promised.

They made their way down the lane. Tom and George were outside by the barn. They stopped what they were doing to come and greet them. "Howdy, Tom........, George," Jackson said, as he helped Ella out of the wagon. "Howdy," replied Tom as he took her suitcase. Georgie tied up the horses as Ella and Tom went inside. He was quiet which was unusual for him.

"Is somethin' wrong, George?" Jackson asked concerned.

"I guess, I've been doin' a lot of thinkin'," he told him. "I've made a decision. I've decided that I'm going with you. It is time for me to join up."

"Are you sure about this?" asked Jackson surprised. "You know this is gonna be hard for the family."

"I know. I figure Tom can take care of the farm and the women and keep an eye out at your place. We still have a few hired hands that can help, too," George explained. "I've stayed out of this war because I thought that Papa would want it that way, but I can't stand by and watch anymore. I figure the sooner the war is over, the sooner we will be rid of the bushwackers and their raidin', the Yankees, and all the fightin' between neighbors. Nobody and no place in Missoura' are safe anymore. This is our home. Not only should men be free from slavery, but Missourians should be free from livin' in fear. I just gotta do my part."

Jackson put a hand on George's shoulder, "I understand, George," he said. "It's a decision that every man has to make for himself. I believe your Pa would understand, too. It seems like none of us has a choice anymore. We didn't ask for it, but the fightin' is right here at our front door."

George nodded his head in agreement. It was obvious that he had thought long and hard about this. He turned quietly and started walking back to the barn.

"Ain't you comin' inside, George?" asked Jackson.

"I'll be in after a bit. You go on," George replied.

George walked away with what seemed like the weight of the world on his shoulders. Jackson stood there thinking. He loved George like a brother. Ella's family had been part of his life since he first came to Missouri. George had always been a good friend to him. Papa O'Connor was always a little tougher on him, but Jackson always suspected it was because his Pa understood him better than anyone else did. George was the one who was most like him.

Georgie questioned everything. He had a hard time doing things just because he was told to. If something didn't make sense to him, it really troubled him. When the war started, to George, it didn't make sense. He believed that all men should be free, but like Papa O'Connor, he didn't think folks should be in other folk's business. He and his Papa believed that local governments should decide for themselves. He felt that folks should be left alone to live their lives and run their homes as they thought best.

As Jackson stood there, looking around at the farm, he wondered, if it might be the last time that he would ever see it again. He didn't usually think like that, but, what if something did happen to him this time? This place had been his second home.

When he was a child, people pitied him and Nathaniel because they had been orphaned so young. But, as he grew to be a young man, the Lord gave him eyes to see how blessed he truly was. Yes, there were many days that he longed for his mother and his father. There were days that he shed many tears over the empty space in his heart that appeared when they left him. However, Jackson believed God and His Word and could see in his own life how God truly does work all things together for good to those who love God and are called according to His purpose (Romans 8:28).

There was a purpose and a plan for the lives of his parents, and he knew there was a purpose and a plan for his life, and Nathaniel's life, and his sweet Ella's life, and the rest of the family. Jackson may not have had the opportunity to be raised by the parents who gave him life, but he could see that he still was blessed.

He knew the amazing love of his Ma and Pa, even if it was for only a short time. Then, the Lord gave him Uncle Richard. He was a good provider who taught him to work hard and be a man. As for Aunt Jane, her love was unconditional, patient, and kind. Jackson owed them so much.

Then, the Lord gave him the O'Connor's. They loved Jackson as if he were one of their own. How many children could say that they had known that kind of love from so many? Yes, Jackson knew loss, but Jackson was blessed because he knew abundant love.

He stood by the wagon and admired the splendor of the O'Connor farm. It was a beautiful place. The lane leading to the farm was surrounded by trees on each side, giving the illusion that the farm was in the middle of the woods, but at the end of the lane was a clearing. Behind the clearing was a hill. The hill was covered by a small forest of mostly maple trees. Papa O'Connor tapped those trees, collected the sap, boiled it down, and made the most delicious maple syrup.

There was a creek fed by a spring that sprung from the bottom of the hill. The creek ran behind the house and the barn along the edge of the clearing. The clearing opened to a wide expanse of sky and land where there was a large section for grazing. The big barn was at the edge where the trees and the field met. In the distance, across the field you could see where each crop had been planted, the corn, the wheat, the beans, and a patch of cotton.

The small cabin that Papa built first for him and Aunt Caroline was at the beginning of the lane that led to the farmhouse. Ella and Jackson stayed there the first winter after they were married. Tom and Anne called it home after they were first married, too.

It was small. Originally there were only three rooms: two rooms for sleeping and a main room where everyone ate and gathered. Later, Tom and George added a proper kitchen and dining room. Then, Tom asked Anne to marry him. They turned that little log cabin into a homey place that always welcomed visitors and had room enough to give them a good meal and a place to sleep if they needed one.

The big house was in the clearing near the barn where you could see for what seemed like miles across the fields. It was a farmhouse, not a plantation house, but it was a gentlemen's farmhouse. It was two stories high, white-washed, and had a whitewashed fence around it. There was a front porch the length of the house with posts from the porch floor to the roof that covered it. Papa had made two rocking chairs that sat on the porch, one for him and one for Aunt Caroline. That is where you would most likely find them both in the evening. Jackson stared at the empty chairs for a moment wishing to see them there again.

Aunt Caroline loved her flowers. The whole porch was adorned with roses and primrose. She enjoyed watching the hummingbirds and the butterflies flutter around them.

The inside of the house, though it wasn't grand, was enough to make any man proud. It had English style and charm with country comfort. There was a foyer and a staircase inside the front door. It wasn't as big or ornate as the one at Caldwell Plantation and there was no chandelier. Still, it was impressive and inviting.

Jackson remembered seeing Tom and Georgie slide down that staircase many times when they were all young. Aunt Caroline would get after them for it. He could almost hear her holler, "Boys, that rail wasn't made for slidin'. Next time use those feet the Good Lord gave you, ya' hear." They would say, "Yes, Ma'am," as they went running out the door. She would smile and shake her head.

The house had a parlor, a proper kitchen, a dining room, and a guest room on the main floor. The parlor had a small table and chairs where the ladies could have tea in the afternoon and the men could smoke a pipe after supper. The kitchen had a cookstove and a cupboard that Papa had made. It also had a wash sink and a farm table and benches. Aunt Caroline would serve breakfast and lunch in the kitchen for Papa, the boys, and the farmhands, calling them in with a bell that hung just outside the kitchen door.

In the evenings, the family would eat together in the dining room. The dining room wasn't as grand as the one at Caldwell plantation, but it was still a fine room. There was a long dining table that fit the family well and still left room for guests. It was covered with a lace tablecloth that Aunt Caroline's mother had given her.

A china cupboard that housed Aunt Caroline's china and her tea service stood on one wall. There was a fireplace on the small wall behind the head of the table. It was only made of brick, but it had a wood mantle that held a modest mirror and some candle sticks which made it look fine.

At the top of the stairs were two big windows overlooking the backyard, the creek, and Aunt Caroline's vegetable garden. There was a bench in front of the windows where Ella's sister, Lila, loved to sit and read her books. There were three bedrooms upstairs each with a small hearth. The girls shared one room. The boys shared another. The other room was for their Pa and Ma. Each room was outfitted with feather beds and pillows, warm handmade quilts, a dresser, and a table with a pitcher and wash bowl. It was a warm, comfortable home.

Aunt Caroline and Papa O'Connor were the heart of this place. It wasn't the same here without them. Jackson prayed that happy times would come here again, and that more good memories would be made in this place.

Chapter 7

Choosing Sides

Jackson was remembering back to when the war started and thinking about all the chaos that followed. It changed everything. Papa O'Connor was determined that neither him nor his family were going to choose sides. "This family has no place in this war," they would hear him say often. And, at first, some Missourians were able to stay neutral because Missouri stayed neutral, but that wouldn't last.

In the beginning, the goal was that Missouri was going to remain part of the Union, but not assist either side. To protect its neutral stand and its people from both armies, the Missouri State Guard was formed. Its primary function was to keep the Union army from moving in and taking control of the state.

Eventually, people started being forced to choose sides. Men started assembling in their districts trying to convince each other which side they should be on. The Guard was supposed to resist any local Union sympathizers (locals who had enlisted in the Union army and their families). The soldiers in the Guard started finding themselves on opposite sides from their friends and even some of their family members.

The victory for the Confederacy at Wilson's Creek placed Missouri under Confederate control, compromising its neutrality. The tide turned. In October 1861, Governor Claiborne Jackson proposed an ordinance of secession that was passed. The Confederate Congress officially admitted Missouri as the 12th Confederate state on November 28th.

Missouri was "plum for the picking" and both sides wanted it. It was the most populated state west of the Mississippi, which meant more soldiers. It was the third highest producer of corn and pork, and, a major producer of grain and livestock, which meant more food to feed the soldiers.

The Guard and the Confederacy were different armies, but they fought side by side. They had a common purpose: resist the Union Army. Many of the men from the Guard started enlisting in the Confederate Army the winter of '61.

Jackson didn't believe in the Cause, but he believed in defending his family and his home. It was an easy decision for him to join up after Uncle Richard, William, Sterling, Robert, and James joined. Nathaniel joined the Guard, too, but not until after Jackson did. Nathaniel was always looking out for his younger brother. He couldn't let him join the fight without him.

With each battle between the Blue and the Grey and each raid from the bushwackers, Jackson's friends and family started choosing sides. It caused deep conflicts. Uncle Richard and his sons gave their loyalty to the Confederacy. Their neighbors, the Whiteakers, would side with the Federalists and join up with the Union.

The Randalls would eventually side with the Union. Jackson, Nathaniel, and George stayed with the Guard and sided with the Confederacy.

A Whiteaker son had taken a Caldwell bride. She would find herself in the middle of a battle, not only between the North and the South, but also between her husband and her father and brothers. Neighbors disagreed with neighbors and communities began to be torn apart by divided loyalties. Some folks around the county didn't like the idea of anyone, including the O'Connors, being neutral.

Chapter 8

The War Makes it's Way to the Farm

J ackson was still standing by the wagon, looking around the farm thinking about how much life had changed here. Ella longed for everything to be like it was before the war. Part of him longed for that, too, but Jackson was a man of faith. He knew that there was a reason and a plan for everything. He believed God and knew that he had to trust Him.

He had seen God at work in his life, in Ella's life, and in the lives of the rest of the family over the course of the years. He had seen firsthand how God can use something that men mean for evil for His glory in the lives of those who are faithful and stand on His promises. Jackson was determined to stand. He couldn't bear it if all the suffering and pain over these last years had been in vain. He had to cast it all at the feet of Jesus and allow the Lord to use it to make him a better man, to change him, and make him more like his Savior.

Papa O'Connor had managed to keep the war away from his family and away from his home longer than anyone else in the county. Most people had their opinion about his refusing to choose sides, but Papa didn't care. He minded his business and expected other folks to do the same. George's decision to join up reminded Jackson about how that all changed one day. His thoughts began to wander back in time to a chain of events that left a hole in many hearts, a time, not that far in the past, that seemed like a lifetime ago.

It all started with a visit to town. George and Tom had gone on some business. They met up with two acquaintances outside the post office, Martin Brown and Hal Babcock. Brown and Babcock had never been up to any good even before the war. Now they used the war as an excuse for their bad behavior. They liked their liquor and they liked to fight, so most people knew to stay away from them, including George and Tom.

Tom saw the two men walking toward them, but he pretended not to notice. George, on the other hand, couldn't help himself and made eye contact with Hal. Tom pulled George by the sleeve and headed for the post office door. Mr. Johnston, the postmaster and a neighbor lady, Mrs. Evans, were inside.

"Well, hello boys. I haven't seen ya'll in ages. How is your Ma and Pa doing?" Mrs. Evans asked.

"We are all fine, Ma'am. Thank you for askin'," Tom replied. George didn't say a word. He stood by the window watching the two men outside.

"We'd like to mail this letter for our Ma, Mr. Johnston. Do you have any letters here for her?" continued Tom.

"Yes, I have a letter," replied Mr. Johnston. "It's from your Aunt Malinda. I think your Ma will be pleased."

"You're right about that. She sure looks forward to letters from Tennessee," Tom said as Mr. Johnston handed him the letter.

Tom turned to Mrs. Evans and said, "Have a nice day, Ma'am."

"Thank you, Tom. Give your Ma and Pa my best, ya' hear?" said Mrs. Evans.

"We will Ma'am." Tom tipped his hat and turned toward the door. Mr. Johnston, all the while, was watching George at the window. He could tell something was wrong.

Brown and Babcock were still hanging around outside when Tom and George exited the post office. Tom walked slowly past them. George was right behind him.

"Howdy, boys," Tom said, "Sure is a fine day."

Hal Babcock locked eyes with George again and scoffed, "Tom, I think your brother was eye ballin' me a while ago. Don't you think he was eye ballin' me, Martin?"

Martin Brown sneered, "Yep, I think he was."

Babcock continued, "I figure that can only mean one thing."

Tom interrupted, "Now wait a minute here. George wasn't eye ballin' nobody. We came to town on business, and we don't want any trouble."

Brown looked at George and said, "If you boys didn't want trouble, you shouldn't have started any."

Tom recognized the look in George's eyes. He was ready for a fight.

Brown kept talking. "You see, we don't have time for folks who won't take up for their neighbors and fight for the Cause. The way we see it, if you ain't for us then you must be agin' us. Or, maybe, you're just too yellow to fight at all."

George didn't say a word. He started towards Brown. Postmaster Johnston flung open the post office door rifle in hand interrupting what was happening.

"Tom...... George........," he said, "is there a problem out here?"

Babcock patted Brown on the shoulder and pulled him back. "Everything is just fine," he said to Mr. Johnston. Then he looked at Tom and George and said, "We'll be seein' you two again." The two men turned around and crossed the road.

Tom and George mounted up and started back toward the farm. Neither of them said anything about what happened when they got back home, but George told Jackson about it the next day.

Jackson remembered warning George not to lose his head, but he was adamant that somebody needed to teach the two ruffians a lesson.

The next week, their Papa went to town with them. He had some business at the blacksmith and a list of some things that their Mama needed from the Mercantile. And, Tom, well, he had his mind set to go calling on Anne Randall over at the local hotel that her family owned and operated. She helped her folks with keepin' up the place and cookin' meals for the people that stayed there.

Papa went off on his own to take care of his business and the boys went in the other direction to go visit Anne and her family. As they crossed the street in front of the barbershop, they saw Hal Babcock and Martin

Brown come riding into town. They were headed toward the tavern.

"George, look the other way and keep walkin'," warned Tom. Hal and Martin didn't seem to notice them. If they did, they weren't interested. Tom and George entered the hotel and didn't think any more about the two men who had threatened them the week before.

Mrs. Randall, Anne's mother, was the first to greet them. She was cleaning off some tables in the lobby.

"Well, hello boys, so nice of you to call," she said, "What brings you to town?"

"Pa had some business to take care of. George and I thought we would come along to keep him company and pay your family a visit," replied Tom.

"I am so glad that you did. How are your Ma and Pa?" she asked them.

"They're doing fine. Thank you, Ma'am," replied George.

"You're just in time," she said, "We were just about ready to sit down for a bite to eat. Come on back and join us for some dinner." She motioned the boys to follow. Tom and George obediently followed her as she called out for her children.

"Anne, Charles, look who's come to visit," she said.

They made their way to a door off the lobby. It led to the place in the back where the family stayed. The door opened into a good size room where there was a cook-stove and wash sink and a place to prepare the meals for the people who rented the rooms in the hotel. In the center of the room was a table where the family ate together. Around the fireplace, there was a rocking chair and three other comfortable chairs. There was a knitting basket on the floor by one of the chairs and a woven rug by the hearth. The family gathered here in the evenings for reading, relaxing, and conversation.

Off to one side of their living space were two bedrooms, one for Anne and one for her parents. Tucked in one corner of the main room was a comfortable bed surrounded by a curtain, the place where Anne's brother, Charles, slept. A door by the cook stove gave them a private entrance. It led to an alley on the side of the building. It was a modest, comfortable home that met the family's every need.

Anne was standing by the stove. Charles was already sitting at the table. Both were obviously pleased to receive their visitors. It was a very pleasant surprise.

"Howdy, Charles, Hello, Anne," said Tom.

"Howdy boys," replied Charles, "Pull up a seat. Anne was just dishin' up some chicken and dumplins'. You're in for a treat. The best dumplins' this side of the Mississippi.'

"I don't know about that," said Anne as she turned to Tom. "It's good to see you both," she said with a thoughtful smile.

Everyone knew that Tom had taken a liking to Anne. Papa and Mama and Mr. and Mrs. Randall approved, and why wouldn't they? Tom was solid. He worked hard. He was loyal, respectful, and family was important to him.

Anne was smart and funny. She had a kind, gentle spirit, but she was not afraid to speak her mind. She respected her Ma and Pa and loved her family. She loved Tom's family, too.

The O'Connor's and The Randall's had been friends for years. Mrs. Randall and Caroline had been friends since the Shaw family first came to Missouri. Anne and the O'Connor girls had been close friends since they were little girls, too. Georgie and Charles were always teasing and pestering the girls while Tom was always coming to their rescue. It was no surprise to anyone that something special would blossom between Tom and Anne, or, that Charles would take a shine to Lila O'Connor.

"How have you been, Tom?" Anne asked him.

"I've been doin' fine. It's sure good to see you," he replied.

"Alright, now, have a seat before the food gets cold," said Mrs. Randall. Tom pulled out a chair for Anne and sat down in the one next to her. Everyone else settled into their places as well.

"Mr. Randall won't be eating with us?" asked George.

"No, Papa, ate earlier," replied Anne, "He's expectin' a stagecoach to come in soon and he wanted to make sure he was ready for it."

"Charles," asked Mrs. Randall, "will you please say the blessin'?"

"Yes, ma'am," he said.

Tom, sitting next to Anne, reached for her hand as they all bowed their heads to thank God for His provision.

"Dear Lord," began Charles, "Thank you for bringing our friends here today. Please be with them on their journey back home. And, Lord, please be with all the folks in our little town. Keep us safe and help us to love our neighbors as ourselves. Help us to honor you during these hard times. Bless this food that we are about to eat and Ma and Anne for preparing it. Bless this fellowship. Amen."

"Thank you, son," said Mrs. Randall as she started to pass the dumplings.

"How are things at the farm?" Charles asked as he reached for a biscuit out of the breadbasket.

"Everyone is doin' fine," Tom replied, "We'll be startin' the harvest soon. So, there won't be much time to come to town until after the fields are taken down." He looked at Anne as he spoke.

"It's good of you to come callin' on us today, Tom," said Anne.

Charles was thoughtful, "Maybe we can find some time to pay a call to you all out at the farm before the winter sets in."

"That is a fine idea, Charles," interrupted Mrs. Randall. "We would all love to visit the farm, but folks gotta be careful travelin' these days. You can't just go off anymore. It just ain't safe."

"Your Ma is right, Charles," said Tom. "Folks are talkin' 'bout all the bushwackin' going on over on the Kansas border. Quantrill and his Raiders are scarin' folks half to death. The bushwackers have been movin' closer and closer in our direction. I heard tell it, that they burned out a farm over in the next county because the folks were speakin' out against secession and against the Confederacy."

Charles interrupted, "It seems like more and more folks are choosin' up sides, even right here in our own town. Did you hear that last week down by the mercantile store a couple of the Caldwell brothers had it out with Jeremiah Whiteaker and a couple of other boys? Someone said that if the women hadn't been there it might have gotten violent."

"What were they all riled up about?" asked George.

"Well, the way I heard tell it was that the Caldwell boys accused Jeremiah of being disloyal to Missoura' because he told them if it came down to it, he would be joinin' up with the Union. Those Caldwell's don't like Yankees much," Charles interjected his own thought.

"Charles," Mrs. Randall interrupted. "You're gossipin'."

"No, I ain't, Ma. This is important," Charles continued. "They told Jeremiah that if he joined up with the Yankees, he'd be nothin' more than a traitor. They said that they wouldn't claim any kin to him and make his life hard any way that they could. It sure is a shame that they did that in front of their sister. She was beside herself, begging them to stop. They finally did, but everyone knew it wasn't over."

"The Caldwell's and the Whiteaker's fuedin' like that. What's goin' to become of all of us?" asked Anne with a look of concern, "Families are risin' up against each other. Neighbors can't get along. I never thought that I would see a day like this."

"You shouldn't worry about such things," Tom told her. "We just gotta' trust the Lord. There is nothin' that can happen to you, or me, or Missoura', that doesn't come through His hands first."

"Tom's right. Now, enough of that," chimed in George changing the subject, "Charles, Lila sends you her best."

"How is Lila?" Charles asked.

"She is doing fine. I know she'd especially be lookin' forward to a call from you anytime that you're able," George told him with a big grin on his face.

"Awe, George, cut it out," scolded Tom.

Then, Tom said, "I know that I speak for Ma and Pa when I say that we would be happy to have you visit." Mrs. Randall smiled as she made eye contact with both of her children.

Everyone enjoyed a good meal and a good visit. Then, George, turned to Tom and said, "Papa will be looking for us. We best be gettin' along now."

Tom agreed. George excused himself from the table and reached to shake Charles' hand. "Charles, it was good seein' you," he said. Then, he nodded his head to Anne and Mrs. Randall. "Thank you, Miss Anne....... Mrs. Randall, for the fine meal and your hospitality."

"You're always welcome," replied Mrs. Randall, "Tell your Ma and Pa hello for us."

"Thank you, Ma'am," said Tom. Then, he turned to Anne and said, "Thank you, for your hospitality." He hesitated as if he wanted to say more, but it wasn't the right time.

Mrs. Randall spoke up and said, "Charles, didn't you say that you had something you wanted to show George outside?"

Charles was confused for a moment and then, said, "Oh, I guess, I did."

Mrs. Randall, George, and Charles left Tom and Anne alone.

"Be careful, Tom, won't you? Anne asked him in a concerned voice. "I have heard stories. People say things."

Tom reached for her hands. "You know better than to listen to gossip," he told her.

"I heard that you and George had some trouble awhile back at the post office. Is it true?" she asked him.

Tom brushed it off. "That was nothin'. Don't you be worrin' about it," he told her.

"I heard that Mr. Johnston came out of the post office with his rifle to break it up. People say that those boys threatened you. That sounds like somethin' to me. I can't help it that I worry for you and your family," she told him. "You must know, Tom, don't you?"

"I know, Anne," he told her. "I feel the same way."

He continued, "It ain't the right time, I know, but if it's alright with you, when the time is right, I'm gonna ask your Pa for your hand." Tom was confident and serious when he spoke.

She gave him a sweet smile and nodded, yes, as she said, "Nothin' in this world could make me happier."

"I've been prayin' about this, Anne. I want the Lord's blessing and I want to be in His will. My family needs me right now, but we will be together. I promise," he told her.

He took her hands in his, put them up to his mouth, and kissed them.

"I best be goin'," he told her.

"I know," she said, with the same sweet smile.

They walked to the door and entered the hotel lobby. Mr. Randall was behind the hotel counter.

"Good day, Mr. Randall," said Tom as he passed by him.

"Bye, now," replied Mr. Randall. "You boys come back again soon."

Tom tipped his hat to Anne and said, "I'll see ya' soon." She smiled and Tom closed the door behind him. George was waiting outside the hotel. The two started toward the Mercantile. George could tell that Tom had something on his mind.

"You alright, Tom?" George asked him.

"I don't hardly know, George," he responded. "All's I know if it wasn't for the North and the South and all this fuedin' going on, I would ask for Anne's hand, and we'd start a life together as soon as tomorrow if I could. But the time just ain't right and I wish it could be different."

They didn't notice, but Hal Babcock had seen them from the tavern window across the street. He jumped out of his chair and stumbled to the door as the boys walked by.

Babcock hollered, "Hey, I told you two that we would see you later."

Tom said, "George, keep walking. He's drunk."

Hal started walking toward them with Martin Brown right behind him. He repeated, "Hey, I said, that I told you that we would be seeing you two later."

Tom turned to him and said, "We heard you the first time. We're in a hurry and we don't want trouble. I think it's best if you just go about your business."

Hal looked angry and lunged toward Tom. George grabbed him and told him, "Get your hands off my brother." Hal hit George. George hit Hal. Tom tried to pull them apart and took a few blows himself. Martin was standing by and started to go for his pistol. He didn't see Papa coming a few yards away.

Papa yelled, "Martin Brown, I wouldn't do that if I were you." Martin froze as he caught a glimpse of Papa, rifle in hand.

"You stay right there," Papa warned.

Papa's arrival and his warning ended the skirmish between Hal and the boys. "Boys," Papa said, "mind what

I say and walk away now, do ya' hear?" He didn't take his eyes off the two ruffians.

Tom and George started to move away.

Papa looked Hal in the eye and said, "Now, you two need to go somewhere and sleep off your liquor. You can thank me later for not firin' this rifle in either of your directions."

He continued, "I don't know what problem ya' have with me boys. But, if ya' have a problem with them, then ya' have a problem with me."

Hal scoffed back at him, "It seems, O'Connor, that your family needs help decidin' what side of this war they're on. Me and Martin and some other folks around here figure you're either disloyal to the South or you're cowardly. What I wanna know is which is it?"

Tom and George could see the fire in Papa's eyes. There had been a day when those would have been fightin' words to Daniel O'Connor, but not anymore. He was not a foolish man. These men were not worth risking harm to his sons or to himself.

Papa pointed his rifle and looked Hal square in the eye. "I will be gracious and forget that you said those words to me, Hal Babcock, but take heed, man. If you bother anyone in my family again, I won't wait to find you stumblin' out of a tavern. I will find you and we will have a reckoning."

"Now", Papa continued, still pointing his rifle at the two men, "We are going to get in our wagon, and we are going to ride out of here, and you two are going to get out of the way." By now a crowd of witnesses had gathered.

Hal smirked and motioned Martin to stand down. Martin put his pistol in his holster. Tom and George moved toward Papa and climbed into the wagon. Papa got into the wagon next, all the while, never lowering his rifle or taking his eyes off the two drunkards.

Papa was quiet and alert as they drove back to their farm. They all knew that this was probably not the last that they would hear of this. When they got back to the farm, Papa didn't speak a word as he walked into the house. Tom and George were serious, not their playful selves when they came inside.

"Daniel, what's wrong?" asked his wife.

He spoke to the whole family when he answered. Ella and Jackson were there along with the rest of the O'Connor family. His tone was serious and the look on his face was grave when he said, "I have feared for some time that the wickedness that has come to Missoura' might touch our family one day. That day has come. The boys and I had a run in with some of the ruffians that I suspect are doing harm to folks and their property around here. They have it in for Tom and George and probably won't be givin' up on 'em anytime soon."

"Papa, what do you mean? We haven't done anything to anybody!" exclaimed Lila.

"Hush, now," scolded Mama. "Hear your Papa out."

"It makes no difference. Some folks don't need a reason to do evil," Papa continued.

"George, why couldn't you have just ignored 'em?" spouted Tom.

George lowered his eyes. He wished he could take it all back, but he couldn't.

"Now, you wait just one minute, Thomas O'Connor," Papa interrupted, "If it hadn't been those two this day, it would have been someone else tomorrow. We all knew there could come a time when the war could come uninvited to this door. The ruffians, the bushwackers, or eventually the soldiers, Union or Confederate, will most likely pay us a visit. We need to be prepared. We need to be ready."

Papa began to give us his instructions. He wanted everyone to know what was expected of them.

"Make sure that you are armed when you leave this house," Papa told them.

He addressed his wife and daughters. "Caroline, girls, do not leave this farm without one of the men."

"And, boys," he told them, "We will not leave any of the women here alone."

"Oh, Daniel, has it really come to this?" asked Aunt Caroline who was trying not to sound frightened.

"Yes, I am afraid it has," answered Papa.

He continued, "We will take turns keeping watch at night. Good neighbors have had their livestock and their horses stolen right out from under them. This family will not willingly aid either the Union or Confederacy. We will not provide horses or weapons or anything else. They will have to take them by force. And, boys, if you must aim your rifles, make sure that you don't miss. Anyone at the end of that rifle is going to be looking to harm you or one of us if they can. Do you all understand?" Papa asked.

George and Tom answered, "Yes, Sir," while everyone else nodded their heads in agreement. Papa put his rifle away, hung up his hat, and turned toward the stairs. He went to his room and closed the door. No one saw him the rest of the evening.

Not long after that, her Mama told Ella that Papa went up to pray that night. She told her that he spent most of that night weeping before the Lord, begging God to protect his family and his home from the war. He asked for the peace that passes all understanding and the courage to lead his family through this trial.

We all had heard accounts of bushwacking in Kansas and Missouri. Mail was being interrupted, telegraph lines were being cut, and farms were being raided. Men like William Quantrill and his raiders had become notorious in just about every county. Small groups of men like him started to band together and engage in the same kind of guerilla warfare, men like Martin Brown and Hal Babcock. The ruffians would steal from the local farmers and kill anyone who got in their way. When they had taken all they wanted, they would burn the farms that they had plundered. Anyone believed to be a Union sympathizer would be a target as would anyone who wouldn't join the confederate cause.

That November, not long after the run in with the two men in town, a storm came through the valley. It was cold, but not cold enough to snow. It was a wild thunderstorm. The winds blew hard, the lightning lit up the sky, and the thunder was fearsome. No one could sleep. The farm and the livestock needed to be protected from the storm and possible raiders.

"I am going to head down to the pasture and check on the cattle," Georgie said, "Tonight is one of those nights not fit for man, nor beasts."

"Yer' right about that George. Wait a bit and I'll go with you." Papa told him. He was cleaning his guns at the table.

"I'll be all right." George told him. "Just come down when you're finished. I'll be careful."

George took his rifle and went on his mission, closing the door behind him.

"Caroline, I think I'll finish cleanin' these later. I'm going to go with George and give him a hand. It would be a good idea to check on the horses, too," Papa told her.

"You best wear your coat and don't forget your hat." Mama commanded.

He smiled at her and gave her a "Yes, ma'am," as he went for his coat. He reached for a rifle that was leaning against the wall by the door, put on his hat, and stepped out on the front porch. The thunder rolled and the lightning flashed bright enough to light up the farm for a moment. In the distance, Papa saw the figure of a man crouched behind the wagon just as Georgie walked around the side of the barn. The man came around the wagon and started to follow George. Papa made haste. He surprised the intruder between the barn and the house with a rifle aimed at his head. Papa demanded that he stop. It was Hal. Georgie didn't see or hear a thing. The sound of the rain and the thunder were too loud. He kept walking toward the pasture.

"You have made a big mistake coming to my home and coming after my son," Papa told him. "Drop your rifle and raise up yer hands."

Hal dropped his rifle and raised his hands. "'Turn yerself around slow," Papa told him. Hal obeyed Papa's command.

"You ain't gonna shoot me, O'Connor," Hal sneered. "Yer too good for that. Always actin' like yer a little holier than everone else. Too good to fight along side yer neighbors."

Papa interrupted him and said, "I don't have to explain myself to the likes of you. You who use war as an excuse to steal and hurt folks just because you think you can get away with it. There will be a judgment someday for the likes of you."

Just then, a shot rang out, the thunder masking the sound. Papa fell to the ground. Martin, armed with a pistol, had been watching from the tree line. Papa had been shot in the back. The two men ran into the storm, the woods, and the night. They left Papa, lying wounded, in the cold rain.

When George got back to the house, quite a bit of time had lapsed. No one knew what had happened out in that storm. He came back by way of the horse pasture, so he never saw Papa lying wounded on the ground.

"Georgie, where's your Pa?" Mama asked him.

"I ain't seen him. I thought he was still in here with all of you," Georgie replied.

"No, he followed right out after you. He wanted to check on the horses and help you with the cattle," Mama told him.

Lila looked concerned.

"Don't look so worried," Georgie told her. "He probably is trying to calm down that mare, so she won't go crazy and bust down her stall. I think that's where Tom is. I'll go down and see if I can find out what's keeping them."

George stepped out onto the porch. Mama followed him. He saw a figure down by the barn. At first, he thought it was Papa. He called out to him, but no one answered.

As he walked closer, he realized it was Tom. He was on his knees leaning over Papa who was lying on the ground.

George ran towards the barn. Mama ran out into the storm after him. The cold rain was pouring down on all of them.

"Help me get him up, George," Tom said frantically.

Is he alright? Daniel, can you hear me?" cried Mama.

"We have to get him inside." Tom told her.

George and Tom carried him to the house. Lucy and Lila were waiting by the door.

"Papa," cried Lila.

"Oh, Papa," cried Lucy.

Both girls were sobbing. George and Tom took him into the small bedroom on the main floor and laid him on the bed.

"You girls, hush," commanded their mother. "Go and fetch me some clean sheets, Lucy. Lila, you start boiling some water. He's bleeding bad. We have to hurry."

Mama could always keep her head, but her children saw a look of fear in her eyes this night that they had never seen before.

She continued with a tone of urgency, "Tom, go down to Jackson and Ella's place. Send them up here and then, you go and fetch the doctor right away."

She tore the sheets to make bandages and started to dress the wound. She tried to slow the bleeding. His clothes were wet, and he was cold from lying in the rain. He tried to speak, but she wanted him to be still and keep quiet. Lucy, with tears in her eyes said, "Mama, he wants to tell you something."

"What is it Daniel?" she asked as she leaned closer to him. Papa was struggling, but managed to get a few words out, "I love you, my darlin', Caroline," he said. "You are a good woman and a good wife. Trust in the Lord." She tried to give him a reassuring smile, but she could hardly find one. "She looked into his eyes and said, "I will always love you, Daniel O'Connor."

Papa looked at Georgie and tried to speak again. Georgie moved closer and heard the words, "Babcock", he said, "Babcock."

George froze. Papa closed his eyes and never opened them again. Those last words were more than George could bear. In that moment, he wore the weight of the world on his shoulders. He collapsed into a chair in the corner of the room, bent over, with his face in his hands. He cried, "This is my fault. It's all my fault."

When Jackson and Ella got there, they heard Lucy and Lila sobbing. George was in the corner, beside himself with guilt, tears running down his face. Mama was sitting next to Papa on the bed, stroking his face and hair. She was silent and showed no emotion.

Ella put her arms around Mama without saying a word. She could only weep. She noticed that she was shivering in her wet clothes. Ella tried to pull her away, "Mama, you're freezin'," she told her, "Please come and warm yourself by the fire." Mama didn't speak, and she didn't move.

When Tom came back with the doctor, it was too late. Papa was gone, and Mama was almost catatonic. The doctor managed to get her upstairs with the help of the girls. They finally got her out of the cold, wet clothes and tucked her in bed.

The next morning, she was delirious with a fever. She kept calling for Papa, but he couldn't come. The doctor stayed for three days, helping Ella, Lucy, and Lila tend to her. It was to no avail. The fever took her. To this day, Ella says that her Mama didn't die from a fever. She says that she died of a broken heart.

Daniel and Caroline O'Connor were an example to their children and to others of what God intended marriage to be. They loved to be together. They loved to talk to each other. They loved to laugh with one another. And, neither could have lived without the other.

Whether they were sitting by the fire or on the front porch or riding to town in the wagon, they were holding one another's hand, or they were arm in arm. They worked together and had a common goal. It was to "love the Lord thy God with all thy heart" (Deuteronomy 6:5a) and "love thy neighbor as thyself" (Matthew 22:39b). Their faith was the foundation that they built their marriage on.

Daniel knew that Caroline was a gift. He knew that God gave him the gift of her, and he was grateful. She respected and adored her husband. Ella said that her Papa and her Mama had one heart. When they took their vows before God, they meant it. God made two hearts into one heart that day. Time spent together, growing in the Lord made the threads of their hearts so intertwined that they could never be separated.

When her Papa died, so did part of her Mama's heart. Their children found comfort in knowing that they were still together for all eternity in the presence and glory of the Lord. Had this not been so, they would have never been able to bear losing them both at once.

It didn't take long for folks to hear what happened at the farm. The next day Charles, Anne, and Mrs. Randall came to help however they could. George and Tom were gone. They had saddled up and rode out that morning almost without a word. Jackson wanted to go with them, but Tom wouldn't hear of leaving the women alone at the farm. They had all made that promise to their Papa.

When Charles got there with his Ma and his sister, Jackson left him to care for the women while he went looking for George and Tom. By the time he caught up with them, they had already found Brown and Babcock at the tavern in town. Jackson was too late.

They two had walked into the tavern, mostly unnoticed, until they called Brown and Babcock out.

"We have a score to settle with you," Tom told them.

Both men stood up from the table with their hands on their guns. Georgie and Tom were also ready to draw.

"Martin, do you see what I see? If it isn't the yellow belly, Yankee lovers," Hal sneered.

Georgie answered angrily, "That's funny coming from someone who shoots a man in the back."

George's words provoked Martin and he drew. Tom beat him to the draw and took him down. As Hal started to draw George lunged toward him and the two men wrestled to the ground. A gun fired and in a few moments time, both Brown and Babcock were dead.

The Provost Marshall arrived right after Jackson. Provost Marshall's had been appointed to keep law and order according to Union regulations. Some were honest and committed to upholding the law, others could be bought and bribed. This Marshall didn't want to be bothered with anything messy. The witnesses said that Martin Brown drew first and that the men were shot in self-defense. The Marshall accepted the testimonies, and nothing more was said to Tom or George again about what happened that day.

Chapter 9

Goodbye Again

Thoughts of that November day had made Jackson's heart heavy. "I have to let it go," he thought to himself. "I have to face today."

He went inside the house where he found Tom and Anne sitting together quietly. Ella sat in the chair by the fireplace with her back to everyone, staring into the flames that were burning in the fireplace. Anne got up and greeted Jackson. Ella didn't move.

"It is good to see you, Jackson," Anne told him.

"Thank you, Anne. I appreciate that," Jackson replied. "Congratulations to you and Tom. Ella told me the news. I will be looking forward to meeting the new addition to the family when I get back."

There had been a lot of changes since the war started. Tom and Anne were expecting their first child after the New Year. Charles Randall, Anne's brother, married Lila back in the spring and Lucy married Amos Whiteaker later in the summer. At first, Charles and Lila and Amos and Lucy stayed at the O'Connor farm. They lived in the big house with George, while Tom and Anne stayed down at the cabin.

They all felt that they owed it to Papa and Mama to keep their legacy alive. They committed to keeping the farm going, at least until the end of the war. However, the war changed things. Charles joined up and Lila moved to the hotel to help the Randalls. Jeremiah Whiteaker joined up, so, Amos and Lucy moved to the Whiteaker farm to help Amos' family. Now, only Tom, Anne, George, and Ella were left to keep their family farm going.

The front door opened. It was George.

"Did you tell them, Jackson?" he asked.

"No, George, I didn't think it was my place to tell them," he replied.

Ella flashed Jackson a look and then fixed her eyes on Georgie as if she already knew what he was going to say.

"Tell us what?" Tom asked with a suspicious look on his face.

"Well, I've been doing a lot of thinking and I have decided that I am going with Jackson. I'm gonna join up," George explained.

"George, No," exclaimed Anne. "Doesn't this family have enough to worry about without having to worry about you, too?"

Tom scolded her, "Anne, hush now. Don't get yerself all worked up."

He turned to George and said, "Anne is right, George. With Jackson gone, we're caring for his place and his live-stock on top of what we do here on our own farm. We are hearing more and more about the bushwackers raidin' farms. They are getting closer and closer all the time. We need you here to help defend our homes and our family."

"That's why I need to go," George answered. The sooner this war is over, the sooner the raidin' and the bushwackin' will be over. There will be law and order again. We will be able to sleep with both of our eyes closed at night and not be in fear of harm coming to our homes, our women, or ourselves.

Ella finally spoke. She was calm and as a matter of fact.

"It's no use, Tom," she said, "Let him go. If there is one thing that I have learned, it's that you can't keep a man from war once he has taken up the cause."

"Ella, that's not fair," scolded Jackson. Her expression turned cold. This wasn't the warm sweet Ella that always looked for good in everything.

"Fair," she replied. "What is fair about any of this Jackson Caldwell? Life is not fair and you of all people know it. Men fighting for a cause that they may or may not believe in. Is that fair? Women losing the men they love, children losing their fathers, families losing their homes, for what? Is that fair?

"Ella, I'm sorry," George told her. "I didn't mean to cause you any harm over this."

"Harm, George," Ella interrupted. She spoke slowly and deliberately, "We have been harmed over... and over........ and over and not because of our own doin'. We had no choice, no say in any of things that have happened.

Ella continued, "I am tryin' to find a way to accept every day how it comes. I am tryin' to believe God at His Word and trust that He has me and you, Anne and Tom, Lila and Charles, Lucy and Amos, and Jackson all in His hands. You men folk and this awful war don't make it easy.

"Ella, you can't blame us for this war," scolded Jackson.

"Maybe not, Jackson," she continued. She began to speak quicker with less control. "But, I can blame greed and selfishness. I can blame the wickedness and pride that lies in the recesses of every man's heart and the devil that feeds it. Don't you see?" Ella tried to make him understand. "I am afraid, and so is every woman like me."

Jackson moved toward her and reached for her hand, but she pushed him away. She turned and stared into the fire as she continued to speak.

"It is not that we can't accept what is done," she explained. "It is being afraid of what is still to come and believing that we can bear up under it."

The fire wasn't only burning in the fireplace, it was burning in Ella's Irish eyes. She turned back to Jackson and fixed them on him.

Then, she said, "Two small children watching their Ma and Pa die like you and Nathaniel did is not fair. Uncle Richard and his family losing Aunt Jane so soon is not fair. You know that things would have been different for them if Aunt Jane had still been alive when this war started. We have all suffered for it."

Then, she turned to George and Tom, "And, what about our Papa and Mama, boys? Papa gave his life to protect us and Mama died of a broken heart because of it. They still had good years left ahead of them, years with us. Their grandchildren will never know them. Is that fair?"

Ella could feel her knees growing weak. It was all so overwhelming, but she was not going to let herself fade. She put her hand on the chair, steadied herself, and calmly said, "George, if you are going to go, then, hurry up and get your things."

She looked at Anne and said, "Anne, please gather some food for George. I only packed enough in Jackson's sack for one person."

Finally, she turned to Jackson, "The day is wastin', Jackson, and I don't want to be worryin' about you not makin' the most of daylight. If you get goin' soon, you may be able to meet up with another regiment before night fall."

Jackson didn't say a word. He slowly walked to the fireplace and started stoking the fire. It wasn't long before George came down the stairs carrying what he would need for their journey. This was it. It was time to say good-bye.

George hugged Tom and Anne.

"Take care of yourself, George," Tom told him. Anne was silent with tears in her eyes.

Then, George approached Ella who was standing arms folded. She didn't respond. She almost seemed frozen. George put his arm around her neck, anyway, kissed her on top of the head and said, "Good-bye, Big Sister. I'll be seein' ya." Ella still didn't move. She just closed her eyes tightly. George turned and walked to the door.

Tom and Anne followed George while Ella and Jackson were left standing alone. Ella took a deep breath. She walked over to the sack on the floor that she had packed for him. She picked it up and approached her husband. She took his hand, placed the sack in it. She reached for his canteen on the table and put his other arm through the strap. "You'll be needin' these," she told him.

Jackson put his arms around her and hugged her, but she didn't hug him back. He let go, kissed her on the forehead, turned, and walked to the door. He only got a few feet out the door before Ella couldn't take it anymore. She didn't say a word. She just hurried as fast as she could to catch him and wrap her arms around his neck.

She whispered, "I love you".

"I love you, too," he said softly.

She squeezed him as if she would never let him go, but she did let go. She let him go and he mounted his horse. George was already mounted, waiting for him. She waved to George and gave him a thoughtful smile. Then, her eyes met Jackson's eyes one more time. She smiled, waved, and blew him a soft kiss. He smiled back at her and the two men rode away.

Jackson and George began their journey in silence. Both men had a lot of things on their minds. Finally, Jackson broke the silence and said, "If you don't mind, George, I'm goin' to take a little detour to my brother's place. I feel like I need to talk to him before I go away again."

George nodded. He understood. He was a good man and a good friend.

Nathaniel Caldwell's place was a good distance from Caldwell Plantation and the O"Connor farm. It was still in the county, but Nathaniel had moved far enough away so that he didn't have much contact with the rest of the family. He lived there with his wife, Rose, and their daughter, Dorie.

Chapter 10

The Battle of Wilson's Creek

Nathaniel signed up for the Guard right after Jackson did. They both fought at the Battle of Wilson's Creek. They both were wounded. They both were sent to the Missouri State Guard Hospital. Jackson's wounds eventually healed so that he could join the fight again, but Nathaniel's wounds were more severe. The doctors said that he was lucky that he didn't lose his leg. Jackson knew that it was because of God's grace and mercy, not luck.

Even though Nathaniel didn't lose his leg, his wounds left him with a bad limp. He was still able to walk, but he couldn't go back to the fight. Instead, he went home to his wife and his little girl.

Nathaniel would have never joined the Guard if it hadn't been for Jackson volunteering first. He was never sympathetic to the Confederate cause, and he had a strong belief that no man should be owned by another man. Because Nathaniel had always felt responsible for his little brother, especially after their Ma and Pa were killed, he couldn't let Jackson go off to war without him.

Jackson wasn't sympathetic to the cause either. He wasn't for the war or for either side. He believed that folks should mind their own business just like Papa O'Connor said. Even so, Jackson knew that the time would come when he would have to choose a side. Uncle Richard and his boys and some of their other neighbors volunteered for the Guard. Jackson would not take up arms against Uncle Richard or anyone else in the family, so he volunteered for the Guard, too.

Jackson and George were rounding a bend, still quite a distance from Nathaniel's place when George asked the question, "Jackson, what's it like?".

"What's what like?" Jackson replied.

"Bein' a soldier. What's it like bein' face to face with other men in a battle?" George asked him.

"I don't know if I can rightly explain it," said Jackson.

He paused and thought about it for a moment.

"I think," he continued, "that it's probably different for everybody. Some don't seem bothered by it, but it bothers me. God is the giver of life. When a man understands the value of life, it is going to get a hold of him when he has to take one."

"Does it ever get easier?" George wondered.

"Maybe for some, those that have had their conscience seared, the ones who want to justify the killin'," said Jackson. "It never gets easier for me. I still see some of their faces in my mind. Others, I still picture falling to the ground off in the distance. I wonder who they are. I wonder if they have a family somewhere. Some of them, George, are just boys, not even men yet."

"Are you ever afraid?", asked George.

"All the time," replied Jackson honestly, "If I didn't have the Lord to help me, I don't know if I could do it. I just remember that nothin's gonna happen to me that is beyond His will, and then, I trust Him."

"What about when you got shot? Did you think that you might not make it?" George was earnest in his questions.

"No, at first I was out cold and didn't know what had happened. When I came to, all I could think about was Nathaniel. If it wasn't for me, he wouldn't have even been alongside that creek that day. He was looking out for me. It was my fault that he got hurt so bad."

Jackson would never forget that day and the battle that would leave his brother lame for the rest of his life. It was August 10, 1861. It happened near Springfield at Wilson's Creek, the beginning of the Civil War for Missouri and the first time that the Missouri State Guard would fight beside the Confederate Army.

His regiment had set up camp just southwest of Springfield by Wilson's Creek. They had been there for about a week scouting for Yankees and bushwackers. It was hot, too hot to sleep. Around midnight, they heard a rumor that were going to break camp and start moving toward Springfield to join up with the Confederate Army there. They never made it. The Confederates joined them instead. Around daybreak, their combined forces crossed paths with Union troops near their camp.

The men were confident, maybe a little too confident. They had been talking about giving the Yankees a good licking and sending them running back up North. Instead, even though they were outnumbered, the Yankees put up a good fight. In the beginning, it looked like they might even win. The fighting only lasted about six hours, but it felt like days to Jackson.

The Yankees surprised them by attacking from behind. There was a lot of panic and confusion. Jackson's group was supposed to hold their ground in a field between the artillery and a tree line along the creek. Nathaniel and Jackson took cover behind some rocks on the right flank. They were taking a lot of heavy fire, but they were giving it right back at them. The Yankees tried to rush them from the trees, but they held their position. Their orders were to hold that line no matter what and they did. But, before it was all over, their group paid a heavy price.

They lost some good men that day. Jacob Johannsen was the youngest, only seventeen. His Pa was sick and couldn't join up, so Jake joined up in his place. He wanted to do his part and make his family proud.

When the fighting started, he froze. Maybe he was trying to find a familiar face to follow, or he was looking for a place to take cover, but he just stood there. Jackson saw him in the distance and yelled his name, but Jacob couldn't hear him. The sound of gunfire, cannons, and soldiers yelling made it impossible. Anderson started out after him, but he didn't stand a chance out in the open like that. He was shot down within minutes.

"I understand why he did it, joined up, I mean," Jackson told George, "But, if you ask me, it wasn't worth it. He was brave and made his family proud, but if it were me, I would rather have my boy back."

Then, Jackson told him about Russell Watkins. He was an old timer, a granddaddy. When their regiment got surprised from behind, Russell reacted the quickest causing a ruckus that gave everyone enough time to take cover. He hollered out and started rushing toward the enemy, firing his guns. He drew fire on himself and saved a lot of men that day.

"Sometimes, I think about his family," Jackson said thoughtfully, "I wonder how they're livin' without him and who's takin' care of them."

George had never seen Jackson like this before. He wasn't angry or anxious. He was grief stricken. The loss of these men genuinely pained him.

Finally, Jackson told him about Joe Peterson. When the fighting started, Joe never stopped. It was like nothing Jackson had ever seen. He didn't set out after any Yankees. It wasn't like that. He was just taking up for their own men. If a Yankee was getting the best of somebody, Joe was right there. He just kept moving from one fight to the next. Jackson couldn't even guess how many men he saved that day, but he knew for sure that there were a lot of men who lived to tell about the Battle of Wilson's Creek because of him.

"Sounds like he was really somethin'," George told him.

Jackson nodded. "He was, but he didn't know it. He didn't think he was worth anything because he didn't have nobody."

One night, Jackson and Joe were both on guard duty, talking, trying to keep each other awake. Jackson asked him where he came from and if he had any family. Joe told him that he was orphaned when he was young and that there was nobody to take care of him. He stayed in a barn at a livery stable, cleaning out the stalls in exchange for a place to sleep and something to eat.

Joe had to grow up fast as a matter of survival. After he had gotten a little older and a little braver, he put what little he had in a sack, hopped a train for St. Louis, and got a job working for the railroad until he enlisted.

Jackson asked Joe what he thought about coming home with him after the war. He told him that they would give him a job and a place to stay. Joe couldn't believe it. He was grateful to Jackson for the offer, but he didn't want to be a burden to anybody or have folks feeling sorry for him. Jackson told him that it wasn't like that. He told Joe that's what friends do for each other, and it was an honor to call him friend.

It was evident how much Jackson cared for Joe as he told George about him. He knew that if it hadn't been for Uncle Richard and Aunt Jane taking care of them, he and Nathaniel might have ended up just like Joe.

"I never figured out why he joined up, George. He didn't have anything at stake. He didn't have any family fightin'," Jackson told him.

"What happened to him?" George asked.

Jackson's tone of voice changed from thoughtful to angry as he said, "He got shot down tryin' to help somebody that was wounded."

Jackson paused a moment, then, he said, "He didn't know how much he mattered to me and to the rest of the men. He thought everyone else mattered more than him, like his life wasn't worth as much. I wonder sometimes if we weren't all entertaining an angel unawares like the Bible talks about. Like, maybe, he was a ministering angel sent to protect all of us."

George didn't have to prod anymore. Jackson's memories of that day started to pour out. He began recalling how he was wounded.

Jackson, Nathaniel, and a few other men got cut off from the rest of the group and were pinned down. They had two choices. They could wait it out knowing they would be sitting ducks after their ammunition ran out, or they could make a run for it and try to get back to the rest of their regiment.

They decided that they didn't want to risk being captured, so they were going to run for it. Bradshaw and Anderson agreed to cover Nathaniel and Jackson, until they got across the field. Once they made it to the next cluster of rocks, they were going to signal and cover Bradshaw and Anderson so they could make a run for it, too.

Nathaniel could run fast. "Remember when we were kids, George?" Jackson asked him. "There wasn't anybody who could run faster than Nathaniel. We both thought we could make it with cover." Jackson could picture it all so clearly in his head. It was as if he were back in that field.

"It was so loud," he told George, "The sound of gunfire and cannons, men hollerin' as they charged, and the wailing of the wounded. There was so much confusion. Nathaniel told me to stay close, no matter what. Then, he took off runnin'. I was right behind him. He ran low, dodging from side to side. I followed and tried to keep up."

Just as Jackson saw Nathaniel land safely behind a large rock, he felt a shock go through him like he had never felt before. It was so bad that it knocked him down to the ground. Nathaniel was safe, and he would have been alright, but he went back for Jackson. That was the last thing he remembered.

Nathaniel picked him up trying to half carry, half drag him to safety. Bradshaw and Anderson tried to cover him, but he got hit and went down, too. Nathaniel didn't give up. He kept his sight set on those rocks. He got hit again, but he kept pulling and dragging until both he and his brother were safe behind them. "We won the battle, George," Jackson told him. "The Yankees retreated. But, if you ask me, no one won that day. Both sides lost well over a thousand men. The Yankees even lost one of their generals. I think, Lyon was his name."

Jackson had no recollection of what happened after he was shot until he woke up in a wagon on his way to a field hospital. He hollered out for Nathaniel, but he didn't get an answer. If anyone knew where he was, they weren't telling Jackson. A couple of days later, at the MSG hospital, he finally found out what had happened.

One of the men in their regiment told Jackson that he saw Nathaniel pick him up and carry him to safety. He also told him that Nathaniel didn't give up even though he was wounded. He pulled and dragged and pulled some more until they both were safe behind those rocks. When the shooting was over, they went looking for the wounded. Anderson said that when they got to the brothers, he was afraid that they both were dead.

George was quiet as Jackson kept talking.

"After I was able to get up and move around, I went lookin' for Nathaniel at the hospital. When I found him, he wasn't doin' very good. He couldn't walk and was still in a lot of pain. I went every day and sat by his bed until they released me. We would talk, and I would read the Bible to him. The men in the beds around him were bad off, too. Some would listen while I read and ask me questions about what they heard. I got to tell them about the Love of

God and about His grace and mercy. Some of them were so open and thirsty for the Spring of Living Water, but not Nathaniel. I was worried about him, George, and I'm still worried. You see, I owe him so much. I just gotta try and reach him somehow.

The two men were both quiet now. Jackson had given George a lot to think about. By this time, they were about halfway to Nathaniel's place.

After he left the war, Nathaniel, with the help of a few neighbors, was finally able to add on to the tiny cabin that was already on his land. It was a comfortable cabin that kept his family safe and warm. He had just enough acreage that he could manage on his own. Even with his bad leg, he would never own a slave or depend on slave labor to make a living. The community of slaves at Caldwell Plantation made an impression on him from the very first day. That impression became a strong conviction for him that all men should be free.

Chapter 11

Nathaniel and Obadiah

J ackson was deep in thought as he remembered back to that day when he and Nathaniel first came down the lane that led to Caldwell Plantation. The boys had just lost their Ma and Pa. They were both sad, afraid, and uncertain about where they were going and who they were going to meet.

They passed by the slaves working in Uncle Richard's fields on their way to the house. They saw mama's and daddy's, old people, and even children who were not much older than they were. As the slaves worked, they sang. Jackson and Nathaniel had never heard songs like the ones that they were singing before. These songs, their Spirituals, were songs of faith and hope. They became special to both the boys.

Nathaniel grew to love many of the men, women, and children that spent their lives in bondage at Caldwell Plantation. In the evenings, he would often sneak down to the cabins where they lived. He felt like he belonged to them more than the family up at the planation house.

There was an understanding, an empathy from these slave people for Nathaniel that no one in the plantation house could ever give him. Some of them understood what it meant to lose someone that they loved. Many of them understood what it was like to have the life that they loved suddenly taken away from them. Others knew what it was like to be thrust into a world that was not their own and be expected to accept it and live in it with no objections.

Uncle Richard and Aunt Jane did their best to make Nathaniel and Jackson part of their family, but Nathaniel wouldn't allow himself to get too close to them. Most of the time, he acted like he didn't want to be there, partly because he was still so angry, and partly because he just didn't want to ever hurt again.

There was one person that could usually get through to Nathaniel when no one else could. Obadiah, or Obie, as some people called him, was a house servant at Caldwell Plantation. He took it upon himself to help an angry little boy find some peace after what had happened to him and his family. Jackson believed that God gave him to Nathaniel to minister to him, and Obie took up the task most graciously. He loved God and loved others, even those who transgressed against him. This was a lesson that he would try to teach Nathaniel over and over throughout the years.

Obie was a slave. He knew transgression. He also understood loss. He knew what it was like to live with an emptiness in his heart, just like Nathaniel. Obie's father, a slave, died before he was born.

Obie only spoke of his father once. Nathaniel never told another soul about it except for Jackson. One day when Nathaniel was having a fit, feeling sorry for himself, he ran to Obie as usual. Obie would find some way to distract Nathaniel from whatever was bothering him and help him feel better. This time was a rare time when Nathaniel didn't want to be comforted. Instead, he lashed out at Obie, acting as if he was the only person in the world who had ever suffered. The usually, patient, Obadiah, gave it right back to him this time. The man of few words stopped Nathaniel in his tracks and told him a story that he would never forget.

"Boy," he said, "now you are gettin' too old to keep feelin' sorry for yerself. You act like you's the only one who ever lost anybody. At least you knew your Mamie and Pappy. There are a lot of folks on this here plantation that can't say that myself included. I didn't know my Pappy, but I don't go around mad at the world over what I missed. You got to stop this. You hear me?"

Nathaniel, surprised by the scolding, pulled himself together. It was obvious to Obie that Nathaniel felt ashamed, so he quietly waited. Nathaniel was quiet for a little while, too. Then, he found the courage to ask Obie the question:

"Obadiah," he said.

"Yes, boy?" Obie replied.

"What happened to your Pappy?"

Obie didn't look at Nathaniel. He thought for a moment. Then, he raised his head and looked off in the distance. He began to tell Nathaniel about his Mamie and Pappy and the story of his Pappy's fate.

"My Pappy died before I was born. I never got to see him, but my Mamie told me everything about him. He was big and tall and strong. She said there wasn't nothin' that he couldn't do. Folks liked him because he was always lookin' out for other people, especially them that wasn't strong like him."

Obadiah had Nathaniel's complete attention. Nathaniel had never heard him speak like this before. Obadiah had always been a man of very few words, so it was evident that this was something that really mattered to him.

Obadiah continued, "Mamie said that he was gentle and kind with children and woman folk, but that he wasn't afraid of no man. He believed that one day he would be free and wasn't afraid to say so. He even had Mamie believin' that someday they would be free together."

The account of his father's death was burned into Obie's mind. He had memorized every detail that his mother had told him. He recounted the events to Nathaniel just the way he heard them.

"My Pappy made a plan to run away and take Mamie with him. Mamie was sore afraid, but she couldn't let him go without her. So, they planned to meet one night in the woods after everyone was asleep. Mamie snuck away without no one noticin', but the overseer found out that Pappy was gone before they got too far away. He went to the other slave shacks to see if anyone else was missin' and found out Mamie was gone, too."

Obie was intense as he continued to tell Nathaniel the story.

"Mamie was waitin' right where Pappy told her to meet him. He took her by the hand, and they ran, and they ran. Before too long they figured out that they had been found out because they could hear a hound dog in the distance. The overseer had taken two men and a hound out after them when he found out Pappy and Mamie was gone. My

Pappy wouldn't give up, though. He had made up his mind that he would never go back. He was gonna be free or he would die tryin'."

"Did they get caught, Obie?"

"Pappy helped Mamie into a tree. Then, he tore off pieces of his shirt and scattered them in different directions, running as fast as he could away from her to try and get that hound dog off their trail. He circled back around, climbed up a tree hisself and hid in the dark up over that trail."

Nathaniel felt his sadness through his words. Obie looked to the ground. He wasn't saying anymore, but Nathaniel really needed to know. He coaxed him just a little with the curiosity of a child.

"Then what happened, Obadiah," Nathaniel asked him.

Obie turned his head, looked away, and said, "Mamie told me that she could hear the sound of the hound dog getting closer and closer. When the men passed under Pappy up in that tree, he jumped one of them. It was too dark to see anything, but she could hear that dog barking and growling. Then, she heard one of the men call the dog off."

More silence, then Obie said, "Mamie heard the sounds of men strugglin', fightin'. She heard a gunshot and knew that they had killed my Pappy."

"What did she do?" questioned Nathaniel.

"She told me she was so scared 'cause she knew that they was going to find her. The dog was gettin' closer and closer until he was barkin' at the bottom of the tree that she was a sittin' in. The overseer aimed his gun up at her in that tree."

"Did they hurt her?" Nathaniel asked anxiously.

Obie shook his head.

"She told me that her heart was pounding so bad that she thought it would pound right out of her chest. She couldn't move, and she couldn't talk. He was almost a laughin' at her when he said, 'Looks like you didn't get too far, now did ya?'"

"When she didn't say nothin' he raised his rifle and he told her, 'Girl, if you know'd what's good for ya', you'll climb down out of that tree, right now, ya' hear?'. Mamie said that she just closed her eyes tight and climbed out of the tree. One of the men grabbed her, tied up her hands, and made her walk back to the plantation."

"What happened to her then?" Nathaniel asked him.

"The master was waitin'. He came out of the house into the dark holdin' a lantern. He asked them where my Pappy was. They told him that he was a lyin' out in the woods."

"What happened to your Mamie, Obie?" Nathaniel asked him.

"They locked Mamie in the shed while they took the wagon out to the woods for my Pappy. It wasn't too long after that night that the master sold her off. He couldn't keep her after she tried to run off because he didn't want the other slaves gettin' ideas. He sold her as a field slave even though she didn't know nothin' 'bout no field work."

Nathaniel felt angry, but it was a different kind of anger than what he felt a while ago. It wasn't anger about himself or his circumstances. It was anger over right and wrong and injustice.

He blurted out, "That ain't right, Obadiah. It just ain't right. Your Mamie didn't deserve that."

"Now you listen here, boy." Obie commanded. "The Lord's ways aren't our ways. What they did to my Pappy and to my Mamie wasn't right, but the Lord was with them. Just like He's been with you and Jackson all this time."

Nathaniel thought for a moment. Obie could tell that it was still hard for him to see the hand of God in such difficult trials, so he continued to try to help Nathaniel understand.

"My Mamie only had my Pappy for a little while, but she accepted that as the Good Lord's plan. She was grateful for what little time they had and praised God for it. They made vows to each other before God and loved one another with their whole hearts even if it was only for a short time. After Pappy died, The Lord gave Mamie strength to endure, and soon after, He gave her a boy child, too. He gave her me."

Nathaniel was trying to understand. Obie wanted him to see the hand of God in the trials of His parents. He wanted Him to see that God was even using what had happened to them to work in the heart of Nathaniel, but the heart of this child was still so broken. He could not find any goodness in the presence of so much pain.

Nathaniel thought some more, trying to make sense of everything that Obadiah had told him.

Then, Nathaniel asked him, "How was it that you and your Mamie came to be here with Uncle Richard and Aunt Jane?"

"When I was a boy, not as old as you, the new master fell on hard times. One day he told Mamie and some of the other slaves to put what they had in a sack and load up in the wagon. Mamie figured that meant me, too. So, we loaded up, and he took us to St. Louis where he planned to sell off as many of us as he could."

"Were you afraid, Obie? Nathaniel wondered.

"Yes, boy, I was real scared. I didn't know what was goin' to happen. Mamie was scared, too, but she tried to not to let me know it. I remember wrappin' my arms tight around her while she stood so still, like she was frozen. We was lined up so folks could look at us. Mamie didn't look at nobody. She lifted her head straight up and stared into the blue sky. It was like she was lookin' for help to fall right down from heaven."

"Is that what happened, Obie? Help came down from heaven?" Nathaniel asked him with an undertone of anger and disbelief.

"Master Caldwell was in St. Louis that day, so I guess, I'll say, yes," Obie answered. Nathaniel looked surprised. "It was no accident that he was needin' some help to build up this here plantation," Obie told him. "He saw us and thought that Mamie might be a help to Miss Jane. I don't think he was lookin' for a boy, but I sure am grateful to the Lord that He kept me and Mamie together. We may not have been what the Master came for, but we was what he got. He looked at me holdin' on to Mamie and the next thing I knew he was a takin' us with him. I don't know why, but I wasn't scared nomore. I knew this Master was a goin' to take care of us."

Obie never knew what prompted Uncle Richard to bring him and his Mamie home, but he knew that something about them struck Uncle Richard that day. Jackson wondered if it was because of what had happened to Uncle Richard and his Pa when they were young. He remembered his Pa telling his Ma about how he and his brothers were separated from their parents when they were boys, sent away as apprentices to help pay off the family debts. Jackson and Nathaniel's Pa seemed to be able to live with it, but Uncle Richard never really got over it. Whatever the reason, Uncle Richard paid a large sum that day to secure both mother and son to his possession.

Obie had said all that he was going to say. Nathaniel had a choice to make. Would he heed what Obie told him and let it change him, or would he stay wrapped up in his own personal pain and continue to be angry about it? His fits happened less often after that, but his anger was redirected. Over time, slave masters, including Uncle Richard and his boys, became the object of his anger. This made life at the plantation an even bigger struggle for Nathaniel.

Life at Caldwell Plantation was better for Cassie and Obadiah than from where they came from, but they were still slaves. Cassie became Aunt Jane's right arm and Obie eventually grew to be Uncle Richard's man servant. He started out taking care of Uncle Richard's horse, fetching his boots and coat, and, running after anything else that he needed. As he grew and gained Uncle Richard's confidence, he was given responsibilities in running the household.

Obie was a grown man by the time that Jackson and Nathaniel came there. Nathaniel soon became Obie's shadow. There was an understanding between the two of them. Neither of them belonged. Each was biding his time, but neither knew when or where they would go.

Even though Obie didn't talk much, he tried to do things to make Nathaniel smile or laugh. Sometimes,

Aunt Jane would send Obie fishing with Nathaniel down at the creek. She was aware of their special friendship and encouraged it when Nathaniel's inner struggles seemed to be getting the best of him. Sometimes, Obie would pack a "surprise" in Nathaniel's fishing basket. Nathaniel would reach in and find a little frog, or a mouse that would make him jump and they would both laugh.

Obie was smart. He didn't have an education, but he was practical and had common sense. He was kind and compassionate. He used his position and privileges as a house servant for the benefit of the other slaves whenever he could. He would make sure that Uncle Richard and Aunt Jane knew what was happening in their slave community. Their overseer didn't always tell them right away if a slave was sick or if one had a need, but Obie would.

Uncle Richard kept his slaves isolated from the outside world. Cassie and Obie were the only exceptions. Obie would sometimes take Aunt Jane and the girls to the mercantile in town. He would wait patiently by the carriage where he would sometimes hear men talking. They would talk about business, the railroad, crops, the weather, politics, and anything else relevant to the day. It was here that Obie first heard about the Underground Railroad.

On Sundays, he would drive Aunt Jane and the girls to church in the carriage while the men would ride along on horseback. There was a gallery in the back of the church where the slaves could listen to the Gospel message delivered by the preacher. The preacher's words pierced Obie's heart and he became a believer.

He shared what he heard in town and in church with the other slaves. It gave them hope, the hope of freedom in this life and in the next. Obie told them about the Underground Railroad and the opportunity for freedom that could be found in the North. And, even more importantly, he told them what he heard from the Word of God, how they could be eternally free from the bondage of sin with life everlasting.

Nathaniel, too, hoped that Obie and the other slaves would someday be free. His convictions about slavery became stronger and stronger as he grew, and he became more and more vocal with his objections about it. When rumors of war began, Nathaniel's objections started to cause conflict within the family.

Chapter 12

The Caldwell Family

J ackson and George were both preoccupied with their own thoughts as they continued riding to Nathaniel's farm. George was wondering about war and pondering the things that Jackson had told him about being a soldier. Jackson, on the other hand, was still thinking about Nathaniel and all the events in their lives that brought them both to this place in time. He knew that it was all part of a bigger plan, but he couldn't help but wonder what would have been different if Aunt Jane were still here. He had many fond memories of her. Days gone by were flooding his mind.

Aunt Jane was the center of Uncle Richard's world. He was a quiet, reserved man who didn't show emotion too readily, but it was obvious to anyone who knew him how much he cared for his wife. He spoiled and pampered her as much as he could within his means. She appreciated his devotion, but she didn't need to be spoiled or pampered. She loved being his wife. She loved him, not his success, his position, or his wealth, just him.

Aunt Jane demonstrated her love and appreciation by running his home efficiently. She took good care of the things that he had worked so hard to give her and their children. They were both proud of their home and they were especially proud of their family.

"I wish things could be different," Jackson thought to himself. "It would break Aunt Jane's heart to know what has happened to her family."

Each of the Caldwell children were a blessing to their mother, a unique piece of a puzzle that made the picture of a family. There was William, the oldest. He was tall and strong. His piece of the puzzle was smart, sensible, and dependable. He was always looking out for the rest of the children.

Next in line was Sterling, tall and lanky, a bit awkward. He was shy and a little unsure of himself because he sometimes stammered a bit. He had his mother's gift for finding the good in most things. His gift, his piece of the puzzle, was a gentle representation of perspective, especially with his brothers, who could be quick tempered.

Then, there was Elizabeth. She was petite and beautiful with dark wavy hair and big brown eyes. She was strong-minded with a good sense of right and wrong. Because she was completely devoted to her family, especially her Ma and Pa, she was the loyal piece of their family puzzle.

Mary Jane was practical and a bit of a mother hen to her younger siblings. She brought to her family the gift of music. This was her piece of the puzzle. When the other children were sad or frightened, she would sing to them. When there was strife in their home, sometimes their mother would insist that the whole family gather around the piano and sing. Sometimes Mary Jane would play a silly song that would eventually make them all laugh. Other times, she might play a hymn as a reminder to them all of love and forgiveness, conviction, and God's eternal promises.

James and Robert were a handful, just a year apart in age. They were clever, courageous, and adventurous and they both liked to show off. Their piece of the puzzle was energy, excitement, curiosity, and a zeal for facing each new day with anticipation.

Joanna was the gentle piece. She loved animals and preferred their company over people. It wasn't unusual to find her alone in the barn in the middle of a batch of kittens talking with them as if they could talk back. Her gentle heart made her especially sensitive to the pain and suffering of others.

Sarah was Uncle Richard and Aunt Jane's baby girl. No one spoke of it, but everyone suspected that she was Uncle Richard's favorite. She was the most like her mother. She looked like Aunt Jane: auburn hair, green eyes, and rosy cheeks. She had her mother's temperament. People were drawn to her just as they were to Aunt Jane. She made people feel comfortable in her presence and had a congenial way about her.

Sarah was proud of her family. To her, she had the strongest, bravest brothers in the whole world, and she admired something about each of her sisters. Sometimes she would try to dress and fix her hair just like Elizabeth. Other times, she would sing and try to make music on the piano like Mary Jane, or fuss over the animals like Joanna. Everyone treated her like a little doll. She was the darling of the family.

Pete was the youngest. He had wild, curly hair and usually a wild look in his eyes. His piece was mischievous and impulsive. He liked to stir the pot, especially where his sisters were concerned.

Uncle Richard had invested his life in making his fortune. Aunt Jane was devoted to making Caldwell Plantation a good home for her husband and her children. Uncle Richard provided safety and security. Aunt Jane was the heart of their home. Uncle Richard was driven and usually on guard. Aunt Jane was open and loving, gracious, and kind.

They were opposites in every way, a source of stability one to another. Together they were strong, unshakeable. With Aunt Jane by his side, there was nothing that Uncle Richard couldn't accomplish. She was the source of his courage.

Aunt Jane appreciated and enjoyed every day. Whether it was sunshine or rain, she would remind Uncle Richard and the children, "This is the day which the Lord hath made; We will rejoice and be glad in it" (Psalm 118:24).

She was eager to offer sweet words of encouragement and a warm embrace for each of the Caldwell children, including Jackson and Nathaniel. Jackson loved her freely. She was his mothers' sister who adopted him as one of her own. Nathaniel cared about her too. Even though he didn't show it. She never gave up on him even when he was being difficult. She loved them both unconditionally.

The other children also accepted Nathaniel and Jackson into the family. Aunt Jane made sure of it. She would not stand for any nonsense or any jealousy out of her children. She was loving but firm. She was a godly woman who taught them God's commands to love the Lord thy God and to love thy neighbor as thyself. Aunt Jane was a good example of devotion to the Lord and loving others, including her neighbors.

Neighbors and friends from town always looked forward to Aunt Jane's hospitality. Her home was always inviting. Her handiwork was in every room. She had good taste and appreciated fine things, but she made sure that the house was still a home, and that people would feel comfortable there.

The Caldwells hosted an annual picnic early every summer and a more formal party just before the harvest. Jackson remembered how much Ella looked forward to her first party. He thought it was silly, but when they were children, she would imagine herself on the way to one of Aunt Jane's parties, all grown up in a beautiful gown, driving up to the plantation in a fine carriage.

"How he wished her life was filled with picnics, parties, beautiful gowns, and carriages," he thought to himself. The war had made that impossible. The war had cast a darkness over their family that he couldn't protect her from.

Chapter 13

Coming of Age

J ackson, still lost in thought, just wanted to remember good things. Naturally, his thoughts were of Ella. He thought back to the day when the dream of her first party finally became a reality. Ella had just turned sixteen and was finally old enough to go along with her Mama and Papa to one of Aunt Jane's parties.

She didn't arrive in a fine carriage like she had dreamed about, but that didn't matter. Ella was too excited to care *how* she got there. She just wanted to get there. Her Papa drove their wagon up the lane toward the house. As they got closer, they could hear the laughter and the music. Papa stopped the wagon by the grand steps and helped her and Mama down. Ella was so excited that she wanted to run to the door. However, she somehow managed to contain herself and not look anxious as she floated up the stairs to make her grand entrance.

Obadiah was waiting by the door and was the first to greet them. As they entered the house, Aunt Jane, of course, approached them with her arms wide open to exchange a welcoming embrace. "So glad you all could come," she said hugging Ella's Mama.

She turned to Ella, took her hand, and said, "Look at you, Ella O'Connor. My, how you have grown to be such a lovely young lady. I hope that this will be a night that you will always remember fondly. A girl's first party is somethin' special."

Jackson remembered how beautiful Ella looked that night. She wore a pink gown and white gloves. Here hair was pulled back and adorned with a few small white flowers and the smile that she wore on her face was the most beautiful of all.

Aunt Jane's parties were lively, yet proper. As a hostess, she knew exactly how to set the standard for propriety yet keep the atmosphere light and merry. The ladies and gentlemen were respectful, but still playful. It truly was a night that Ella never forgot. She recounted every detail to Jackson on more than one occasion, even though he was there, too.

There were fiddlers tucked away just behind the stairway, so as not to take up any dancing space. A modest chandelier was lit high above the dancers. The music was lively and loud. There was a table with punch on the right side of the room. The piano was pushed behind it. There were pockets of people socializing everywhere. The double doors to Uncle Richard's library were wide open as was Aunt Jane's parlor doors on the other side of the gathering space. Guests mingled in both spaces, drinking punch, laughing, and visiting. On the left side of the room halfway up the stairs, observing all the festivities, were the young gentlemen, including Jackson. Some were sitting. Some were leaning over the stair rail. The younger Caldwell children in their night clothes were at the very top, peeking through the banister so as not to miss out on the merriment. Jackson smiled at her from above the crowd and greeted her with a nod of his head. She smiled up at him and started to make her way through the room.

Ella was on a mission to find her dear friend, Elizabeth Caldwell. Although Elizabeth was a little older than Ella, the girls had been friends since they were little girls. Ella found her sipping punch with Anne Randall. Elizabeth and Anne were both excited to see her. They greeted each other with quiet squeals and a squeeze of each other's hands.

"I am so glad you're finally here, Ella," Elizabeth told her. "He's here."

"Who's here?" Ella asked her.

"Oh, Ella, how can you ask such a question?" Elizabeth said to her, almost a little annoyed.

Anne answered for her, "Jeremiah, who else would she be so excited to see?"

"Yes, I saw him when we came in, sitting up on the stairs, with the other boys," Ella said.

"You mean the other young men, Ella," Anne corrected her. "We are not little boys and girls anymore."

"That's fine, Anne," Ella told her as she motioned for her friends to look at Amos Whiteaker standing behind the parlor door at the bottom of the stairs, "But, someone should have told that to the boys." The girls giggled at the sight of Amos leaning on the wall, one hand in his pocket, and the other tossing a small ball up in the air.

Elizabeth had set her affections on Amos' older brother, Jeremiah Whiteaker. The Whiteakers were neighbors of the Caldwells and the O'Connors. Each family had worked hard to build their homes, their families, and make a living off working their land. Each family had been in Missouri before it became a state. Each family was well known and respected in the county.

Even though these families shared a love for the land and the territory, they did not always share the same political views. More than once, a festive gathering was interrupted by men, cigars, and a heated political debate. The women folk could usually use their charms to diffuse their disagreements, but evenings were still sometimes cut short because of it.

The Whiteakers would become strong supporters of the Union which would cause a strain between that family and the Caldwells. Uncle Richard didn't like the idea much of Elizabeth taking a fancy to Jeremiah, but at that time, he didn't have reason to forbid it. The night of the party, romance started to bud between the two of them along with a few other couples in the room.

The girls were still busy chatting by the punch bowl when Ella's brother, Tom, started walking towards them. He seemed a little nervous, but he tried to look confident as he approached the girls. Anne thought for sure that he was coming to talk to her, but he stopped and addressed Elizabeth instead.

"Miss Elizabeth, my friend, Jeremiah, was wondering if you would mind if he asked you for a dance. You see, he never asked anybody to dance before and wanted to make sure that you would say yes."

"Well, then, I think that he should try and see what happens," she said with a big grin on her face.

Anne, a little annoyed, addressed Tom directly and said, "What about you Mr. O'Connor? Are you plannin' to ask anyone to dance tonight?"

"Well, Miss Anne, now that you mentioned it, I don't think I could leave tonight without takin' home the memory of a dance with you," he responded quite confidently. "Would you give me the honor?"

Anne couldn't disguise how pleased she was. "Why yes," she said, "I think I will." Tom took her by the hand and escorted her to the dance floor.

He motioned to Jeremiah who hesitantly approached Ella and Elizabeth still sipping their punch. Jeremiah hardly got the words out before Elizabeth gave him her hand and started moving toward the dance floor, too.

Ella stood there mesmerized by everything she saw and heard around her. On the dance floor, she saw her Pa twirling her Ma round and round. Uncle Richard and Aunt Jane were doing their best to give them some competition as many of the guests gathered round to watch. All the while, Jackson was still watching from above.

This night was becoming everything that Ella hoped it would be and more. The large entry way of Uncle Richard and Aunt Jane's home was "the ballroom" to her from that day forward. She would always think of it filled with people, music, and laughter just as it was at that moment.

Ella began to move about, curious about every detail of the festivities. Jackson, still watching from the staircase where the young men were congregating, made his way up the stairs, across the second story hallway, and down the servant's staircase at the back of the house. He was on a mission to meet up with Ella and ask her for a dance.

Meanwhile, Ella wandered into Aunt Jane's parlor where some of the older folks had found some comfortable chairs and good conversation. She let the smell of warm apples and pumpkin lead her through the parlor to the dining room. The table was full. She wouldn't expect anything less at one of Aunt Jane's parties. There was ham, bread, sweet potatoes, pie, and pudding. She reached for a plate, ready for a sampling, and felt a tap on her shoulder. She turned and saw Jackson standing there with a playful grin on his face.

"Good evening, Miss Ella," he said with a bow.

They both laughed and started to chat as Jackson reached for a plate, too.

"This table is somethin'," Ella told him impressed.

"Sure is. Aunt Jane had Cassie and the girls cookin', bakin', and getting ready for this for two days," Jackson told her.

They filled their plates and then, Jackson said, "Follow me."

Ella obliged and followed Jackson out of the dining room, back through the parlor, behind the old folks, and quietly out the parlor door onto the front porch without anyone noticing. They sat down on the edge of the porch with their feet dangling off it like they used to do on the rocks by the creek when they were little. Ella had been doing her best since she arrived at the party to be ladylike and grown up, but with Jackson she could just be herself. The two were somewhere between being a man and a woman to missing the simpler times when they would play ball together, climb trees, and race each other to the creek. Sitting on the edge of the porch in the moonlight they were just Ella and Jackson.

"Do you ever wish we were kids again, El?" Jackson asked her.

"Sometimes, but mostly I look forward to doing the new things that we get to do because we're growin' up. Like this party. I have been lookin' forward to this for so long," she told him.

"I haven't cared too much for parties," Jackson told her, "At least not until tonight." Ella gave him a puzzled look.

"You know what I'm talkin' about, El," he said, "you said it already. We ain't kids anymore. I was lookin' forward to spendin' time here with you."

Ella giggled a bit and started to blush.

Jackson scowled. She recognized the crinkle of his eyebrow and tight-lipped look on his face.

"Come on, Ella," he scolded, "This is me you're talkin' to. Why you actin' like that?"

Ella apologized, "I don't know. I guess, I thought I was supposed to, bein' it's my first party and all. I'm sorry."

"It's alright," he said. Jackson was quiet. He seemed to be searching for the right words.

Ella could feel her heart start to race. "Could this be it? Is he really going to say it?" She thought to herself.

He looked at her for a moment. Then, he reached for her hand, turned away, and didn't make a sound. He said everything that he wanted to say without a word and a squeeze of his hand. When she squeezed his hand back, he turned and looked at her again. The gentle smile on her face told him that she loved him, too.

The two sat quietly in the bright moonlight for a while. The moon was so big and so bright that it seemed as if they could reach out and touch it. It was almost as if it were hung there especially for the two of them, as if they were the only two in the whole world who could see it.

Finally, Jackson spoke, "I guess I've always known, El, even when we were kids, that I wanted us to be together."

"I know," she told him, "I feel the same way."

He looked relieved. They had never hidden their feelings for each other, but they had never acknowledged them either. For some reason, talking about it changed everything, but for the better.

The two were interrupted when some of the other guests stepped out onto the porch for some air. Jackson smiled at Ella, jumped up, and said, "We best be getting you back to your first party. Could I have this dance, Miss Ella?" he asked as he reached for her hand again to help her up.

"Why, I would be honored, Mr. Caldwell," she replied.

Jackson led her back in the house and pulled her through the crowd to the dance floor. Ella was floating on air. She had never been so happy. She and Jackson danced and laughed the rest of the night.

They didn't notice that Tom and Anne danced together all night, too, or, that Elizabeth and Jeremiah were stealing away in the corner of the room to talk and get to know each other better. They also didn't notice Nathaniel and Rose Whiteaker sneaking out the back door and wandering down the hill by the slave cabins. Nor did they know that Nathaniel opened his heart to Rose about how much he longed for the slaves to be free and how much he cared for so many of them. They were not aware that Nathaniel was proposing to her out under their moon that night. Jackson and Ella simply stayed fixed on each other, as if there was no one else in the room.

The two were also oblivious to the heated political debate that had erupted in Uncle Richard's library. Uncle Richard and Mr. Whiteaker had disagreed over political matters many times, but this was different. Times were changing. Missourians weren't just talking about what side of the slave debate they were on. Many were beginning to act, taking matters into their own hands.

Chapter 14

The Lines Are Drawn

T he Kansas-Nebraska Act of 1854 split the Nebraska Territory into two regions for the purpose of preparing both Kansas and Nebraska for possible statehood. This wasn't a problem for most Missourians. The problem was that the act repealed the Missouri Compromise of 1821, which, for more than three decades, had guaranteed that any new states west of Missouri would be free. The new act would give the new territories the right to decide for themselves whether they would be pro or antislavery.

Some proslavery Missourians began taking matters into their own hands. The Border Ruffians, as they were called, were furthering their cause through acts of violence. They were intimidating Kansans living along the Missouri/Kansas border to vote in favor of slavery. Other proslavery Missourians slipped over the Kansas border themselves, posing as Kansans to illegally vote in favor of slavery.

Some Missourians like Uncle Richard were in favor of the act and the possibility of more slave states. Others, who were antislavery, like Mr. Whiteaker, were against it. The two men drew a line in Uncle Richard's library that night. It was no longer a disagreement between neighbors. They were choosing sides over what had become a border war.

Meanwhile, Nathaniel and Rose were on their way back to the house from their walk under the moonlight. It was the happiest that Nathaniel had been since before his parents died. Rose was delighted and obviously excited as Nathaniel was going to ask her father, Mr. Whiteaker, for permission to marry her. The joy and excitement of the moment was quenched by what they heard as they passed by the library window. Nathaniel motioned for Rose to be quiet and the two stopped to listen to what was being said.

"So, you believe" Mr. Whiteaker asked Uncle Richard, "that it is acceptable for Border Ruffians to intimidate Kansans, influencing them to vote in favor of slavery and pose as Kansans to cast their own proslavery votes?"

"Whether I think it is acceptable or not isn't the issue. Quite frankly, I don't have to explain myself," replied Uncle Richard. "My point is that it is about time for Congress to stay out of folks' business and leave the issue of slavery alone."

"With all due respect, Richard," interrupted Mr. Randall, "You know that it's not that simple."

"I disagree, Sir," snapped Uncle Richard. "It is plainly simple. The government should not meddle."

Mr. Randall, attempting to shed light on the bigger issue, said, "You aren't the only one who has strong feelings about a man ownin' another man. This division has caused lots of folks throughout the South to start talking about secession. It's gonna get worse before it gets better."

"I am well aware of the differences in opinion regarding slavery," argued Uncle Richard. "However, people have been able to live side by side with those differences for many years. We have done it right here in our own county."

Uncle Richard continued, "Folks in the South have owned slaves for generations. It's our way of life. No one, not the Yankees or Congress or anyone else, has the right to tell us what we can and can't do with our own property." Uncle Richard was adamant.

"Property. That's the problem," repled Mr. Whiteaker. "There are those of us that don't believe that a person should be property. Folks are standin' up for slaves that can't stand up for themselves and they are willing to fight so that all people can be free."

Papa O'Connor spoke up. "Now hold on. Not all Missourians are takin' sides. Me and mine will fight for no such cause. Richard is right about one thing. We have all done well these past years to agree to disagree and respect one another's views about how to live and work our own land. It seems that it would benefit us all to continue to do so."

"Don't you see, Daniel, that looking the other way all these years has made the problem worse," scolded Mr. Whiteaker. "No man wants to be owned. Slaves will eventually find a way to be free and people who are sympathetic to the cause will help them."

Uncle Richard was getting angry when he said, "Are you referring to the so-called Underground Railroad?" He didn't give anyone time to reply. "I have suspected for some time now that even some of our own good citizens have helped runaway slaves escape. And, as far as I am concerned, these do-gooders are nothing more than thieves, stealing property from their neighbors in the name of freedom."

"Now wait just a minute," Mr. Whiteaker interrupted.

"No, you hear me out." Uncle Richard demanded. "Congress already ruled in the case of Dred Scott deciding that slaves do not have rights and that they have no citizenship. That includes mine. I dare any man to meddle in my business and try to aid any of my slaves to run. I give a warning this day, this night that anyone who does will pay and pay dearly."

"Gentlemen," said Papa O'Connor, "We have been neighbors for many years. We have helped one another. We have looked out for each other. This part of Missouri is what it is today because of our hard work. We should not let our differences divide us. And, truly, we should not let our differences ruin such a wonderful evening. For the sake of everyone, let's put this conversation to rest and enjoy the festivities."

Mr. Whiteaker and Uncle Richard were quiet. Uncle Richard moved toward the fireplace, resting his arm on the mantle staring into the flames. Mr. Whiteaker nodded, and said, "Yes, Daniel, you are right. I will leave you now." Then, he left the room.

Uncle Richard still said nothing. Everyone knew that this was not the end of it. It was no longer men just talking over brandy and cigars. It had become neighbors choosing sides.

Mr. Randall, changing the subject, said, "Daniel, we haven't seen you over at the hotel for a while now. Next time you're in town, come over and have some lunch with us."

"Thank you for the invitation. I will be sure to do that," Daniel told him. "But, as for now, gentlemen, I think that I should find my dear wife, and see if she has saved a dance for this old Irishman."

Nathaniel and Rose were still on the porch by the window. Quietly, Nathaniel reached for Rose's hand and led her away from the window to the parlor door. Before they went back inside to join the party again, Nathaniel said, "Rose, I don't think this is the best time to be talkin' to your Pa about us getting married. With him and Uncle Richard disagreeing about things, he might think twice about it. It might be better to wait until things settle down some."

Rose didn't say anything. She was holding back the tears as she nodded in agreement. Nathaniel pulled her close and hugged her tight. "I'm sorry, Rose," he said. "It will happen. I promise, just not tonight. Come on, now, and let's have a dance." Rose managed a smile and Nathaniel escorted her back to the dance floor.

Rose loved Nathaniel, but she didn't always understand him. Her love for him would bring her great joy, but it would also bring her great pain. This night was her first taste of that. There would always be dissension between her family and the Caldwells.

At the time, no one understood how important the events of that night were in the lives of so many. It began simply as one of Aunt Jane's parties, but it was a spark for change in the lives of many of the people who attended. The relationship between Mr. Whiteaker and Uncle Richard would never be the same. Mr. Randall became more adamant than ever that he would not stand idly by while men, women, and children were held in bondage. He was ready and willing to do something about it. Daniel O'Connor became even more resolved that he would not take a side.

As for the young people, the party was a catalyst for change for many of them, too. Jackson and Ella spoke aloud for the first time about their feelings for one another. Jeremiah and Elizabeth began courting and Nathaniel asked Rose to marry him.

Nathaniel did finally ask Mr. Whiteaker for permission to marry his daughter, but it was some months later. Mr. Whiteaker was reluctant, but still gave his consent. Uncle Richard didn't approve, but he knew that Nathaniel had made up his mind, so he conceded.

Nathaniel and Rose decided to be married on New Year's Day. Jackson remembered it well. It was cold and overcast, as was the overall tone of the day. Everyone tried to be happy for the couple, but Mr. Whiteaker and Uncle Richard had never made amends.

The couple was married in the parlor at the Whiteaker farm. Only the two families and Obadiah were there to share the special day. Nathaniel insisted that Obadiah be allowed to attend. Uncle Richard agreed to let him witness the wedding from inside the parlor doorway. Obadiah was hopeful that this would be the beginning of a fresh start for his young friend.

Rose was beautiful in a blue satin dress. She wore white gloves and carried a bouquet of pink camellias. The couple exchanged their vows. Then, the guests enjoyed cake and punch. There was no talk of politics, and everyone tried to be cordial. The union of the two families was complicated, but Jackson had high hopes at the time that everything would work out.

Nathaniel and Rose's wedding was the first union between the Caldwell and the Whiteaker families, but it wouldn't be the last. Not long after Nathaniel and Rose were married, Rose's brother, Jeremiah, paid a call to Caldwell Plantation.

"Good evenin', Mr. Jeremiah," said Cassie as she greeted him at the front door.

"Good evenin, Cassie," he replied.

"Shall I go get Mr. Nathaniel and Miss Rose for you?" she asked him.

"No, actually, I am here to see Mr. Caldwell. Is he here?" he asked.

"Yes, sir, I'll go and fetch him," Cassie told him. "You can wait in Master Caldwell's library." She motioned toward the door.

Jeremiah went to the library and waited patiently for Uncle Richard. Jackson came in from the barn, noticed Jeremiah, and stopped to greet him. He was curious. The Whiteakers didn't usually make calls at Caldwell Plantation.

"Howdy, Jeremiah. You lookin' for Nathaniel and Rose?" he asked.

"No, I just have some business with your uncle that I need to take care. Cassie went to fetch him for me," replied Jeremiah. He was looking anxious.

"Is there something I can do for you? You don't seem like yerself." Jackson replied.

"Naw, there ain't nothin' you can do," Jeremiah paused. "I've come to ask your uncle for Elizabeth's hand, and I am worried that he might say no," Jeremiah explained honestly.

"It's about time," Jackson told him with a smile. Then, he offered some friendly advice. "I wouldn't worry too much. One thing that I know for sure is that Uncle Richard loves his girls, and he wants them to be happy. He knows that you make Elizabeth happy. Just don't let him know that you're nervous."

Jeremiah nodded. "I appreciate that, Jackson," he told him. It ain't that I'm afraid of him or anything. It's just that my Pa and your Uncle Richard haven't been on good terms for a while now," he explained.

"Yeah, but, look at Nathaniel and Rose. Things seem to be working out alright for them," Jackson told him.

"Well, I just hope that your uncle agrees," said Jeremiah.

Jackson left Jeremiah to go clean up and find some supper. He met his uncle on the way upstairs.

"Evenin' Uncle Richard," Jackson said as he passed by.

"Evenin' Jackson," replied Uncle Richard, "Did you get that hitch on the wagon fixed?"

"Sure did," Jackson told him. "It won't be givin' us no more trouble."

"Alright then," Uncle Richard said as he disappeared into the library.

"Good evening, Mr. Caldwell," said Jeremiah.

"Hello Jeremiah. What can I do for you?" Uncle Richard asked him.

Jeremiah had practiced this over and over in his head a dozen times. He decided the best thing to do was to just say it and not beat around the bush.

"Well, Sir, I think you know how I feel about Elizabeth." Jeremiah told him.

"Yes, I am aware." Uncle Richard responded.

"Well, with that said," Jeremiah was direct and to the point, "I would like your permission to ask her to marry me."

"Jeremiah, I'm sure you know that I have concerns about my daughter marrryin' into the Whiteaker family. It is nothing personal against you. It's your Pa. He and I have our differences," Uncle Richard explained.

"Yes, Sir. I know," Jeremiah told him.

"However, I know that you make Elizabeth happy, and I don't think it is right to hold anything against you because of my disagreements with your father. So, I will say, yes." Uncle Richard agreed.

Jeremiah shook Uncle Richard's hand with gratitude and said, "Thank you, Sir. Thank you."

As Jeremiah was leaving, Uncle Richard called to him and said, "Jeremiah."

"Yes, Mr. Caldwell," replied Jeremiah.

"Don't make me regret my decision," Uncle Richard told him.

"You won't, Mr. Caldwell. You won't."

Uncle Richard called for Cassie who answered him quickly, "Yes, sir?"

"Go fetch Miss Jane and Miss Elizabeth and send them to the parlor," he told her. Cassie obeyed.

Jeremiah stood by the parlor door, watching, waiting. Uncle Richard waited in his library until he heard his wife and daughter coming down the stairs. Both ladies were surprised to see Jeremiah.

"Why, Jeremiah Whiteaker, how nice of you to call," said Aunt Jane.

Elizabeth, obviously excited to see him, reached for both of his hands and said, "Oh, Jeremiah, it is so good of you to come."

Everyone followed Aunt Jane into the parlor where she offered Jeremiah a comfortable chair.

"No, thank you, Ma'am. I would rather stand." He explained.

"Jane, Jeremiah would like to ask Elizabeth a question," Uncle Richard told her.

Aunt Jane didn't seem surprised when he got down on one knee, took Elizabeth by the hand and said, "Elizabeth Caldwell, will you marry me?"

Elizabeth beamed. "Yes," she said. She hardly waited for him to get back on two feet before she threw her arms around his neck and hugged him tightly. Then, she turned to her Pa and hugged him, too. Quietly, she said in her Pa's ear, "Thank you, Pa. I love you."

And, so it was, that the Caldwells and the Whiteakers would be brought together for another wedding. This one would be much more difficult for Uncle Richard than Nathaniel and Rose's wedding. This time it was his daughter to be given away, and to a Whiteaker. The couple was married in the little country church where all the local families gathered to worship. This time the O'Connors and the Randalls were invited to the ceremony, too.

Elizabeth, who was known for her beauty, looked especially lovely on her wedding day. Her gown was handmade from white satin and lace that Aunt Jane had sent from New Orleans. It was off the shoulders with a v shaped neckline adorned with a silk ruffle. The bodice was fitted at the waistline and the skirt was full in keeping with the style of the day. There were layers of ruffles and small silk flowers adorning the entire gown. Her veil was a wreath of flowers with shear cloth attached that was half the length of her gown. She carried a bouquet of wildflowers.

The guests were invited to a reception at Caldwell Plantation after the ceremony. It was the most magnificent of all the Caldwell galas. The fiddlers were tucked away in their usual fashion under the stairs in the grand entry. The piano was pushed back into the corner to make plenty of room for dancing. There was a feast laid out on the dining room table that made all the previous ones look light. This time a wedding cake was the centerpiece. It was a delicious dark delicacy, flavored with fruit, large enough to feed all the guests.

It was a joyous day for the couple even though Uncle Richard and Mr. Whiteaker were less than enthusiastic. When Nathaniel married Rose, it was a good change for him. He fit in well with his new family. They shared the same beliefs and convictions. The transition wouldn't be as easy for Elizabeth. Even though she loved Jeremiah, she was still a Caldwell.

"It was a good year," Jackson recalled, "two weddings and the annual picnic at Caldwell Plantation. The planting season went well. Everyone in the county was anticipating a good harvest. The political climate had been unusually calm and to top it off, Aunt Jane was making plans for her annual fall party.

Jackson's mind continued to wander back. "We all make plans for tomorrow," he thought to himself, "never knowing if we have tomorrow or what tomorrow might bring.

Chapter 15

Scarlet Fever

It was late August when young Sarah Caldwell became ill. She hadn't been herself for about a week or so, somewhat listless without much of an appetite. Jackson remembered her wandering downstairs barefooted in her night gown with her cheeks looking flushed one day. Aunt Jane immediately scooped her up and carried her back to her room.

Joanna had been feeling poorly, too. Uncle Richard told Jackson to hitch up the wagon and take the younger children, Petey, Mary, James, and Robert to the O'Connor's. Jackson knew that whatever this was, it was serious.

The O'Connor family gladly took them in. Aunt Caroline knew that the children were frightened, so she and the rest of the family did everything they could to put them at ease. They wanted to help them take their minds off what was happening back home.

"You children are just in time. We were just fixin' to put supper on the table. Lila baked a couple of apple pies special for ya'll. Come on in now. We'll be eatin' soon," she told them. She turned to Jackson and asked, "Will you be joinin' us, Jackson?"

"Thank you, Ma'am. I wouldn't mind, but I think it would be best if I get on back home," Jackson spoke with concern.

"We understand," said Papa O'Connor. "Is there anything that we can do?"

"You have already done enough, takin' the children in. I"ll be back to get them just as soon as I can." Jackson promised.

"You don't worry about that and don't worry about the children. We'll take good care of them. They can stay as long as you need them to," Aunt Caroline assured him.

"We are real grateful to have such good neighbors," said Jackson.

He turned to the children and said, "Now you children mind what these kind folks tell you. Be good. I promise that I will come back for you just as soon as I can."

"Tell Ma and Pa not to worry, Jackson. I'll make the boys mind," said Mary, always the little mother hen. She was trying her hardest to be grown up.

"Do you have to go?" asked Petey. He wanted to be brave, so he was trying not to cry.

Jackson leaned over and told him, "Remember all the times that you told me that you were big and strong like the other boys?" Petey nodded. "Remember how you told me that you wasn't a baby no more and you could do anything that Robert and James could do?" Petey nodded, again. Jackson continued, "Well, this is your chance to show everyone that you are a little man now. So, go on. You'll be alright." Petey obeyed.

Robert and James were angry about being sent away. They thought that they were old enough to stay.

"You boys help out while you're here," Jackson told them, but both boys ignored him. Neither said a word. He gave Petey and Mary one last reassuring smile and left them in the care of the O'Connors.

While Jackson was safely delivering the children, William went to town to fetch the doctor. After examining the girls, his diagnosis was Scarlett Fever. It was just as Uncle Richard suspected. With so many people living on the plantation, the doctor feared the possibility of an epidemic. He instructed Uncle Richard to keep the younger children away until the girls were better. The slaves were not allowed anywhere near the big house. He thought it best if no one in the family see the girls except for Aunt Jane and Cassie.

They cared for Sarah and Joanna day and night. Folks prayed and prayed until, little by little, their condition started to improve. Finally, it was safe to bring the children home. Everyone was relieved. They were all anxious for things to get back to normal. A few days after the children came home, everyone was gathering around the table for breakfast, everyone except Aunt Jane.

"Where is your mother?" Uncle Richard asked Mary.

"I don't know, Pa," she answered, "I'll go and find her."

Sara interrupted, "No, Mary, I'll go find Mama." She was bouncy and bubbly and so glad to have her energy back.

Everyone continued with their breakfast. The boys were chatting about getting ready for the harvest and Mary was talking to her Pa about going to visit Elizabeth at the Whiteaker farm. A few moments later, quiet as a little church mouse, Sara entered the room. She stood in the doorway and didn't make a sound.

"What's the matter, Sara? Where is Mama?" Mary asked her.

Sara looked a little frightened when she answered. "She's upstairs in her room. She's in bed, Papa, feelin' poorly, like me and Joanna."

Uncle Richard hurried from the table and went to check on his wife. William didn't wait for instructions. He immediately saddled his horse and went to town to find the doctor.

The children were frightened.

"Don't you children be frettin'," Jackson told them. "Your Pa will take good care of your Ma. Now go on and eat your breakfast."

They quietly obeyed. After they finished their breakfast, Mary started them on their morning chores. Cassie made a breakfast tray to take to Miss Jane. Jackson met Cassie on the stairs when she was coming down from her room. The look on her face was grave.

"How is she?" asked Jackson.

"Looks to me like Miss Jane's got the fever, too, Master Jackson," she told him fighting back her tears and trying to not look worried.

"William went to fetch the doctor. You go on now and don't be worryin' yerself. Doc will fix her up, just like he did Sara and Joanna," he told her.

Soon after the doctor arrived, he confirmed what everyone feared. Aunt Jane had Scarlett Fever. The younger children packed up and went back to the O'Connor farm. Uncle Richard and Cassie tended to her day and night. Folks were prayin' and prayin' just like they did for Sara and Joanna. Only this time, Aunt Jane wasn't' getting better. Instead, little by little, she was getting worse.

The doctor came every day for more than a week. Finally, he told them that there wasn't much hope that Aunt Jane would recover. She was too weak, and she was just getting weaker.

Early one morning, she managed enough energy to reach for Uncle Richard's hand. She smiled at him and said, "The sunlight's nice." She could see the rays of the morning sun shining through the gap in the bedroom curtains. She always loved mornings. He obliged his wife and opened the curtains.

She spoke slowly and softly, "I love you, Richard."

"Don't talk, Jane," he told her. "Be still, so that you can get better."

She spoke softly, "You know, I'm not gonna get better."

"Don't say that." he said.

"Listen to me. I got somethin' to say that's important," she tried to be firm, but her voice was weak. "You are a good man, but I don't think that you have ever believed it. You've always acted like money and nice things was what made you important. None of this makes you important, Richard. You are valuable because you are God's creation, because you were created in His image, and you matter to Him."

Richard began to sob with his face in his hands sitting by her bed.

"Don't go," he cried, "What will I do without you?"

Jane put her hand on his head and softly said, "Hush now." She paused for a moment, "It pains me so that I can't tell the children good-bye. Promise me that you'll take good care of them."

Richard looked in her eyes and said, "I promise."

Then she said, "This body may be dyin', but I'm gonna live forever. I'm goin' to my forever home where I will rest in the arms of my Savior. Look to Him, Richard. You will find Him, and we will be together again."

Aunt Jane closed her eyes. Uncle Richard held her hand and sobbed.

Jackson heard Uncle Richard sobbing and ran to her room. When he opened the door, he knew that Aunt Jane was gone. He remembered the overwhelming feeling of grief and how everything changed that day at Caldwell Plantation. How he wished she were here. "I miss you, Aunt Jane," he thought to himself and then he thought about it no more. It was too hard. Jackson brought his thoughts back to the here and now and continued to ride.

Chapter 16

Nathaniel and the Underground Railroad

Nathaniel's place was finally in sight. Jackson wasn't sure exactly what he would say, but he trusted the Lord to give him the words. For a minute, it looked as though there was no one there. Everything was quiet and still. Then, he saw Dorie run around the corner of the house from the barn. Rose was right behind her. She saw the two men riding in from the distance. She and Dorie went inside. By the time Jackson and George reached the cabin, the door opened, and Nathaniel stepped onto the front porch.

"It's good to see you, Nathaniel," Jackson said as he approached him.

Nathaniel's response was less than warm.

"You shouldn't have come here, Jackson," he said.

"Last I knew, we're still brothers. You tryin' to tell me I ain't welcome here?" Jackson asked.

"You're welcome here if you came as my brother, but if you came here to talk to me about the war or what happened with Robert and James, you're wastin' your time," Nathaniel told him adamantly.

George stayed where he was. He didn't say a word. He knew how to mind his own business.

"I gotta go back to meet up with the rest of the boys, Nathaniel. I wanted to see you before I left," Jackson told him.

"You make it sound like you have to go. Nobody's makin' you," Nathaniel told him.

"We've been through this," Jackson said. "I've tried to help you understand that I don't see it that way."

Nathaniel was unsympathetic when he said, "Understand? I can't understand why you would fight with an army who wants to keep people from bein' free."

"I ain't no Confederate and you know it. It ain't about any of that for me," Jackson told him.

"It should be," Nathaniel snapped back.

The two had chosen sides. Jackson knew that they would not agree. The very thing that Jackson tried to prevent from happening was happening between him and Nathaniel. The reason he joined the Guard in the first place was so that he wouldn't be fightin' against his Uncle Richard and the boys. He never thought that he and Nathaniel would be on opposite sides. This wasn't supposed to happen.

"I didn't come here to argue with you," Jackson was almost apologetic.

"Then, why did you come?" Nathaniel asked him.

"I was just hopin' that maybe I could make things right before I go. I did a lot of thinkin' on the way here. I was rememberin' back before the war. I was rememberin' your wedding and Jeremiah and Elizabeth's wedding, and I was thinkin' about when Aunt Jane got sick. You know this would break her heart to see her family divided like this." Jackson told him.

"It's too late. Those Caldwells ain't my family anymore. They made their choice. Nobody has a right to own other human beings. And, you know as well as I do that James and Robert have been doin' what everyone's sayin' that they're doin'."

Jackson's demeanor immediately changed. He looked at Nathaniel, then to George, and back to Nathaniel. Nathaniel knew what Jackson was thinking. He didn't want to talk about the rumors in front of George. Nathaniel said no more about it.

"What about you Nathaniel? People think you have somethin' to do with the slaves that have been runnin' off around the county." Jackson was concerned for his brother, but Nathaniel was silent.

Jackson mounted his horse and then continued, "If you're helpin' runaway slaves, I hope you know what you're doin'." Nathaniel still didn't speak. "Good-bye, Big Brother. I'm mighty grateful to you for always bein' there for me. I wanted you to know that before I left.

As Jackson turned to ride away, Nathaniel finally spoke. "You take care of yerself."

Jackson nodded. Nathaniel sat down on the bench by the front door and watched as the two men disappeared in the distance. He had always been there, looking after Jackson. This time, Jackson was on his own.

Nathaniel thought about what Jackson said to him before he left. He was right about him helping runaway slaves, but he could never admit to it. Not because he was afraid or because he didn't trust Jackson, but because he wanted to protect him. He didn't want the rest of the Caldwell family holding Jackson accountable for the things that he was doing. Jackson was better off not knowing.

So many things had happened that led Nathaniel to what folks were calling the Underground Railroad. He knew why he did it. That was clear. How he got there, on the other hand, was a little harder to sort out. He started thinking about the chain of events that started him on the track to help runaway slaves escape to freedom.

Right after they were married, Nathaniel and Rose made their home at Caldwell Plantation. The Caldwells welcomed her with open arms, Aunt Jane being especially excited to add Rose to the family. The first few months were a blessing. The family treated her like one of their own. Then, Sarah and Joanna got sick. Nathaniel thought it would be best if Rose went to stay with her family until the sickness passed. She was expecting their first child in early spring.

Nathaniel stayed behind to help on the farm. His job was to oversee the field work and make sure that the crops were delivered after they were sold. Even with slave labor, there was still a lot of work that had been done and every Caldwell did their fair share.

Nathaniel had saved the money that he earned working on the plantation and bought his own land right before he proposed to Rose. There was a small cabin on it that he had planned to add on, but things didn't happen the way that Nathaniel planned.

After Aunt Jane died, he just couldn't leave. It was because of his attachment to the slaves on the plantation not because of any attachment to the family. He didn't know if Aunt Jane's passing would change how the slaves were treated or provided for. He felt obligated to watch out for them, at least for a little while. His dream of working his own land would have to wait.

William and Sterling managed the fields along with Nathaniel. They also supervised the overseer and managed the slaves. Jackson was responsible for making sure that things were kept up, the fencing, the wagons, the tools, and such. James and Robert cared for the livestock. And, Pete, since he was the youngest, usually ended up with the jobs that no one else wanted. And, of course, Uncle Richard was the final authority on all things relating to the plantation and the Caldwell family.

After Aunt Jane died, Uncle Richard got lost in his grief. He never found himself again. Everyone suffered, but the younger children were affected the most. William, Nathaniel, Jackson, and Sterling were already grown. Elizabeth had married the summer before and moved to the Whiteaker farm to be with her husband.

Mary Jane was next in line, so she stepped into the role of mothering the other children and running the house. It was natural for her, but a heavy burden for someone her age. Joanna, already an introvert, withdrew from people even more. Robert and James were at the age where they really needed their father, but Uncle Richard didn't seem to notice. They often acted out to get his attention, but he grew more and more distant with each passing day. Their acting out caused all kinds of trouble in the family, with neighbors, and even with some of the people in town.

As the two boys got older, they started spending more and more time away from home. They had gotten acquainted with some men who were rumored to be running with a group of bushwackers. Jackson and Nathaniel suspected the rumors were true but couldn't prove it.

Robert and James were not the only ones who didn't always account for their whereabouts. Though it mostly went unnoticed, Nathaniel had some secrets of his own. No one knew, not even Jackson or Rose, that Nathaniel had been helping runaway slaves. With Rose safe at her family's farm, Nathaniel and Obie were getting ready to try and help some of the slaves from Caldwell Plantation find their way to freedom.

Mr. Randall helped Nathaniel make his first contact with the Underground Railroad. He approached Nathaniel one Sunday after the church service. Nathaniel was waiting by their wagon for Rose who was visiting with some of the ladies, sharing the good news that she and Nathaniel were expecting. Mr. Randall took advantage of the opportunity to speak to him alone.

"Nathaniel," he said, "I've gotten acquainted with somebody that you might like to meet."

"Is that right?" Nathaniel replied, "And who might that be?"

"Well, the funny thing is, I can't tell you his name, but I can tell you that he feels mighty strongly about some of the same things that you and I do," Mr. Randall kept talking. "He needs help gettin' some friends out of trouble, some folks that can't help themselves."

Nathaniel was confused and curious at the same time.

"If you can't tell me his name, can you tell me how you know him?" Nathaniel asked.

Nathaniel listened as Mr. Randall began to tell him about how he got to know the mysterious stranger. The man had come to the hotel one day and rented a room. It wasn't long until he became a regular customer. He kept to himself and never said much, but Mr. Randall noticed that he often changed his name in the guest registry. He didn't question the man about it, but he kept an eye on him.

One morning, as he was tending the front counter, a Marshall from the next county came around asking some questions. He told Mr. Randall that he was investigating some rumors that were going around back where he came from. There was talk that some folks around our town were helping runaway slaves make their way through the county to the Kansas border. He wanted to know if Mr. Randall knew anything about it.

Nathaniel listened intently as Mr. Randall continued to tell him the story. "My new friend was sitting at a table by the front door eating his breakfast. He didn't look up, but I could tell that he was paying close attention to what was being said. I told the Marshall that I hadn't heard about anything like that and told him that I was sorry that I couldn't help him."

The Marshall told Mr. Randall that he would be around for a couple of days and that he would be obliged if he thought of something or heard something that might be a help. Mr. Randall offered him a room, but he declined. He was planning to check in with the sheriff to see if he had an extra cot at the jail. Mr. Randall left the invitation open. The sheriff thanked him and left.

The stranger got up from the table and climbed up the stairs to his room. Within a few minutes, he came back down with his saddle bag in hand. When he stopped at the counter to turn in his room key, Mr. Randall asked him if he would be seeing him again soon.

He said, "I'm not sure."

"That was curious," said Mr. Randall, "that Marshall comin' around here askin' questions about the Underground Railroad."

Nathaniel was paying close attention to everything that he was hearing.

Then, Mr. Randall said, "He told me, 'I don't know about that. I didn't pay him any mind.' Then, I reassured him that folks around here mind their business. He thanked me for the hospitality and was on his way."

"I'm guessin' he came back," said Nathaniel.

"Yes, he came back a few weeks later. This time he signed in under the name Jones," Mr. Randall told him.

"'Mr. Jones?' I asked him," said Mr. Randall.

"'That's right. Jones.' He told me," Mr. Randall continued.

This time the stranger lingered by the counter. He never did that before. Then, he asked what happened with the Marshall.

"Nothing," said Mr. Randall to the stranger.

The stranger still lingered. Then, Mr. Randall said, "That Marshall was barking up the wrong tree."

"How do you mean?" asked the stranger.

"There are a lot of folks around these parts that don't much like the idea of slavery," Mr. Randall told him. "They'd be happy to hear about some of them makin' it to free territory."

The story was getting better and better. Mr. Randall had Nathaniel's complete attention.

"Do you know anyone like that," asked the stranger.

"If I think hard enough, I might think of one or two," he answered.

"I'll keep that in mind," the stranger told him.

Then, he left. He made two more visits to the hotel after that without a word about their conversation. However, the third visit was different. He rented a room as usual and checked out the next morning just like he always did. But this time, he came back again the very next day. When he came down for the noon meal, he approached Mr. Randall.

He said, "Say, I was wondering if you remember that talk we had awhile back?"

"Yes," Mr. Randall told him, "As a matter of fact, I do."

He seemed a little nervous when he asked, "Did you think about it?"

Mr. Randall didn't speak. He reached for a piece of paper and wrote a note. It said: "The edge of town, behind the livery stable, ten o'clock, tomorrow night." The stranger took the note, nodded, and went to his room.

"You want me to meet him?" asked Nathaniel. Now he understood.

"Only if you want to," Mr. Randall told him.

"You think you can trust him?" Nathaniel asked him.

"Somethin' tells me that we can. I feel like I gotta try and help him somehow or I won't be able to live with myself. The Lord has blessed me with so much, while all around me there are folks living in bondage. It pains me to know that some are mistreated, and others live in fear every day," Mr. Randall sounded passionate.

"You gotta be careful talkin' like that," Nathaniel warned him. "You'll get yourself into trouble."

"You heard the preacher. Christ came to set our spirits free. He paid the price for everyone who would believe. He paid with His life. He is the only One who has the right to be called Master," Mr. Randall told him.

Nathaniel didn't hesitate. He said, "I'll be there. We'll both just trust that the Lord knows what He's doing and see what happens."

Mr. Randall nodded.

By this time, Rose was walking toward the wagon. Mr. Randall greeted her.

"Good day, Miss Rose," he said as he passed by her.

She smiled and said, "Good day, Mr. Randall."

Nathaniel helped her into the wagon, and they were on their way. She was still staying with her parents at the Whiteaker farm. It didn't feel right bringing her to the plantation in her condition. Nathaniel thought it was better for her to stay with her own family a little while longer.

Nathaniel spent the rest of that Sunday with Rose and her family at their farm. They had a fine meal and good fellowship. Mr. Whiteaker liked to recap the morning message after dinner and discuss it with his sons. They all gathered in the parlor while the men talked about Bible doctrine and the ladies read books, embroidered, or just listened to conversation.

It was hard for Nathaniel to concentrate. He could only think about his meeting later that night with the mysterious stranger. It was getting late in the day. it was time to say his good-byes. He kissed Rose, told her that he would see her in a couple of days, thanked Mrs. Whiteaker for the fine meal, and climbed up in the wagon to leave.

He would have to stop at Caldwell Plantation on his way to town. He needed to take the wagon back and get his horse. No one at the plantation went to church that day. Uncle Richard hadn't gone since Aunt Jane died. Jackson would sometimes take the children to church with him, but he had been staying in the bunkhouse out at the O'Connor farm the last couple of days. Jackson was good at fixing things, and he was always willing to help the O'Connors with a special project now and then.

Jackson hadn't said anything, but Nathaniel suspected that there could be another wedding in the spring. He was sure that Jackson was going to ask Ella's Pa for her hand soon. She was almost eighteen and it was time for them to start thinking about starting a life together.

When he got back to the plantation, Nathaniel unhitched the wagon and went to see Obie. He didn't tell him about his meeting. He just always found comfort in Obadiah's presence. They visited awhile. Then, he went to the barn to saddle his horse. James walked in as he was saddling up.

"Where you goin'?" he asked Nathaniel.

"Since when do you care where I go?" Nathaniel asked him.

"I don't care," James smirked.

Nathaniel mounted his horse and started riding to town. As James was watching him leave, Robert happened by.

"Where's he going?" he asked James,

"I don't know, but we probably wouldn't like it," James told him. James was always suspicious of Nathaniel, tonight, more so than usual.

Nathaniel got to town right at night fall. He waited anxiously until it was time for his meeting. It was hard to believe the Underground Railroad was running right past their little town to Kansas all this time and he didn't even know it.

At ten o'clock sharp, Nathaniel was waiting behind the livery stable. The stranger got there right after he did.

"Howdy," said Nathaniel.

"Are you alone?" asked the stranger.

"I'm alone," Nathaniel replied, "What can I do for you?"

"I'm lookin' for someone who might be interested in helping me move some cargo. I need someone who knows the county and knows some good places to stop along the way. Do you think that you might be the right man?" the stranger asked.

The man was obviously nervous. Nathaniel knew that he must be in a desperate situation to reach out to Mr. Randall for help. Nathaniel also knew that if he said yes to the stranger there would be no turning back. He didn't hesitate.

"Yes, sir," he said, "I think that I can help you."

It turned out that the man was a conductor on the Underground Railroad line. He had reached the usual "depot" the night before and found no "cargo", the reason that he came back to the hotel the next morning. The depot had been discovered, so the contact that he was to meet hid the "cargo".

The man needed someone familiar with the county to help him. He needed someone that he could trust, someone who would know the best route to get them to where they needed to go. Mr. Randall thought that Nathaniel was the right person to help him.

That night, Nathaniel made his first trip for the Underground Railroad. The mysterious stranger explained where the "cargo" was hidden. Nathaniel knew exactly the shortest and best way to get there.

It wasn't what he expected. He found a family hiding in a barn, a daddy, a mama, and two little girls about five and six years old. He never forgot the fear he saw on their faces when he opened the barn door where they were hiding. The daddy was standing ready holding a pitchfork. The mama was holding her hand over one of the girls' mouth so that she wouldn't scream.

"Stop right there," said the man with the pitchfork.

"It's all right," said the mysterious stranger. "We're here to help you."

The man still didn't put down the pitchfork. Then, the mysterious stranger said, "Next stop, Kansas."

There was a look of relief on the man's face. He slowly put down the pitchfork. Tears started to fill his eyes. The mysterious stranger hugged him and told him that it would be all right. Then, they set out to make it to the next county by daylight. The safest way to travel and be undetected was by foot. Nathaniel had never traveled so far on foot before. His war injury made it especially diffi-cult, but it was worth it.

He and the stranger helped carry the girls when their little feet couldn't walk anymore. They were both so brave even though they were so scared. The stranger and Nathaniel gave them a sack of food that Mr. Randall had sent for them and then they left them at the next "depot" never to see them again. Nathaniel's first run for the Underground Railroad was a success.

Mr. Randall's hotel became the Underground Railroad base for all Nathaniel's "trips". It was not a "depot" or "station". Runaway slaves never actually came through the hotel. However, Mr. Randall gathered supplies, passed messages, and did anything else to help the "conductors" as they passed through the county.

Nathaniel, knowing the county so well, was instrumental in helping each load of "cargo" reach their designated "station" safely and undetected. They would be able to rest and get the supplies that they needed for the next leg of their journey. Mr. Randall would tell Nathaniel when the next "train" was coming through. Then, Nathaniel would meet the "conductor" and the "cargo" and help them reach their next destination.

The reason that they were a "line" and not a "station" was because it was just too dangerous. There was too much support for the Confederacy and too many pro-slavery activists all around their town and the rest of their county. It just wasn't safe.

Nathaniel and the mysterious stranger had to trust each other with their lives. Yet, they never knew each other's real names. It would be too dangerous if either of them ever got caught. The less they knew about each other the better off they were.

Nathaniel helped the stranger make three trips. Now, he was ready to plan his own. The mysterious stranger agreed to help Nathaniel and Obie send some of the slaves from Caldwell Plantation down the line. Moses, Little John, and Jeruselah had been very dear to Nathaniel since he was a child. He always told them that he believed that one day they would be free. That day finally came.

Chapter 17

The Underground Railroad at Caldwell Plantation

N athaniel. still sitting on his front porch, continued to remember back to that day and the details of the plan that would help his friends become free. If Uncle Richard and the boys would have found out, they would have seen it as the ultimate betrayal. Nathaniel didn't care. By then, any loyalty, any affection that he felt for any of them was gone.

William and Sterling would never stand up to Uncle Richard. They were content with their way of life at the plantation, so they had no reason to. Nathaniel didn't respect either of them. Robert and James were up to no good and Nathaniel knew it. He felt only contempt for them. As for Uncle Richard, he was physically present, but the loss of Aunt Jane had changed him. In a way, much of him died with her, as did any affection that Nathaniel had for his uncle.

The plan was that he would sneak the three slaves out in broad daylight. Obie would cause a distraction that would require the attention of the overseers. He would claim that he saw some men, possibly bushwackers, sneaking around the plantation. The threat of bush-wackers would be taken seriously. Uncle Richard and the overseers would arm themselves and go out searching for whomever was trespassing. This would leave Sterling and, possibly William, in charge of the slaves while they continued with their field work. William and Sterling would not question Nathaniel when he left with the wagon, nor would they be as attentive to the slaves as the overseers would be.

Early that morning, Nathaniel put the slaves to work loading the wagon with cotton sacks. The wagon was stationed next to two sheds that housed the field tools and the sacks used for gathering the crops. Moses and Jerusaleh usually helped with the morning chores up by the house: hauling water, milking the cows, feeding the chickens, and picking garden vegetables for the day's meals. They would not be missed by William or Sterling. Little John, however, would have to escape quickly just before Nathaniel was ready to leave or he would be missed out in the field.

It was late morning and time for Nathaniel to take the cotton to town. Moses and Jerusaleh were waiting behind the shed. One at a time, they hurried into the wagon. Nathaniel covered them with bags of cotton without anyone noticing.

The other slaves stopped for the noon break. It was while they were all moving about that Little John also boarded the wagon and covered himself with cotton bags. Nathaniel climbed into the wagon and started to roll away towards town.

There was a small dugout a few miles away from the plantation house. When Nathaniel was a child, he used to go there whenever he was angry or sad. Only Jackson and Obie knew about it.

They called it his cave. It was much too small to be a real cave. However, it was big enough to provide a hiding place for his precious "cargo" in the wagon.

Nathaniel would hide them there, deliver his cotton to town, bring the wagon back to the plantation, and hear that Moses, Little John, and Jeruselah were missing. He would offer to help find them. All the while, knowing that his mysterious "conductor" friend would pick up his "cargo" after dusk and take them to Nathaniel's cabin on the other side of the county. They would hide in the cellar until the next night when Nathaniel would meet them and the "conductor" and help them reach safety.

Everything went as planned. Just as he expected, Nathaniel came back from town with the wagon to hear that three slaves were missing. He did his best to seem surprised. He was told that Robert, James, William, and the overseers were out looking for them. When the search party returned, Nathaniel was relieved that they came back empty handed.

The next evening just after dark, Nathaniel was leaving to meet the "cargo" and his "conductor" friend. He didn't know it, but James was watching him. James had stepped back behind some bushes by the front porch and watched while Nathaniel went into the barn, saddled up his horse, and left into the night.

James was curious. He knew that Nathaniel was up to something. It even crossed his mind that Nathaniel might have had something to do with the slaves running away the day before. Everyone knew how much Nathaniel cared for the slaves at Caldwell Plantation, but James was up to his own mischief, so he chose not to investigate. He saddled up and rode off to meet up with Robert who was waiting for him at the saloon in town.

Nathaniel rode to his farm, left his horse in the small barn, and collected the "cargo" from the cellar. The group would have to travel on foot to the next county where they would find shelter at the first "depot". This was a new route for the "conductor". He was not as confident about this trip, but he felt that he owed it to Nathaniel to help him and the "cargo" get to the next stop.

Nathaniel's farm was on the county line. His neighbor, Sam Alton, owned a large amount of land along the border on the other side of the line. Sam was a strong supporter of the Union and was vocal about his antislavery beliefs. Nathaniel was confident that they would be safe passing by his place.

The small group set out on the first leg of the journey. It was a cool fall night. There was no moon which made it very dark. Nathaniel was familiar with their surroundings, but it still took them longer than expected because of the darkness. He was sure that they were getting close to his neighbor's farm when they heard noises in the distance.

They followed the sounds, carefully and quietly. As they got closer, they saw some light. Nathaniel was right, they were at Sam's place. The group stayed quiet and hid in the woods not too far from the house. His friend, Sam, holding a rifle, was standing in front of the porch talking with a group of men on horses. Two of the men were holding torches. Nathaniel, the "conductor", and his "cargo" watched and listened intently.

"I won't be sayin' it again," Sam told the men, "Yer trespassin', and it's time that you be gettin' off my land."

"We ain't goin' anywhere 'til we're good and ready, Old Man," said one of the men.

Another one of the men interrupted, "See, we've been hearin' rumors about you bein' a Yankee lover. Folks around Missoura' are mighty tired of Yankees and take offence to anybody that might be a helpin' them."

It was too dark to see clearly, but it looked to Nathaniel like the men on horseback were wearing scarves over their faces. This would be his first encounter with bushwackers. He had heard stories. They had a fearsome reputation which made Nathaniel afraid for his friend, Sam.

"It ain't none of your business, but I ain't helped nobody," Sam told them.

"What if we say that we don't believe ya', Mister?" said the man on horseback.

"I don't care, what you believe. Get off my land," Sam told them.

Sam was going to defend himself and his home. Nathaniel had a hard decision to make. He felt compelled to help his friend, but if he did, it would endanger those that were with him. Nathaniel put his hand on his pistol contemplating if he would rush to Sam's aid, but, the "conductor' put his hand firmly on Nathaniel's shoulder and pulled him back.

Then, just like that, one of the men on horseback drew his gun, not a word, not a warning. He shot Sam down in cold blood. Jerusaleh started to scream, but Moses quickly covered her mouth. They all froze from fear that someone could have heard her.

Only one of the men looked toward the sound of the muffled scream. It was too dark for the gunman to see anything in the woods, but Nathaniel could see the men by the light of their torches. He recognized the scarf that one of the bushwackers was wearing and the markings on his horse. He knew the man and he knew the horse. It was James Caldwell.

Sam's wife came out of the house, screaming, crying, running to her husband's side. One of the bushwackers, hollered out, "Burn it," and the men carrying torches threw them through the windows of the house. They took the two horses in the barn and three of the bushwackers quickly rode away. James lingered a moment staring into the woods. Then, he turned his gaze to the burning house. Finally, he looked a moment at Sam's widow who was crying over his lifeless body. Then, he, too, quickly rode off into the dark night.

Nathaniel quietly told the "conductor" and the "cargo" to wait for him. He wanted to go to Mrs. Alton's side. The "conductor" stopped him again and whispered, "No, Nathaniel. They could come back and kill us all. You can't help her. It's too late. We promised to take these people to freedom. We need to finish what we started."

Nathaniel knew that his friend was right. He could not help the Altons, but he could help the slaves that had put their lives in his hands. It caused him great pain, but he turned and slipped away into the darkness, leaving Mrs. Alton there alone.

Nathaniel and the "conductor" successfully delivered their "cargo" to the next station just before daybreak. Nathaniel was confident that his friends would get the help that they needed to make their way to freedom from there. Jerusaleh put her arms around Nathaniel's neck and hugged him tightly.

"God bless you, Master Nathaniel," she said to him. "We's never gonna forget all that you did to help us. Thank you."

Nathaniel gave her a thoughtful smile and said, "Ain't nobody your master anymore. You and Moses and Little John are soon to be free and I'm glad that I had a part in it."

Moses approached him with his hand extended. Nathaniel shook his hand and then Moses pulled him in for a firm embrace.

"I wish that there was somethin' I could do to repay you for all you did," Moses told him.

"Just make somethin' of yourself, Moses," Nathaniel replied. He turned to Little John and said, "Do you hear that, Little John? This is your chance, your chance to be free and have a good life. That's how you all can repay me. Make somethin' of your life."

Little John nodded. Nathaniel turned and left his friends in the care of his Underground Railroad acquaintances. His "conductor" friend followed him outside and walked him to the stable. The "station" would loan him a horse, so that he would not have to make the journey back on foot.

The "conductor" spoke with concern, "I can see that what happened out on the line tonight has been eatin' at you."

Nathaniel led the horse out of the stall, making no eye contact, he said, "And, what do you know about it?"

"I know more than you think," the "conductor" explained. "My sister and her family were killed a while back at their home along the Kansas border." Nathaniel made eye contact. His friend had never told him anything personal before. They kept to business. It was safer that way.

The "conductor" continued, "By buswackers, just like your friend last night. It wasn't your fault. If you would have tried to help, you could have gotten all of us killed."

The familiar rage that he felt as a boy had made its way to the surface again. He remembered what it felt like to see his Pa, his Ma, and many others killed during the raid on their wagon train so many years before. The difference this time was that he was no longer a boy. He was a man who would not stand by and do nothing about it.

"I did what you said, and I didn't help," Nathaniel told him, "But, that don't mean that I can't make 'em pay for it."

"You best be careful," the "conductor" warned him. "Men like them don't have a conscience and if you go and get yourself dead, you won't be able to help anybody."

Nathaniel threw the saddle up onto the horse and mounted. He looked at the "conductor" and said, "Thank you for helpin' my friends. I'll be seein' ya'." Then, he rode away.

Chapter 18

A Family Divided

Nathaniel arrived at the plantation house late that afternoon. He had not told anyone that he would be gone during chore time. His absence that morning did not go unnoticed. He met Jackson as he rode in who was fixing a wagon wheel down by the barn.

"Where you been?" Jackson asked him. "William and Sterling have been fit to be tied wonderin' where you were at."

Nathaniel said nothing. He tied up his horse and pulled off the saddle. Jackson continued to work on the wagon, but kept talking, "Everything's been upside down around here because of Moses, Jerusaleh, and Little John runnin' off. James told Uncle Richard that he thinks somebody on the farm helped 'em. He was even sayin' that Obie was actin' suspicious, remindin' Uncle Richard that Obie was the one who saw the trespassers that they went out lookin' for."

"Obie didn't do nothin'. He didn't help nobody run off," Nathaniel told him adamantly.

"That may be so," Jackson told him, "But Uncle Richard gave him a harsh talkin' to. He told Obie that he had done a good job servin' him all these years and that he appreciated him. Then, he told him that it didn't mean nothin' when it comes to helpin' slaves run off. Uncle Richard said that if he found out that Obie helped 'em, he would pay for it."

Jackson could see the anger in Nathaniel's eyes.

Nathaniel said, as a matter fact, "If anyone lays a hand on Obadiah, they'll be answerin' to me."

"You better watch yourself, Nathaniel," Jackson warned. "I know how much Obadiah and the other slaves mean to you, but, what about the family? Have you forgotten all that they've done for us?"

"As far as I'm concerned, you're the only family I got, Jackson," Nathaniel told him. "This family here ain't doin' right. I don't understand how you can look the other way while folks livin' right down the hill from where you sleep every night are kept there against their will."

"It ain't like that and you know it," Jackson said as he tried to reason with him. "They don't know any different and most of 'em wouldn't change things even if they could."

"You can keep on believin' that if it makes you feel better, Little Brother, but deep down you know that it ain't true," Nathaniel replied.

"All's I know is this is how it's been since we came here and nothin' has changed," Jackson told him.

Nathaniel was cool and deliberate when he spoke and said, "Everything has changed. Missoura' has changed. I've changed, and the folks livin' right here on this farm have changed. They ain't the same as when we were kids."

"I don't know what you're talkin' about, but the one thing I do know is that I won't forget what Uncle Richard and Aunt Jane did for us. And, as for the boys and the girls,

I love all of them as if they were my own brothers and sisters. I can't go against 'em," Jackson explained.

"So, you won't go against *them*, but you'd go against me?" Nathaniel asked him.

Now Jackson was angry. "You know better. I ain't choosin'. You are my brother, and you will always come first. I just hope that you ain't doin' somethin' that you shouldn't be doin'," Jackson warned.

Nathaniel really didn't doubt his brother. He knew that Jackson was loyal. "Enough talk," he told Jackson, "I got things to do." Then, he turned and left Jackson standing by the barn.

Nathaniel entered the house through the back door and found Cassie in the kitchen. Her demeanor changed when she saw Nathaniel standing there. She looked concerned.

He calmly said, "Anything left to eat?"

"Yes," she told him. "There's some cornbread and beans on the sideboard. They might still be warm."

Nathaniel helped himself and sat down to eat. Cassie poured him a glass of milk and set it down next to his plate. Neither of them said a word.

As Nathaniel was finishing his supper, Uncle Richard came into the kitchen. Nathaniel looked up and said with a low voice, "Howdy."

"Where you been, Nathaniel?" Uncle Richard asked him with a piercing gaze.

"I mean no disrespect, but I don't think that I have to account for where I go or what I do," Nathaniel told him.

"There was work to be done and you weren't here to do your share. Worse yet, we've been lookin' out for trespassers and huntin' for runaway slaves. You should have been here," Uncle Richard told him.

Nathaniel's reply was less than apologetic, "I've always done more than my share of the work around here. I stayed on this past year to help out because of all that has happened, even though I should have been with my wife. Now you're sayin' that's not good enough."

"Maybe, since you choose not to bring your wife here and you've got better things to be doin', it's time for you to be movin' on," Uncle Richard told him.

Nathaniel stood up from the table. This was his way out. He would not stay in the same house with Robert and James anymore after what happened at Sam Alton's farm, but he didn't want his leaving to look suspicious. "I think you're right," Nathaniel agreed. "It's time for me to be on my way."

Cassie, a silent witness to the conversation, was heartbroken. She loved Nathaniel. She always would, but she knew, too, that it was better for him to leave. It would be safer for everyone.

Nathaniel walked out on Uncle Richard, went to his room, and packed up the few things that he still had in the house. Robert and James saw him leaving and followed him down to the barn.

"It's about time you showed up," Robert told him.

Nathaniel ignored him.

"Where do you think you're goin' now?" sneered James.

"I ain't one of your slaves, James," Nathaniel told him as he kept walking. "I do as I please and don't have to give account to nobody."

Nathaniel's response incited him. He lunged at Nathaniel, grabbed him, and threw him against the side of the barn. Nathaniel offered no resistance.

"You may not be one of my slaves," James told him, "But as far as I'm concerned you ain't no better. Pa should have sent you down the hill to live with them when you got here. You ain't never been part of this family and you never will be. If you was really a Caldwell, you'd be loyal to Pa and the cause and stand with the rest of the family."

Nathaniel, pinned to the side of the barn by James, was calm and as a matter of fact with his reply, "It's you that's a disgrace to the Caldwell name, not me. You think nobody knows what you've been doin", but you're wrong. I am MY father's son and proud of it. My Pa would never own another man or build a fortune off the hard work of men, women, and children who don't have a choice. You're right, I ain't part of this family and I never wanted to be."

Nathaniel saw hate in James' eyes as the two men faced off. James did not possess the same control that Nathaniel did in the moment. He pulled out his pistol and held the barrel to Nathaniel's head. James was shaking, sweat rolled down his face, and his breathe was labored.

"You think you can talk to me like that and get away with it?" James asked Nathaniel.

Robert interjected nervously, "James, what's gotten into you? Yer takin' this too far."

"You shut your mouth, Robert," James retorted. "You know he's been askin' for this for a long time."

Jackson happened by on his way up to the house. He saw James restraining Nathaniel and holding a pistol to his head. Alarmed, he ran toward Nathaniel and James and hollered out, "James, what are you doing? Have you gone crazy?"

James didn't answer.

"Put that gun away," demanded Jackson.

"This ain't your business, Jackson. This is between me and Nathaniel," James retorted.

"C'mon on now, James," Jackson told him. "You're makin' this my business. I said put your gun away."

"He's right, James," Robert told him. "Pa wouldn't like this. Leave him alone. Let's go to town and cool off."

Everyone paused a moment and then, James slowly put his pistol in his holster. He released Nathaniel. Then, he and Robert rode off.

"Nathaniel, what in the world is goin' on?' Jackson asked him still shocked by the whole situation.

"It ain't your business, Jackson," Nathaniel told him as he picked up his hat.

"What do ya' mean, it ain't my business? Nathaniel, talk to me," he pleaded as Nathaniel walked away.

Nathaniel mounted his horse and took one last look at the plantation. There were no good-byes. He felt no sadness. Instead, he only felt disdain. The beautiful house, the sprawling fertile fields, and the big barn were all a representation of a way of life that he loathed, wealth built by the hands of men, women, and children who were in bondage.

"No more," Nathaniel said to himself, "No more." He never belonged here. It had been an anchor around his neck for so many years, dragging him down. He rode off quickly with no regret.

Nathaniel's memories of the night that he left Caldwell Plantation were interrupted by little Dorie who came running out of the cabin.

"Where did Uncle Jack go, Papa?" Dorie asked him.

"He had some things to do that he believes are important?" Nathaniel answered.

"I didn't get to show him the new doll that Mama made for me. Will he be comin' back?" she asked her Pa.

"I hope so, Dorie, I truly hope so," he told her.

Chapter 19

Ella Remembers

While Jackson and George continued their journey to meet up with Jackson's regiment and Nathaniel reminisced on his front porch, Ella was doing her best not to worry about her husband and her brother. She wanted to be obedient to God's Word. She knew that she should trust the Lord in all things. However, there were days that she struggled desperately within her heart. These were the times when she was overcome by the fear of losing yet another person that she loved.

There had been so much loss and so much pain in so many lives. Some days, she wondered if she could bear it all. Then, she would read God's Word or hear something that the preacher would say, and she would be reminded to cast her cares at the feet of Jesus. It was too much for her to carry by herself, but she knew that her God was able. It was the only way that she could make it from day to day without Jackson by her side. She longed for a simple, normal life, with her husband, in her own home, working their own farm, raising a family together, and praising and worshipping God. Ella didn't get what she wanted.

After Jackson and George left that morning, she tried to stay busy. She helped Anne with some house chores, all the while trying to not think about the 'what if's'. "What if Jackson were hurt again? What if he were captured? Would he be the same? Would the war change him forever? What if he didn't come back at all?"

Ella, with broom in hand, was sweeping around the fireplace as if she were swatting mice. Anne was sipping a cup of tea, working on some sewing, all the while, watching Ella fret.

"Ella, your're gonna wear out those boards if you keep that up," she told her.

"I know," Ella agreed, "I just have to keep myself busy or I'll go crazy." It was hard for Ella to get used to the emptiness. The O'Connor farm had always been so full of life.

While she continued to fret and Anne continued her sewing, the front door opened, and Tom came in from the work shed carrying a beautiful cradle. Anne rose to her feet with joy and excitement.

"What have you been up to, Thomas O'Connor?" She asked him.

"What does it look like?" He told her with a mischievous grin on his face.

"Oh, Tom," Anne said, as she threw her arms around his neck and hugged him.

"Does that mean you like it?" he asked her as he kissed her on the forehead.

"Quit you're teasin'," she warned him. "I love it," she said as she ran her hands over the rails, admiring his workmanship. "Thank you."

Ella was determined to be happy for her brother and Anne even if she could not be happy for herself. She went to her room and came back with a baby blanket that she had made especially for Tom and Anne's new baby.

"I was savin' this for when the baby came, but I want you to have it now. Then. the cradle will be all ready when he or she gets here," Ella said with a smile as she handed the blanket to Anne.

"Oh Ella, it's just beautiful. Thank you for thinking of us," Anne told her.

"You're welcome. I'm pleased that you like it," Ella replied.

"It's mighty thoughtful of you, El," Tom told her, "We appreciate your thinkin' about us especially when you've got so much on your own mind."

Ella managed a half-hearted smile and a nod as Tom continued, "You know that we were sorry to see Jackson and George go, too. Don't you?"

"I know," she told him, "But don't either of you be worryin' about that. You just think about gettin' ready for the new addition to the family. I'll be alright and Jackson and George will take care of each other. The Lord is teaching me to trust Him. That's what we all need to do."

"Of course, you're right," Anne explained, "It's just such troublin' times that we're livin' in. It's frightenin' knowin' that I am bringing a child into it when there is such uncertainty."

"Just remember," Ella told her, "It may be uncertain for you and me, but the Good Lord knows exactly how it will all turn out. He's not surprised by any of this. He's got Jackson, George, and your sweet baby in his hands. He's gonna take care of us, Anne. I just know it."

Anne hugged Ella and put the blanket into the cradle. Tom, not knowing what to do to ease Anne or Ella's burden, tried lightening the moment when he said, "I'm thinkin' we should find a place for this here baby cradle. Why don't you show me where we should put it, Anne?"

She smiled and said, "I know just the place," and she followed him up the stairs.

Tom and Anne had moved from the little cabin at the end of the lane to the farmhouse after Lucy and Amos and Lila and Charles left. Ella was glad to have them here with her. She could have never stayed in her Pa and Ma's house all alone.

Standing by the fireplace, Ella thought about what she said to Anne. "I know in my heart that what I told Anne is true, Lord," she quietly prayed, "but, even though I know that it is true, I am so afraid. Dear God, please take care of Jackson and George. Bring them back home to us safely."

She sat down in the rocking chair and closed her eyes. She wanted to feel Jackson close to her. She would have to hold him tightly in heart and her mind.

She thought about how much she loved him. She thought about how they both knew, even as children, that they would always be together. She believed that God had given them to each other.

She remembered the day when he asked her to marry him right outside this room on the front porch. It was a day much like today, right after the harvest. The sun was shining, but the air was crisp. The leaves were beginning to fall, making a blanket on the ground full of color: yellow, orange, and red. The smell of wood burning in the fireplace filled the air. Jackson came here to her family home to pay a call. He knocked on the door and Ella's Mama greeted him.

"Hello, Jackson. We weren't expectin' to see you today. Won't you come in?" her Mama asked him.

He said, "Thank you ma'am, but if it's alright, I'll wait here. I came to see Ella. I was wonderin' if she could come out on the porch so that we might talk alone?" he asked her.

Mama was a little puzzled when she said, "I think that'll be alright. I'll go and fetch her for you." And, in just a moment, Ella greeted Jackson on the front porch.

"Hello, Jackson," Ella said rather surprised to see him.

"Howdy, El," he said. They stood there looking at each other. Jackson was nervous and awkward. Ella was confused.

Finally, she said, "Mama said that you wanted to talk to me."

"Yes, I do. I've got somethin' that's been on my mind. I think you probably already know, but I need to tell you anyway. You see......... well............. it's time," he told her.

Ella interrupted, "Time for what?"

"Well," Jackson was trying to explain, "Ya' see, Nathaniel's left the plantation."

She interrupted again, "Left? Where did he go?"

"He went and got Rose from her Ma and Pa's place and took her home to their farm, but never mind about that," he continued. "What I'm tryin' to tell ya' is that I feel like I've done my best to help Uncle Richard and the children get back on their feet since losing Aunt Jane, but things are never gonna be the same there. It may never be right again. Now that Nathaniel's gone, it seems like it might be a good time for me to start thinikin' about what I'm gonna do next. I think I need to find my own way, be my own man."

Ella interrupted again, "Jackson Caldwell, you didn't come here to tell me that you're leavin' did you?"

"Awe, El, would you let me finish?" Jackson said, annoyed this time. "No, it's nothin' like that."

"Well, then spit it out," she nervously demanded.

"I'm tryin'," Jackson told her. "I'm thinkin' that it's time for.........well, for you and me, ya' see................to be together all the time."

Ella's eyes opened wide in disbelief. She didn't know if she dare hope for what she thought that he might be trying to say. "What are you sayin', Jackson?" she asked him.

"I want to know if you'll marry me," he blurted out.

She couldn't believe her ears. She was stunned. She froze, composing her thoughts. She wanted to remember this always.

Jackson, waiting nervously for a reply, studied her face, looking for some sort of reaction to his question.

Then, she gave him a gentle smile, moved toward him, and put her hand on his cheek. Softly, she said, "Yes, Jackson, I'll marry you."

Jackson, relieved, smiled, too, as she wrapped her arms around his neck, and he lifted her off the ground twirling her round and round. He kissed her sweetly as he set her down. She let him go and he reached for her hand to lead her into the house.

"We best go see what your Pa has to say about it," he said as he pulled her toward the door.

"Papa," Ella called as she and Jackson came into the house. Her Mama was in the parlor.

"Mama, where's Papa?" Ella asked her.

"Last I knew, he was down by the barn," Mama told her.

"I'll be right back," Jackson told her as he ran for the door.

He was off to find her Papa while Ella and her Mama waited.

"Ella, what's gotten into that boy?" Mama asked her.

"Oh Mama, Jackson asked me to marry him. He's going to ask Papa's permission right now." Ella had never looked so happy as she told her Mama the news.

Tears filled Mama's eyes as she hugged her girl. "Oh, Ella," Mama said. "I know that you and Jackson will be just as happy as your Papa and I have been for all of these years."

"I love him so much," Ella told her.

"I know that you do, and I believe that he loves you, too," said Mama.

Meanwhile, Jackson found Papa in the barn.

"Hello, Jackson, what brings you here on this fine day?" Papa asked him as he continued about his work.

"Well, Sir, I have a question that I have been wanting to ask you for a while now," Jackson replied.

"And what might that be?" Papa inquired.

"I've been thinkin' that it's time for me to be on my own," Jackson explained.

"You have now?" Papa asked as he stopped what he was doing. "Are you lookin' for a job?"

"Not exactly," Jackson continued.

"I've been thinkin' about the future," Jackson paused, searching for the words. "And, sir, I think you must know how I feel about Ella," Jackson told him with a lump in his throat.

Now he had Papa's undivided attention.

Jackson continued, "I want Ella to be a part of my future. I'm asking you for permission to marry her."

Daniel O'Connor knew that there would come a day when he would be giving his girls away. He could not know that Ella would be the only one that he would see walk down the aisle. The thought of her leaving the family weighed heavy on his heart, but he could not ask for a finer young man for his sweet Ella.

"I see," replied Papa. "Have you prayed about this decision, and do you believe that it is the Lord's will?"

"Yes Sir, I have. And, yes, Sir, I do," Jackson said confidently.

"And do you have a plan to take care of a wife?" Papa asked him.

"I've worked hard for my Uncle Richard and saved near all the money that I've earned workin' at the plantation. I mean to buy some land before we marry, so we can work our own farm together," Jackson explained.

"I expected you to come askin' me this very question one day, so, I am not surprised. I speak for her mother and meself when I say, yes, to your request," Papa told him.

Jackson was relieved. "Thank you, sir," Jackson told him as he reached to shake Daniel O'Connor's hand.

Jackson hurried back to the house without another word. The door flew open as Ella was nervously waiting for her Papa's reply. Jackson blurted out, "He said yes." Ella laughed with delight and Jackson picked her up and twirled her around again.

"Woo hoo," he hollered, "He said yes."

Daniel could hear Jackson all the way down by the barn. A bittersweet smile appeared on his face. Meanwhile, Mama, a witness to the goings on up at the house, laughed with Ella and Jackson, too. Her heart was so full of joy and thankfulness to the Lord for answering her prayers for her daughter. She had prayed since Ella was a little girl that the little boy who would grow to be her husband would be raised in the nurture and admonition of the Lord. She prayed that he would love her and lead her as the Lord commands in His Word. Mama believed that Jackson was that man.

Chapter 20

The Wedding

Once Jackson and Ella had her parent's permission, they were determined to not let any grass grow under their feet, or, rather, snow fall under their feet. They decided they were going to be married before the first snow fell. The next Sunday they asked the preacher if he would do the honor of marrying them in their little country church.

Plans were soon underway. Mama insisted that Ella have a proper wedding dress, so mother and daughter went to town to select fabric so she could start making one right away. Lucy and Lila helped write invitations and Papa decided that they would host a reception at the family farm. It would be a day that Ella and Jackson would always remember.

Ella remembered waking up on her wedding day still in disbelief that she was finally going to marry Jackson Caldwell. She felt like she was dreaming as she laid there in her warm feather bed in the room that she had shared with her two sisters. Lila and Lucy were already awake. They both seemed to be waiting for her to open her eyes. They each grinned and giggled as they leaped onto Ella's bed.

"Oh, Ella," Lucy said, "I can't believe that you're really getting married today."

Ella was giddy. "I can't believe it either. I feel like I've been waiting for this day my whole life."

"I'm so happy for you, Ella, but I am going to miss you so much," Lila told her.

Ella sat up and hugged her. "I'll miss you, too, Lila, but we will always be sisters. Not even Jackson can take the place of my sisters. Besides, I'm only going to be a few steps away down at the end of the lane, at least for the winter. I'm sure we're still gonna see each other plenty," Ella told her.

Papa O'Connor had given Ella and Jackson the land on the edge of his property as a wedding gift, but there was no house there yet. Ella and Jackson would stay in the small cabin that Papa and Mama first lived in until Jackson and the boys could start building their new house in the spring.

There was a knock on the bedroom door and Mama entered with Ella's wedding dress draped over her arms. "It's time to rise and shine, sleepy heads. We have a weddin' to get to," Mama told them.

The girls jumped up and Mama carefully placed the dress on the bed. Ella was in awe of Mama's handiwork. She pulled the ribbons through her fingers and fluffed the lace around the neckline as she admired it. "Oh, Mama, it's so beautiful," she told her.

Mama was pleased as she said, "I'm so glad that you like it," choking back the tears.

Ella knew how much love went into making the beautiful gown that lay in front of her. It was white, with a rounded neckline that was trimmed in lace from shoulder to shoulder. The dress had no sleeves, but long satin gloves would cover her arms and a matching cloak would keep her warm on the way to the church. There was a sash around the waist that was tied into a bow on one side. "So, simple," she thought to herself, "and, so beautiful."

Lila and Lucy scurried downstairs to start some breakfast while Mama helped Ella dress. Mama was already wearing her blue Sunday dress. Ella thought how lovely and young her Mama looked. She looked much too young to be the mother of the bride.

"I can't believe that I am standing here in front of a bride," Mama told her. "It seems like yesterday that you were just a little girl, singing with me and helping me weed the garden."

Ella reached out to her and hugged her tight. "Thank you, Mama," Ella told her, "For my dress and for your help, but mostly for loving me and taking care of me all these years. I love you so much."

Mama spoke no words. She just smiled as tears slowly flowed down her cheeks. There was so much love on her face. Ella reached for hands and continued, "Now don't you worry. Jackson is going to take care of me now, just like you and Papa did all these years. I hope knowin' how happy I am will make it easier for you to let me go."

"Yes, my darling girl. I couldn't part with you if that weren't true," Mama told her. "Now, no more tears," she said as she wiped her cheeks. "This is happy day. My, you are the most beautiful bride that I have ever seen."

Ella turned to look at her image in the mirror, admiring her lovely gown.

"Jackson loves me. He's been waiting for this his whole life, too," she thought to herself as she gazed into the mirror.

Lucy and Lila, back from breakfast, interrupted. "You look beautiful," Lucy squealed.

"Do you really think so?" Ella asked her beaming.

"Of course, you do," Lila interjected.

"You two better be getting ready, too," Ella instructed. "Don't you be making me late for my own weddin'."

Each of the sisters put on their best Sunday dresses. Then, it was time to go. Papa looked so proud as he saw the lovely bride walking down the stairs. Mama was waiting by the door with three bouquets of pink asters that she had lovingly picked that morning, one for each of her daughters. Mama, Lila, Lucy, Tom, and George took the wagon and left for the church. Ella and Papa would take the small carriage the long way to the church so that the bride would be the last to arrive.

It was a beautiful sunshiny day, a little cool, but normal for this time of year in Missouri. Neither father nor daughter spoke at first. Each preoccupied with their own thoughts. Today, Ella was seeing the countryside that had been so familiar to her with new eyes.

"I never realized how truly lovely the country is in the fall, Papa, the trees beginning to change colors, the sun shining on the hillside, and the asters all still in full bloom," she told him as she smelled the aroma of her own bouquet.

"Ah," said Papa, "You're seeing it as a young woman today. You are no longer seeing life through the eyes of a child."

Ella thought for a moment. Then, she asked him earnestly, "Am I ready, Papa?"

"Yer as ready as anyone can be," he assured her. "No one ever really knows what to expect when joinin' their life with another's, but if you build your new life on the foundation of the Lord Jesus Christ and use His Word as your guide, you cannot fail."

Ella slipped her arm through her Papa's arm and laid her head on his shoulder as she thought about what he told her. "Papa is right," she thought to herself, "He is so wise. This is God's plan, and I am so blessed."

Papa and Ella soon arrived outside their little country church. Wagons, horses, and carriages surrounded the building indicating that the church house was full. The Randalls, the Whiteakers, the Caldwells, and the O'Connors were all in attendance.

George was waiting by the door. When he saw Ella and Papa, he went inside and announced the arrival of the bride so that everyone could take their places. Lucy and Lila went to the front of the church, bouquets in hand, and took their places by the alter. Nathaniel and Tom took their places, too, as did Jackson who was nervously waiting to see his bride.

Papa helped Ella out of the carriage and escorted her to the front doors. George was waiting there to open them for her grand entrance. Ella gave George her cloak. He opened the doors. The music began to play, and all eyes were on Ella as Papa walked her down the aisle to meet Jackson. Ella noticed nothing in the room except for her groom. She was fixed on him, and he was fixed on her.

Papa reached for her hand, placed it in Jackson's hand, and took a seat next to Mama. Jackson smiled at her and softly said, "You're beautiful."

Ella blushed and smiled back at him. Jackson was handsome in his new suit, but it was the smile that he wore on his face that Ella remembered the most. They turned their attention to the preacher who began to address the couple standing in front of him. They exchanged their vows and were pronounced man and wife.

The newlyweds hurried out of the church and climbed into the carriage that had brought Ella there. Their guests hurried out behind them and threw rice as Jackson and Ella wheeled away in the carriage. Then, each family followed behind them for the reception at the O'Connor farm.

The reception was so festive. Papa played his fiddle, and everyone danced. Lucy and Lila served punch and Mama sliced the cake that Mrs. Randall had made.

Ella was grateful as she thought back to her wedding day. She was grateful to have had all her friends and family together, and she was grateful for Jackson. The Lord reminded her that she was blessed, and, for a moment, she was at peace again. She started thinking about their first Christmas.

Chapter 21

A New Life

The newlyweds settled into the little cabin that her Papa had built so many years before, looking forward to their first Christmas together. Ella remembered the morning that Jackson woke her up, excited to go hunting for their first Christmas tree.

"Wake up, sleepy head. The day's a wastin'," Jackson said as he wiggled her toes that were peeking out from beneath the quilt.

She opened her eyes and gave him a smile as she stretched and said, "What are you up to?"

"C'mon on now," he told her. "Get dressed. You and me are goin' to go find us a Christmas tree."

She was as excited as she was when she was a child at just the thought. She leaped out of bed, hurriedly got dressed, found her coat and her boots, and was ready to go.

"Hold on," Jackson told her, "Don't you want a bite to eat, first?

Skillet in hand, Jackson was already serving up some eggs.

"You thought of everything, didn't you?" Ella told him as she sat down at the table.

They quickly devoured their breakfast and hurried off in search of the perfect tree. It was a lovely winter day even though there was no sunshine. It wasn't too cold and there was a light dusting of snow on the ground. It wasn't long before they stumbled upon what Jackson thought was just the right tree.

"What do ya' think?" he asked her.

"It's perfect," she told him.

It was a beautiful pine, just the right height. Jackson cut it down with the saw that he had brought along and dragged it back to the cabin. He stood it up in an empty corner while Ella pulled out her sewing basket. They decorated it together with ribbon and yarn.

When the work was all done, they stood together and admired their finished tree.

"It's beautiful." she told him.

"Just like you," Jackson told her as she put her arms around his neck to hug him tightly.

"Thank you for thinking of this," she said.

"You're welcome," he said with a gleam in his eye.

They planned to spend Christmas with the O'Connor family. Ella wanted to do something special for everyone, so the couple spent Christmas Eve making popcorn balls together. Ella was surprised at how handy Jackson was in the kitchen. He didn't even seem to mind. They talked as they worked. They laughed. They sampled the delicacies and enjoyed every moment.

Christmas Day was perfect, even though all the snow had melted. It was sunny and the air was crisp. The family enjoyed a fine meal, sweet potatoes, ham, and fresh baked bread. They opened their gifts: wool socks for the men, scarves for the ladies, an embroidered handkerchief for Mama, and a new book for Lila. The family was blessed.

Papa played the fiddle. They all sang hymns and worshipped God. Then, they gathered around the fireplace. It was an O'Connor tradition to read the account of the birth of the Savior from God's Word and praise Him for His precious Gift.

After Papa finished reading from the Scripture, he turned to his family and said, "You see, my dear sons and daughters, we can never out give the Lord. The Bible says in John 3:16, 'For God so loved the world that He gave His only begotten Son that whosoever should believeth in Him should not perish but have everlasting life'. The Father sent his only Son to be born in a manger, a King with a lowly birth, to live, and then, to die in our place so that we might have eternal life. There is no greater gift, no greater love."

Then, he raised his head and look upward. It was as if he was looking into heaven. With tears in his eyes, he reached for Mama's hand, speaking slowly and precisely, "Lord, I give you glory...... and honor........and praise. Thank you....... for the precious gift of your Son. Thank you, Dear Saviour, for your sacrifice, for giving your life, so that those in this family and all others who would repent of their sins and believe on Your name, could have forgiveness of sins and life everlasting. Thank you for saving me, Dear Lord. And, if there be anyone here in this room that is not in your fold, I ask that you shine your light in their hearts and birth them into your kingdom. Amen."

The words that Papa had shared from God's Word and his prayer, made an impact on Jackson. He had never heard anyone pray with such honesty and purity before. He remembered his Pa praying before meals when he was a young boy. He remembered his Ma praying with him when she tucked him into bed at night. He remembered Aunt Jane praying in her parlor for her husband and each of the children.

Each prayer was sincere, but Papa O'Connor's prayer was different. He honored. He petitioned. He expected an answer from Someone that was in their midst. It was almost uncomfortable, in a good way, in a reverent way. It was powerful. Jackson desired to meet God that way, to be able to offer prayers so sincerely, so earnestly. He would never forget that Christmas. He would never forget what he learned from Papa O'Connor that day.

Christmas came and went, as did winter. Then, came the first signs of spring. Jackson and Ella worked together to plant their first crops. Once the planting was finished, Jackson built a small shed, a chicken coup, and with the help of Pa, George, and Tom, a small barn that was finished by early summer.

With the crops in the field, a shed and a barn complete, Jackson and Ella would begin building a home of their very own. It was small, only two rooms, but it was built with love and their very own hands. There was a small bedroom in the back and one large room in the front that was multipurpose. It served as kitchen, dining room, and parlor.

Tom and George helped Jackson with the large fireplace that kept the cabin warm. There were two rocking chairs sitting side by side that Tom had made. In front of the fireplace between the two chairs lay a large rug that

Ella had woven herself. Mama made curtains and gave Ella a quilt that her grandmother had made many years before. Little by little and with help from their family, that tiny little cabin felt more and more like home.

The summer was good. There was so much accomplished. Then, Fall came with ample goodness of its own. The harvest was plenteous. Jackson and Ella celebrated their first anniversary and they marveled at the blessings. God had been so good to them.

Then....... tragedy struck. Their faith was tested. It was right after this harvest that Babcock and Brown came to the O'Connor farm and killed Ella's Pa. Life as she knew it changed forever. She faced great pain. She faced great loss, the loss of both her parents. And soon, she would be face to face with war.

Chapter 22

War is Declared

Word traveled quickly around the county about what happened to Daniel O'Connor. Many folks decided it was time to take measures to protect themselves and their property. The threat of bushwackers and the threat of war were looming. Many of the local men, including Jackson, joined the Missouri Volunteer Militia.

Ella remembered the day that Jackson joined all too well. It was the morning after her Papa and Mama's funeral. Grief-stricken, she got out of bed that morning, made some coffee, and stared out the window, wondering to herself, "What will we all do now?".A voice in her head said, "Just do what you would do any other day. Papa and Mama would expect you to." So, she got started on her morning chores.

As she busied herself in their tiny cabin, Jackson was nowhere to be found.

"I wonder what he's up to," she thought to herself.

Soon the door opened, and Jackson came in from outside.

"There you are," she said to him. "I was wonderin' where you were at."

"I was just gettin' the chores done a little early today. I was plannin' on goin' to town," he told her.

"To town? What for?" Ella asked him.

Jackson turned and looked out the window. He was quiet.

"Jackson, what are you goin' to town for?" She pressed him for an answer.

He looked back at her, and said, "I know that you have been through a lot and I don't want to add to your burden, but we're livin' in such troublin' times and I just got to do somethin' about it if I can."

"What are you sayin'?" she asked with an anxious voice.

"I've decided that I'm joinin' the militia, El," he told her.

"Jackson, No!" she exclaimed.

"Hear me out," he told her.

She was quiet, but Jackson saw the fear in her eyes.

"I've been thinkin' about this for a while now," he told her. "Folks are choosin' sides and fightin' for what they believe in. If we all do our part maybe this will all be over quick like and we can go about livin' our lives again. I need you to understand that I'm doin' this for all of us, for you, for me, for the rest of the family, and the family that you and me might have some day. And, after what happened to your Pa, El, I feel like I got no choice. It's all right here at our front door."

"There's always a choice. I need you, Jackson. What am I going to do if you leave me here all alone?" she asked him earnestly.

"That's why I'm joinin' the milita. They're right here in our own county where I can train close to home. Uncle Richard and the boys joined up with them months ago and they ain't had to go anywhere. They've just been watchin' out for things around here and trainin' in case war does break out. If the war doesn't come to Missoura, there won't be anything to worry about. Besides, I wouldn't leave you all alone. I already talked to Tom. If I do have to go away, I'm gonna take you back up to your Papa and Mama's place," he assured her.

"And what about our place, our home right here?" she asked him.

"Tom said I could bring him our livestock and that him and the hired men would watch out for our place, too," he told her.

"You'll be runnin' down bushwackers," she told him. "You know what their like. You know what they did to Papa."

By now there were tears streaming down her face.

"Don't you see that's why I'm doin' this? I want to try and make a difference, before it gets any worse," he explained.

Now Ella was frantic, "You're going to do what you want to do, and I can't stop you, but I won't forgive you for this," she told him.

He walked over to her and hugged her tightly. He kissed her on the top of her head and said, "Yes, you will. You'll forgive me, and one day you'll understand why I gotta do what I'm doin'."

He let her go, picked up his hat, left for town, and did exactly what he said that he was going to do. He signed up for the Missouri State Militia.

Jackson's regiment did stay close to home at first. Then, in early May, everything changed. Missouri Governor Claiborne Jackson claimed Missouri for the Confederacy. The federalists would not give it up without a fight. The

Governor ordered the militia to camp outside of St. Louis. They were told that they were going there for training. However, rumors circulated that they were really on a mission to seize the federal arsenal located there.

Between 700 and 900 soldiers were camped there. The Union Army surrounded them and disarmed the soldiers without any violence, but when they marched back to town, the Union Army was attacked. During the attack, twenty-eight civilians were killed. Missourians were outraged. As a result, Governor Jackson presented a new military bill before the Missouri Legislature calling for the militia to be abolished and for it to be replaced by the new Missouri State Guard.

Ella was thankful that Jackson came home unharmed, but the incident influenced his decision to join up with the Guard. He didn't believe in the Confederate cause. He had joined the militia to protect his home and his family. But, because he refused to take up arms against his family, he had no choice. He would fight alongside the Confederacy.

As a member of the militia, he was serving his family and his neighbors. As a member of the Guard, he was choosing a side in the war. Now he would be on the opposite side of many of his neighbors. He never wanted that to happen.

When the rumors of war started, Ella had convinced herself that somehow, they could escape it. They would be safe, in their own little world on their own little farm. She understood now that there was no escape. The Lord had been working in her heart during the past months. He was teaching her to accept her circumstances and to trust Him in all things. She had to be brave for her and for Jackson.

All these memories, Jackson's proposal, their wedding, their first Christmas, losing her Papa and Mama and the beginning of the war, made Ella feel guilty for not supporting George's decision to join up.

"Why did I make it so hard on him, this morning? Why didn't I hug him and tell him how proud I am of my little brother? Why didn't I tell him that Papa and Mama would be proud of him, too? Why didn't I tell him that I love him?", Ella thought to herself.

She was so wrapped up in Jackson's leaving again that her emotions had gotten the best of her. The fear of possibly losing her brother or her husband had overwhelmed her. She realized that she was only thinking about herself. "Lord, please forgive me for being so selfish?" she prayed.

Ella's thoughts were brought back to the present as she heard Tom and Anne coming down the stairs. They were talking about the cradle and talking about the baby. They were so happy despite everything that was happening around them.

"Did you find a good place for the cradle?" Ella asked them.

"Yes, we found the perfect place," Anne replied with a glow on her face.

"I guess it's time to be thinkin' about some supper," Ella told them. "I'll go and see what I can fix for us."

"I'll come and help you in a bit," Anne told her.

Ella was off to the kitchen. She made a promise to herself that she would do her best to make it through each day, brave and strong, until Jackson would come back to her again. She had no idea how much her resolve would be tested in the months to come.

Chapter 23

The Caldwells and the Confederacy

Times had changed for everyone since the sweet days of innocence when all that Ella had to worry about was what she would wear to one of Aunt Jane's parties. Times were still changing. Jackson and George were gone for who knew how long, fighting a war that neither of them believed in, a war that had affected so many people, so many families.

Charles Randall was fighting for the Union, leaving Lila behind at the hotel to help his Ma and Pa manage their business. Elizabeth Caldwell Whiteaker was now the wife of a Union army captain, while her father and her brothers had taken up the Confederate cause. Her family home, the beautiful plantation, the place that had always been so full of music, laughter, hospitality, and life was now quiet, sad, and uninviting. And, as for Nathaniel, the war had left him maimed, bitter, and estranged from many of the people that loved him.

Richard Caldwell's decision to stand with the Confederacy, would be costly. It would cause his family much heartache. The Caldwells were vocal about their support of the Confederacy, often criticizing and arguing with anyone who sided with the Union.

At first, it almost seemed noble. They were holding to a belief about their way of life and acting on their desire to protect it. Their beliefs, however, evolved into a conviction that was rooted in pride and prejudice. The result was hatred and contempt that led to violence. The raid at Sam Alton's farm was just the beginning of Robert and James Caldwell's involvement in bushwacking.

At first, the two brothers distanced themselves from any raids in their own county or close to their own home. However, with each raid their consciences became seared. They became more and more callous to the suffering that they caused. They even justified it.

No one knew if Uncle Richard was aware of James and Robert's involvement with bushwackers, but there was no doubt about Uncle Richards involvement in aiding the Confederacy. Caldwell Plantation became known as a haven for Confederate soldiers looking for food, shelter, supplies, and fresh horses. He acted as if no one could touch him, as if no one could reach into his world, including the Yankees. Some thought he was brave. Others thought he was full of pride, thinking that he was above the law.

It became common for Confederate soldiers to sneak onto the plantation. Mostly, those caught on the wrong side of the line after a battle or the brave ones who were on their way back to battle after checking on their homes and families. Cassie and the Caldwell daughters were instructed to give any Confederate soldier in need a hot meal and a comfortable place to rest before they continued their journey.

As the war progressed, Uncle Richard's aid increased. It began to take a toll on his finances. His fortune was dwindling. He lost interest in running the plantation. Aunt Jane was no longer there to manage the household finances. William and Sterling had their hands tied in managing the farm because their father would not give them any control. Both sons decided that they could be more useful fighting for the cause and eventually joined the Confederate Army.

The war raged on, and the Confederacy needed more and more help. The more that Uncle Richard got away with, the bolder he became. He started sending Robert and James south from St. Louis with wagons filled with supplies to aid the Confederate soldiers. They even started smuggling ammunition.

Many people owed Uncle Richard favors because of his financial investment in building up the Missouri Territory. They had made their fortunes with his help. His business had been important to merchants, shipmen, lumber suppliers, etc., many of them loyal Confederate citizens. Uncle Richard did not hesitate to call in favors, even though it was becoming increasingly dangerous for any citizen who was a rebel sympathizer.

The Caldwells had become the topic of conversation for the local gossips. The rumors about Uncle Richard and the boys aiding confederates were numerous. Many folks supported their endeavors, but there were plenty of others who did not. It was not uncommon for Uncle Richard or the boys to be confronted by a neighbor or acquaintance about something that they heard. Amos and Jeb Whiteaker, particularly, had many confrontations with Robert and James about loyalty and choosing sides.

One altercation was especially intense. Robert and James were at the local saloon and got wind of some town gossip.

"Howdy, boys," said the bartender, "What'll it be?"

"Whiskey," James told him.

The bartender put up two glasses and poured both boys a glass. Robert placed the money on the counter while James looked around the room. There were many eyes on the two Caldwell's as they settled in at the bar. A few of the patrons got up and left. Other than the usual card game going on in the back corner, it was a quiet night in the saloon.

After a while, one of the locals approached James and Robert.

"Howdy," he said as he positioned himself by Robert.

"What do you want?" Robert asked him.

"I was just wonderin' how things have been goin' on your side of the war?" the man asked him.

James flashed him a look and asked, "What business is it of yours?"

"Well, there's been talk about Yankees settin' up camp around here," he told them.

Robert with a voice of disdain, "Yeah, we heard. What's that got to do with us."

"I don't rightly know if it has anything to do with you," the man said, "but, I thought that you might want to know that Amos and Jeb Whiteaker were over at the mill talkin' about it."

"So," replied Robert.

This got James' attention. He looked at the man and asked, "What were they sayin'?"

"It seems that Jeremiah Whiteaker might be headin' up one of the regiments that's supposed to be comin' to town. They was braggin' about how the Yankees was gonna be takin' care of bushwackers and anybody in the county that was helpin' the Rebs," the man told them.

The man's comments incited James. "I think those Whiteaker boys don't know what their talkin' about," James told him with a tone of disgust.

"Yeah," Robert interjected, "Me and my brother ain't afraid of no Yankees."

"That may be so," said the man, "but, you boys better be careful and get ready for when they get here. Jeremiah Whiteaker knows this county and he knows the people. He'll be watching anybody that he knows sides with the Confederacy."

The man walked away, and James turned back toward the bar. He quietly finished what was in his glass, tapped Robert on the arm, and said, "Let's go."

Robert followed and asked, "Where we goin'?"

"We're gonna pay Amos and Jeb a visit," James told him.

The Whiteaker farm bordered the O'Connor farm on one side of the road and Caldwell Plantation on the other side of the road. Though not a proper plantation, it was a respectable rival to the splendor of Caldwell Plantation. There were multiple dwellings on the farm: a small house for Amos and Lucy, another one by the pond for Jeremiah and Elizabeth, a bunk house for the hired men, and the main house.

The main house was where Mr. and Mrs. Whiteaker raised their large family. Jeremiah and Elizabeth had been staying there since Mr. Whiteaker took ill from a stroke. There was plenty of room and Mrs. Whiteaker appreciated the help. She also appreciated the company of her daughter in law. She had been the only lady in the house since Rose had left with Nathaniel to move to their own homestead. Elizabeth was equally appreciative of Mrs. Whiteaker's company since Jeremiah was away fighting in the war.

Elizabeth had made the little house that she shared with Jeremiah an inviting home, but the main house was more of what she was accustomed to coming from Caldwell Plantation. Mrs. Whiteaker had good taste and had collected some fine things of her own over the years. She hung blue velvet draperies over the tall windows in the parlor and a fine hand carved mantel hung over the fireplace. There were two portraits on the wall, one of her and one of Mr. Whiteaker. A small table with two small chairs in the French style were positioned in front of the fireplace. It was the place that Mrs. Whiteaker enjoyed entertaining a guest or two for afternoon tea.

The parlor was also the place where the family would gather in the evening to hear Mrs. Whiteaker read. She loved literature. Mr. Whiteaker took credit for the fine library that they had built in their home, but it was really Mrs. Whiteaker who collected the books.

When Lucy was a young girl, Mrs. Whiteaker had always been very generous to loan her fabulous tales to get lost in. They had a special friendship because of their mutual love of literature. Now, Lucy as a young woman, was blessed to be Mrs. Whiteaker's daughter in law.

Lucy enjoyed stealing away to the main house in the evenings. Her favorite room, of course, being the library. There were shelves from floor to ceiling that were filled with books of every kind. She would curl up on the big rug in front of the fireplace on chilly nights to read, while Amos worked at his father's desk.

Since Mr. Whiteaker had become ill and Jeremiah was in the army, Amos, who was next in line, managed the farm. The Whiteaker Farm was a lot to manage. They grew crops, but they also did their fair share of ranching. They owned a large herd of cattle and horses.

Amos was working at his father's desk by oil lamp and Lucy was reading a book, when Robert and James quietly rode up to the main house. Mrs. Whiteaker and Elizabeth were seated at the table in the parlor. Elizabeth was working on some embroidery while Mrs. Whiteaker looked on. The house was well lit as the two men approached it on horseback. Newt and Henry, two of the hired men, saw James and Robert ride in.

"Can we help you boys?" Henry asked them.

"Maybe. We're lookin' for Amos and Jeb," Robert told them.

"What do you want with em'?" Newt asked.

"None of your business," James sneered.

"We think it is," Newt told them.

Just then, Jeb, who had also seen the two men riding in, came walking up from down around the corral.

"It's alright," Jeb told the hired men. "What do you two want?" he asked Robert and James.

"We heard that you and your brother have been talkin' around town," James explained.

"What's it to you?" Jeb asked him.

Robert jumped off his horse and darted towards Jeb, "You know you've been runnin' your mouth about me and James," he said as he stood almost nose to nose with Jeb.

"I think you two should be leavin'," Newt told them.

"Robert, that's enough," James scolded, and Robert backed away.

"We came out here to warn you," James told him.

"Is that so?" Jeb asked him.

"You know there's a bunch of folks in this here county that don't like Yankees," James told him. "You Whiteakers have turned on your neighbors and you've turned on Missoura'. People don't appreciate it."

"People, James, or you Caldwells?" Jeb accused him.

"You know we ain't got time for no Yankees," Robert interrupted.

"That don't give you or the likes of you the right to break the law," Jeb told him.

Then, he didn't hold back. He told them what he had wanted to say for a long time.

"We know you two have been ridin' with the bush-wackers, raidin' farms in neighborin' counties and so does everyone else. It's an evil thing that you've been doin' and you need to answer for it."

"You can't prove it," Robert told him.

"Are you threaten' us?" James asked as he put his hand on his holster. "Even if we done what you say we done, who do you think's gonna make us pay? You? Jeremiah?

191

the Yankees?" It's you Yankees that are gonna pay," James threatened.

Jeb was unarmed. Newt was wearing his holster and placed his hand in the same position as James. He watched James carefully.

"You need to be leavin'," Jeb told them with a loud voice. "You don't belong here. Who are you to come on my land and make threats to me?"

Elizabeth, having heard the loud voices, curiously stepped out onto the porch. She saw the five men. Recognizing her brothers, she approached them.

"James, Robert, what are you two doin' here this time of the evenin'?" she asked them. As she got closer, she could tell that something was wrong.

"What's the matter?" she asked.

No one answered at first. Jeb didn't look at Elizabeth. His eyes were locked on James.

Finally, James spoke, "Jeb and Amos have been talkin' in town about Robert and me," James told her.

"What does he mean, Jeb?" Elizabeth asked him.

Jeb still didn't take his eyes off James. He still didn't answer.

"We been hearin' that your new family here, Lizabeth, has plans to make Robert and me pay for bein' loyal to Missoura'," James told her.

"Jeb, what's this about? What does he mean?" she was earnest as she reached for his arm and prodded him for an answer.

"You might as well know," Jeb told her, "They've been up to no good."

"If you mean sidin' with the Confederacy, everyone knows that my Pa believes in the Confederate cause and that James and Robert are in the Guard. None of this is new," she told him.

"What's new is the Yankees are comin' and their gonna be cleanin' up the county. The Guard and Confederate sympathizers ain't gonna be able to keep causin' mischief or come and go as they please anymore," Jeb told her.

"A person should have the right to decide which side they want to be on," Elizabeth told him.

"Even so," Jeb told her, "They don't have the right to steal, burn farms, and kill people."

Elizabeth was shocked. Robert, enraged, knocked Jeb to the ground. The two men fought.

Elizabeth screamed. "Stop this! Do you hear me? Stop this now!" She demanded.

The hired men pulled Jeb and Robert apart and the two men composed themselves.

Amos, having heard the skirmish, came out onto the porch rifle in hand. He didn't speak. He just watched intently. Lucy followed and stood behind him.

"Jeb, you don't really think that my family has any part in bushwackin'?' she asked him.

Jeb didn't say anything. Instead, he locked eyes again with James.

"James," she said, "tell them it's not true. Pa would never be a part of somethin' like that."

"Lizabeth, you made your choice when you married a Whiteaker. We've made our choice, too. You're our sister, but we ain't on the same side anymore." He looked at Robert said, "We're done here. Let's go."

Robert mounted his horse and Elizabeth continued to plead with her brothers.

"Robert, what is he sayin'?" she asked him.

Robert said nothing, but he looked ashamed.

"James, please. We're family. You're my brother and I care about you," she told him.

"Everything's different now," he said as he started to ride away.

She ran after them calling their names, "James, Robert, please come back. We need to settle this."

Her brothers rode away, hastily into the night.

Elizabeth turned to Jeb, looking for an explanation. Then, she turned and looked up at Amos still standing on the front porch.

Jeb walked past her to go into the house.

"Jeb," she said. He kept walking.

She turned to Amos.

"Amos, you don't think that my Pa and my brothers are bushwackin', do you?' she asked him.

"Elizabeth, you are my brother's wife, and I promised to look out for you while he was doing his duty, but right is right and wrong is wrong. Anybody caught bushwackin' needs to pay for it," Amos told her as a matter of fact.

He went back inside, and Lucy followed. What Elizabeth saw and heard that night troubled her deeply. She knew that Jeremiah would clear everything up when he got back. She just needed to be patient and wait.

Chapter 24

A Family Broken

I t had been a week since Jackson and George had left for the war. Ella needed a distraction. Tom decided that a trip to town was just what they all needed. They would take care of some business and pay one last visit to Anne's family before the baby came. Their first stop was the post office where they bumped into Sarah Caldwell.

"Hello, Sarah. It's so good to see you," Ella said as she greeted her with a warm embrace. "How is your family?"

Sarah seemed anxious, almost preoccupied when she said, "We're all fine, Ella. Thank you for asking."

Tom tipped his hat and said, "Hello, Miss Sarah." Anne greeted their neighbor with a smile and the two of them proceeded into the post office.

Ella attempted to continue the conversation.

"Jackson told me that Sterling and William joined up with the Confederacy," she said.

"Yes, that's right," Sarah told her.

"George left with Jackson just last week to join the Guard," Ella said.

"I didn't know that." Sarah replied, "I'm sure you worry over both them."

"Yes," Ella explained, "But, I'm learning to trust the Lord more and more every day."

Sarah looked nervous as folks passed by. Finally, she pulled Ella by both her arms around the corner of the post office building.

"Sarah, whatever is the matter with you?" Ella asked her.

"Mary was out to visit Elizabeth at the Whiteaker place yesterday. We've been missin' her so much and knew that she was probably lonesome with Jeremiah gone. Not to mention, how worried we were after the run in that James and Robert had with Amos and Jeb." Sarah told her.

"Run in? What are you talkin' about? Ella asked her.

"James and Robert paid a visit out at the Whiiteaker place. They heard a rumor and went to settle it," Sarah told her.

"What rumor?" Ella asked her.

"It ain't no rumor. Elizabeth was tellin' Mary that Jeremiah got promoted to captain and about how proud she was of him. She said that she was so thankful because he was gonna be assigned right here," she explained to Ella.

"Here?" Ella asked confused. "Yankees are movin' in here?"

"Yes, because of all of the bushwackin' goin' on and all the people sidin' with the Confederacy. They call us rebels and say that we are a threat to the security of the Union," Sarah told her.

"I thought that was what the Provost Marshall was for, to keep law and order," Ella said.

"Evidently, he can't do it by himself. There are too many of us that have chosin' to stand with the Confederacy and they want to know who we are," she continued. "Jackson and George can't come back here until this war is over," she warned. "You have to tell them."

"How would I do that? I don't even know where he's at right now." Ella told her.

"I want to tell you somethin', but you can't tell a soul, not even Tom and Anne. Do you promise?" Sarah asked her.

"Yes, I promise," Ella replied.

Sarah continued, "I just sent a letter to St. Louis to some people that my Pa knows. We have a mail line goin' from there. We use it to get word to our soldiers about what the Yankees are up to back here and anywhere else that we hear about."

"That sounds dangerous, Sarah," Ella warned her. "Are you sure you know what you're doin'?"

"We gotta do somethin' to help the cause. We just can't sit around and wait." Sarah told her.

Ella reached out to her and gave her a firm hug. She was worried.

"I won't tell a soul," Ella told her, "But, you promise me that you will be careful."

"I will," Sarah promised as she rushed back to the wagon where Obie was waiting for her. Ella made eye contact with Obie. He gave her a thoughtful smile and tipped his hat from across the way.

As Sarah and Obie drove away, Tom and Anne had finished their business at the post office.

"Ella," Tom said, "I'm goin' to take you and Anne over to the hotel, so you can start your visit. Then, I'll go on over to the store and get the things on our list. I'll meet you both when I'm through."

"Ella and I can walk, Tom," Anne told him.

"Walk! You shouldn't be walkin' in your condition," Tom told her.

Anne laughed. "Thomas O'Connor, I'm not sick. I'm perfectly capable of walking three blocks. The fresh air and the exercise will be good for me. It will be good for both of us," she told him.

"I'll take good care of her. We'll go straight there and meet you real soon," Ella reassured him.

"Alright," Tom conceded, "I ain't gonna argue with the both of you."

The two ladies enjoyed their stroll to the hotel. Mrs. Randall was behind the counter when Ella and Anne opened the door. Anne's mother was obviously glad to see them.

"Anne, Ella, what a wonderful surprise," Mrs. Randall said as she approached the girls with arms wide open. "What brings you to town?" she asked them as she hugged them both.

"Tom had some business, so Ella and I thought we would come along to visit with you and Pa and Lila," Anne told her.

"I'm so glad that you did, but I'm not sure you should have made the trip in your condition," Anne's mother told her a bit concerned.

"This was probably my last chance before the baby comes, besides I'm not due for a few more months. Don't you fret. I feel fine, just a little tired," Anne told her.

"Well, come along and let's find you a soft chair and somethin' to eat," Mrs. Randall said as she escorted the two ladies back to the family's living quarters.

"Is Lila home?" Ella asked Mrs. Randall as she followed along.

"As a matter of fact, she is," Mrs. Randall told her. "Your sister is out back hanging some sheets on the line. She'll be finished in just a little while."

Ella was so looking forward to seeing her. Lila understood how she felt and what she was going through with Charles off fighting for the Union somewhere. "Oh, how strange it all is," Ella thought to herself. "Charles in blue and Jackson in grey. How did this happen?"

Anne's father was just as surprised to see her as her mother was. "Hello, Pa," she said with a smile as she hurried across the room to hug him.

"It's so good to see you, Anne. You as well, Ella," Mr. Randall said obviously glad to see them both.

"Tom had some business, so Anne and Ella came with him," Mrs. Randall told her husband. "Isn't this a wonderful surprise?"

"It is indeed," said Mr. Randall.

"Can I get you some tea?" offered Mrs. Randall.

"Yes, thank you, Mother, that would be lovely," Anne told her.

"I'd love some tea," said Ella.

"Come sit down," said Mr. Randall as his wife went to get the tea.

The back door opened before Ella got to her chair. It was Lila. She was so surprised and excited to see Ella that she dropped her empty basket with a squeal and hurried to greet her sister.

"Ella, I didn't know you were coming. I'm so happy to see you. How have you been? Hello, Anne. It's so good to see you, too. Where's Tom? How is he? How long can you stay?" All three women started to laugh as Lila realized that she left no opportunity for either of them to reply to anything she asked.

"I'm sorry. I'm just so happy to see you both," she said as they made themselves comfortable for an afternoon visit.

"We're glad to see you too, Lila. I know you've only been gone a little while, but it seems like forever," Ella told her.

"Mother and Pa Randall are taking good care of me, so don't you be frettin'." She turned to Anne and said, "I hope you don't mind, Anne, but I've settled into your old room."

"Of course, I don't mind. I think you and I have traded places. Tom and I moved up to the big house and we have taken over your old room," Anne told her.

Lila laughed and said, "Who would've ever thought?"

They all continued with some good conversation. The Randall's talked about business at the hotel, some colorful characters who had visited, and how everyone was keeping busy. Ella and Anne talked about the weather and the plenteous harvest and how thankful they were to get most of the work done that they needed to before winter set in. They had a cup of tea and some pie. Then, there was a knock on the door. It was Tom.

"Come in, Tom," said Mrs. Randall, "Would you like to join us for some tea?"

"Thank you, ma'am, but no tea for me," Tom said. "Hello, Pa Randall. Hello, Lila. These ladies have sure been anxious to see you all."

"Thank you for bringing them with you, Tom," said Mr. Randall. "We've missed you all so much."

"Ella and Anne were just tellin' us about the farm. How is everything out there?" Lila asked her brother.

"We're managin'," Tom told her. "We do the things that are important and don't worry about the rest. That's all you can do in times like these. Big Sister, here, has been a blessing," Tom said as he looked at Ella. "She has been doin' as much work as any of the hired men."

Ella smiled, a little embarrassed, and said, "I'm not doin' any more than my share. We all have to pitch in."

"I know exactly what you mean, Tom," Mr. Randall told them all. "If it wasn't for Lila, Mother and I couldn't keep this hotel running. We are mighty grateful to your little sister."

Lila, too, a little embarrassed said, "That's what families do, we help each other and take care of one another, right Ella?"

Ella smiled and nodded.

Mrs. Randall turned to Ella and asked, "What news do you have from Jackson, Ella?"

"He's fine. Thank you for askin'. He was just home about a week ago," Ella replied.

Surprised, Lila interrupted, "Jackson was home!"

"Yes, only for a few days, but I was so grateful. I think you should know, though," Ella said addressing Lila, "that George went with him."

"No," Lila exclaimed, "Tom, what would Papa say?"

"He'd tell him that a man has to do what he thinks is right and he would promise to pray for his son while he was gone. That's what we're going to do," Tom told her.

"Yes," Lila said, "I suppose you're right."

"Have you heard from Charles, Lila?" Anne asked her.

"I got a letter yesterday. He said not to worry and that he was doin' fine, but you know he wouldn't tell us if he wasn't," Lila told her.

"Don't you be worryin'," Tom told her. "I'm sure he's alright. Folks say that the Union Army is way better off than the boys in grey. The confederates have had their supplies intercepted, and food is scarce for the soldiers fightin' in the deep south.

"I'm mighty thankful that the Guard isn't fightin' down that way," Ella told him.

"We all are," Anne told her thoughtfully.

Ella turned the attention to Mr. Randall. She had to ask. She had to know. "Mr. Randall, have you heard the rumors about the Yankees movin' in right here in our county?

Mr. Randall took a deep breath, and, let out a sigh. "Yes, I've heard. It is not a rumor. We are expecting a regiment to arrive early next week. It's been told that they'll be settin' up camp near Hope Creek."

"Hope Creek!" Anne exclaimed. "Why, that's near Whiteaker land and not that far from our homestead."

"There have been rumors that the rebel army has been getting a lot of aid from Confederate sympathizers around here," Mr. Randall told them. "The Provost Marshall has been watching, but he can't keep track of everything on his own, and the bushwackin' against anyone sidin' with the Union has gotten out of control. Some say that the bushwackers are local, right here in this county."

"Somethin's got to be done," Mrs. Randall said. "It ain't safe for anybody."

"Of course, you're right," Ella agreed, "but, I don't know that Yankee troops here is gonna help. What about our

Confederate neighbors, what about the Guard? It won't be safe for any of our men. It won't be safe for Jackson or George in their own homes."

"I'm sorry, El," Tom told her, "But, Jackson knew that when he left. So did George. They knew that it was coming down to this."

"And, what about, Charles, Ella?" Lila asked her, "Bushwackers hate the Union and anyone who supports them. That makes most of us in this room a target for their violence. I'm sorry, but I'll sleep a little better knowin' that the army is close by."

Ella didn't know what to say. She hated all of this.

Mrs. Randall changed the subject, "Let's talk about happier things, shall we? Anne, your father and I are sure anxious to see our first grandchild. We are mighty thankful to the Lord for his good care of the both of you."

"Thank you, Mother. Tom and I are anxious, too," she said.

"Have you picked out any names, yet?" Lila asked her.

"As a matter of fact, we have, but you will have to be surprised like everyone else," Tom teased his sister with a grin.

"Thomas O'Connor, you're terrible," she grinned back at him.

"You're right," he agreed, "and, it's time that I should be gettin' my terrible self and these two lovely ladies back home. We don't want to be travelin' when it's dark.

"So soon," Anne said, "It feels like we just got here."

"I know." Ella told her, "But, Tom's right about travelin' after dark. It just ain't safe."

The visitors said their good-byes and started the journey back to their farm. Ella was quiet. Her heart was heavy over the things that she heard in town. She was afraid for Sarah. She was afraid for Jackson. She was afraid for George. She was afraid for herself. It seemed like there was nobody and no place safe in Missouri anymore.

This was soon to be proven true. Her family, friends, and neighbors had seen trouble. Many of them knew grief, but no one anticipated what was coming in the days ahead. One day, one chain of events would change everything forever. Not one family who was dear to Jackson and Ella would be untouched. The wounds would be so deep, that they would leave scars that would last a lifetime.

Chapter 25

Family Loyalty Tested

The Provost Marshall had heard the rumors about bushwacking and local citizens aiding the Confederate Army. He paid many a visit to Caldwell Plantation inquiring about the things that he heard. Of course, the family denied any involvement. Without proof, the Marshall could only watch and wait.

The rumors about Yankee regiments coming to town were true. Captain Jeremiah Whiteaker's unit arrived a week later and set up camp at Hope Creek. They started scouting the county, looking for rebels and bushwackers. The Caldwells were on the top of the watch list.

Uncle Richard, James, and Robert were smart. It was their county. They knew the terrain and they knew the people. They had been getting away with aiding the enemy, wartime treason. James and Robert had even gotten away with murder, the murder of Sam Alton. No one knew how many other raids they had done, how much property they had destroyed or stolen, or how many other lives they had taken.

After James and Robert joined the militia, their bush-wacking activity slowed down. However, the methods that they used in bushwacking carried over into their military activities. This was not condoned by any of their leadership, but James and Robert, like Uncle Richard, also seemed to think that they answered to no one. Their ruthless methods earned them both a discharge from the Guard and the brothers returned home. They remained loyal to the cause, though, helping Uncle Richard further it anyway that they could.

One night, while James and Robert were in town, four confederate soldiers visited Caldwell Plantation looking for help. Uncle Richard would never turn one of them away. He fed them and gave them each one of his best horses to go back and join the fight. The men were caught just over the county line. Not only were the men caught, but so was Uncle Richard. They told their apprehenders who had helped them.

Now there was proof. The Caldwells were aiding the Confederacy. The Provost Marshall made another visit to Caldwell Plantation. This time to arrest Richard Caldwell.

Petey saw the Marshall riding up the lane and called out to his Pa. Mary, Joanna, and Sarah hurried down the stairs as Uncle Richard came out of the library. He met the Marshall on the front porch.

"What do you want, Marshall?" Uncle Richard made it obvious the Marshall wasn't welcome.

"Mr. Caldwell, I came here to arrest you," the Marshall told him with his hand on his pistol.

"For what?" Uncle Richard asked him.

"For aiding confederate soldiers. Last time I checked that is considered treason," the Marshall told him.

"I didn't help anyone," Uncle Richard told him.

"Well, I'm holdin' four confederate soldiers who have supplies and four fresh horses that came from your place. They said that you helped 'em," the Marshall explained.

"Papa, no," cried out Sarah.

"Hush now, Sarah. It'll be alright," her father told her.

The Marshall with his hand still on his holster said, "It would be a good idea to get your horse and come with me without any trouble."

Uncle Richard turned to his children and said, "Now don't you girls worry. Petey, go and tell Elizabeth what happened. She'll know what to do."

Uncle Richard mounted his horse and went with the Marshall. Sarah made haste. She called for Obadiah.

"Obie, get the carriage, we need to go see Miss Elizabeth, right now." Sarah told him.

"What's wrong, Miss Sarah?" Obie replied.

"It's Pa. The Marshall came and took him. We have to hurry, Obie, now go," Mary told her.

"Yes, Ma'am," Obie hurried to get the carriage.

He hitched up the carriage and Petey drove his sisters to the Whiteaker farm. Mary and Sarah hurried to the front door calling for Elizabeth. Petey and Joanna waited in the carriage. Elizabeth hearing the ruckus met them at the door.

"Mary, Sarah, what on earth is the matter?" Elizabeth asked her sisters.

"It's Pa, Elizabeth," Sarah told her.

"Pa, what's wrong?" she asked concerned.

"The Marshall came, Elizabeth. He came and he arrested Pa for helping the soldiers that came to the house last night," Mary told her desperately.

"Arrested! Where did they take him?" Elizabeth asked her.

"We think that he took him to town," Sarah told her. "Papa told us to come and tell you. He said that you would know what to do."

Lucy and Amos in the library heard the ruckus, too, and joined Elizabeth by the front door.

"What is goin' on?" Lucy asked Elizabeth.

"It's my Pa," Elizabeth said. "I need to go to the camp and see Jeremiah. I can't go alone. Amos, please go and find Newt. Ask him if he will take me.

Then, she said, "Now, you girls go with Petey and get on home and don't you fret. Don't do anything until you hear from me and that goes for Robert and James, too. Do you hear me?"

Petey and the girls did as they were told while Newt took Elizabeth to camp to find her husband. They were met by two guards.

"Good evenin', Mrs. Whiteaker," said one of the guards.

"It's urgent that I see my husband," she told the guard.

"Who do you have with you?" the other guard asked her.

"One of the hired men from our farm," she told the guard.

"Please wait here, Ma'am. I'll tell the captain that you're here," he said.

It only took a minute and Jeremiah exited a large tent at the end of the row. Elizabeth didn't wait. She ran to her husband.

"Elizabeth, what are you doing here?" Jeremiah asked her.

"I'm sorry, Jeremiah. I need your help," she told him.

As he was leading her by the arm into the tent, he said, "Come in here where we can talk."

Jeremiah could tell that Elizabeth was fighting back tears. "What happened? Are you alright?" Jeremiah asked her.

"It's my Pa," she told him, "The Provost Marshall arrested him, Jeremiah, for treason. You know what that means. They'll hang him. They'll hang my Pa." She grabbed a hold of him and sobbed into his chest.

"Shhh," he told her as he stroked her hair. After she composed herself, he asked her again what happened.

"They caught four confederate soldiers last night. The soldiers told the Marshall that Papa helped them and gave them horses," Elizabeth told him.

Jeremiah's demeanor changed. This was a serious offence, but he wasn't going to borrow trouble. He had just as much jurisdiction as the Provost Marshall. Surely there was something that he could do.

"Can you help him?" Elizabeth asked earnestly.

"Don't you worry. I'll go see the Marshall in the morning," Jeremiah reassured her. "Now, you go home and wait for me. Do ya' hear?"

She nodded, "Yes, Jeremiah," she said. "Thank you. I'll see you soon." She kissed him good-bye and left for home. There, she waited.

Jeremiah left camp early the next morning and went to see the Provost Marshall.

"Hello, Captain Whiteaker. What brings you to town this fine morning?" the Marshall asked him.

"I think that you probably already know why I am here, Marshall. We should get right to the point," Jeremiah told him.

"All right," the Marshall replied.

"I understand that you're holding Richard Caldwell in one of your cells back there," Jeremiah told him.

"Yes, that's right. He is being held for treason," the Marshall told him.

"Do you have proof?" Jeremiah asked him.

"I have the testimony of four men who said that they were at Caldwell Plantation a few nights ago where they were given food and horses," the Marshall told him.

"What does Richard say?" Jeremiah asked him.

"He denies it, of course. Do you think he'd admit to something like that? Look here, Captain. Everybody knows that the Caldwells have been helping the Confederates. You know it and I know it," the Marshall said as a matter of fact.

"You and I have both heard the rumors." Jeremiah told him. "I'll give you that, but I don't think that you have enough evidence to hold Richard for treason. It is his word against four rebel soldiers."

"And, as for the horses, how do you know that those rebels didn't sneak on the plantation and steal those horses?" Jeremiah asked him.

"I think there is enough evidence to not only hold him, but to also put him on trial. We need to make an example around here. The Confederate sympathizers and the bushwackers need to know that we aren't playing around with them," the Marshall explained.

"What if I vouch for him?" Jeremiah asked.

The Marshall looked surprised. "What do you mean?" he asked Jeremiah.

"I mean, what if I take responsibility for Richard? What if he signs an agreement that he won't aid any rebels for the remainder of the war, and I promise to be responsible for him keeping his promise?" Jeremiah was earnest.

Jeremiah almost couldn't believe what he was hearing come out of his own mouth, but he had to do something. He loved Elizabeth. Nothing was more important to him than she was. He had to help her Pa.

"That sounds mighty risky since you know the Caldwells are Confederate sympathizers. Do you really want to do that for a rebel?" the Marshall asked him.

"Not for a rebel, Marshall, for my father-in-law," Jeremiah corrected him.

"All right. I will accept a written statement from Mr. Caldwell promising not to help any rebels or aid any bush-wackers," the Marshall told him.

"Thank you, Marshall," Jeremiah told him relieved.

"Wait a minute, that's not my only condition," interrupted the Marshall. "I also need a written statement from you agreeing to take responsibility for Mr. Caldwell."

"I am willing to do that," Jeremiah told him.

"There's more," continued the Marshall, "I need you to post bond."

Jeremiah didn't speak. He thought for a moment. There was a war going on which caused most folks to be short on money. Jeremiah was no exception.

"Treason is a serious offence. The amount would be substantial," the Marshall told him.

"I see," Jeremiah said, "In other words, you don't want me to be able to post bond, so you're gonna make sure that I won't be able to get the money."

"I don't appreciate what you are implying," said the Marshall.

"I think that you are underestimating me and my family, Marshall," Jeremiah told him. "This is not a game. A man's life is at stake.

"Richard Caldwell has repeatedly aided the rebels," the Marshall told him, "There is no guarantee that if I turn him lose, he won't keep it up. For all I know, he might run off and join 'em."

"You don't have proof!" Jeremiah shouted.

"That may be so," the Marshall told him, "But without proper bond, he is going to stay right here and face trial."

Jeremiah only hesitated a moment. He knew what he had to do.

"I'll post the deed to my farm," Jeremiah said abruptly.

The Marshall was taken back for a moment. Then, he said, "A deed?"

"You heard me," Jeremiah said, "The deed to my farm. It's more than enough to post ten bonds. Will you agree to it?"

"Yes, I'll agree," the Marshall told him.

"I need to see Richard and explain what we have discussed," Jeremiah told him.

The Marshall reached for the keys and opened the big metal door that led to the cell block. Richard, in the last cell, looked relieved to see Jeremiah.

"Hello, Richard," Jeremiah said.

"Hello, Jeremiah," Richard replied.

"I've been talking with the Marshall about the predicament that you're in and I think we have come to an agreement," Jeremiah told him.

"That's good news. How long do I have to be in here?" Richard asked.

"Well, that's up to you," Jeremiah explained. "The Marshall is willing to release you, if you will sign an agreement that you won't help any rebels or bushwackers anymore," Jeremiah told him.

"He just wants me to sign a paper?" questioned Richard.

"No, I have to sign one, too," Jeremiah replied, "They will only release you if I vouch for you and take responsibility for anything that happens after they let you go."

"You're willing to do that?" Richard asked him.

"If you promise me that you won't help the rebels anymore, I'll do it," Jeremiah told him, "But, there's somethin' else. He wants me to post bond," said Jeremiah.

"Bond? How much?" Richard inquired.

"I have to put up my farm," Jeremiah told him.

Richard was silent. He stared at the floor and thought for a moment.

He looked Jeremiah in the eye and said, "I promise."

Jeremiah told the Marshall to write the agreements. Jeremiah signed one and Richard signed the other. The Marshall unlocked the cell and let Richard walk away a free man. The Marshall agreed to allow Richard to claim his horses. There were listed as stolen property claimed by the rightful owner. Jeremiah silently rode with Richard back to Caldwell Plantation, delivering him and his horses to his family.

Petey saw them coming up the lane. He hollered for the girls. They came running out of the house calling for their father. They all hugged him as he got down from his mount and welcomed him home.

"Oh, thank you, Jeremiah," Sarah said. "Thank you for helping our Pa."

Richard turned to Jeremiah, "Thank you," he said.

"Just don't make me regret it," Jeremiah told him as he turned his horse to go back up the lane and rode away.

Jeremiah's next stop was the family farm. He had to tell Elizabeth about her father. He also had to somehow explain to his family that he posted the farm as bond in exchange for his release.

When Jeremiah's father got sick, he divided the farm between his sons. Since Jeremiah was the oldest, he got the main house, most of the land, and most of the livestock. Jeb got eighty acres on the north side of the property, some of the cattle and horses. Amos and Lucy got the small house, eighty acres on the south side, and some of the cows and horses, too.

How was he going to tell his mother that he posted the deed on their home as bond for a Confederate sympathizer? She loved Elizabeth, but she had no affection for any of her family. His brothers were going to be angry. They cared for Elizabeth and had no ill will toward her sisters, but they despised the Caldwell men. Now, the fate of their farm was in the hands of Richard Caldwell.

Jeremiah quietly road up to his family home. He went in the house and found Elizabeth in the parlor working on some mending. She got up and approached Jeremiah immediately when she saw him.

"Jeremiah, I didn't hear you come in. I've been going crazy waitin' to hear about my Pa," she told him.

"Where is everyone?" Jeremiah asked her.

"Your mother is seeing to your Pa. Jeb and Amos are down by the barn and Lucy is down at the little house. Jeremiah, what about Pa?" she asked him anxiously.

"Your Pa is alright. I rode with him to the plantation on my way here. He's safe and sound," Jeremiah reassured her.

She threw her arms around his neck and said, "Oh, thank you, thank you."

"Don't thank me, Elizabeth. The Lord was merciful to your Pa," Jeremiah told her giving glory to the Lord.

"How did you get him out?" she asked her husband.

"I want to tell everyone what happened at once," he told her.

She had no idea what this had to do with the rest of the family, but she was concerned. She could see that Jeremiah was troubled.

"Go and fetch mother, Elizabeth, while I go and find Jeb and Amos," he told her.

Elizabeth did what he said. Jeremiah went looking for Jeb and Amos. They were working down by the corral.

"Hello, Jeremiah," said Amos. Both men stopped their work. They had been waiting to hear what happened at the Provost Marshall's office.

"Can you boys come up to the house? I have something that I want to tell you. Amos, you might want to get Lucy and bring her up to," Jeremiah told them.

"What happened, Jeremiah?" Jeb asked him.

"I'll tell you everything up at the house," Jeremiah told him.

Jeb followed Jeremiah back to the house while Amos went down to the little house to get Lucy. Mrs. Whiteaker was waiting in the parlor with Elizabeth. She was happy to see Jeremiah.

"Hello, Son," she said sitting in her chair. Jeremiah walked over to her and gave her a one-armed embrace and a kiss on the cheek.

"Hello, Mother," he said. "How's Pa?"

"He is the same, good days and bad days," she told him.

Lucy and Amos arrived and joined the family in the parlor.

"What's this all about, Jeremiah?" Jeb asked him.

"I have somethin' I need to tell you all and I thought telling you together was best," Jeremiah explained.

"It sounds important," said Mrs. Whiteaker.

"Yes, it is," Jeremiah told her. "I went to see the Marshall about Richard Caldwell this morning. The charge he was being held on was treason, punishable by hanging," Jeremiah explained. "I couldn't let Elizabeth's Pa hang without trying to do something about it."

"What did you do, Jeremiah," Jeb asked him suspiciously.

"I asked him to release Richard to me. I volunteered to sign an agreement that I would be responsible for him, if he would sign an agreement that he wouldn't aid rebels for the rest of the war," Jeremiah continued.

"Why would you go and do a fool thing like that?" Jeb asked him angrily. "No offence, Elizabeth, but the Caldwell men have been up to no good since before this war started. You know they are as guilty as they can be, proof or no proof. They help the same army that your fightin' against, Jeremiah. Have you lost your mind?"

Elizabeth was stunned. She was hurt. She said nothing. She only listened.

"Jeb's right," Amos told him. "You can't trust a Caldwell."

"And, what if he lied," Jeb asked him. "Will they come and get you if he gets caught again? You will lose your career and your good name."

Elizabeth had to speak, "My Pa would not do that to my husband!" She was adamant.

"I mean no disrespect, Elizabeth," Jeb told her, "But, your Pa and your brothers can't be trusted."

"Jeremiah," his mother asked, "What will they do to you if Richard doesn't keep his promise?"

Jeremiah hesitated for a moment. Then he answered, "I had to post bond, Mother."

"Bond?" said Amos, "You don't have enough money for bond."

"It wasn't cash," Jeremiah continued.

"Then, what did they take for the bond," Jeb asked even more suspicious.

Jeremiah finally blurted it out, "I had to give them the deed to my share of the farm."

Lucy gasped. Mrs. Whiteaker looked ghostly. Elizabeth exclaimed, "Oh Jeremiah, No!"

Jeb and Amos were angry. Neither one had ever been this angry at their brother before.

"The farm!" exclaimed Amos.

"I didn't have a choice. I couldn't let my wife's father be hung for something that was his word against someone else's. Jeb, you would have done the same thing if you was in my place," Jeremiah told him.

"Jeremiah, you are wrong," Jeb told him. "I would not have done the same thing because there are other people involved. You are my brother and I love you. I care for your wife, too, but you've gone too far. What if Richard doesn't keep his promise? Where will Mother and Pa live? They built this house with their own hands. We were all born here. Pa worked this land and made a good living to share with all of us. Now, you have turned over the deed for the best part of it," Jeb scolded him.

"I'm sorry, Jeb, but I tell you I didn't have a choice," Jeremiah was earnest.

"There's always a choice, Jeremiah," Jeb said. He was still angry. "Richard Caldwell made a choice, and you should have let him live with the consequences. It's not even just about your dragging the family into this. It's bigger than that Jeremiah. You're a soldier. The Caldwells are rebels. The rebels are killing Union soldiers. You could come face to face with the very same men they're helping, and they wouldn't hesitate to shoot you down."

"Boys," cried their mother, "What's done is done. We can't let this, or this war, tear our family apart. The Lord is in control. Your brother felt he had good reason to do what he did. Now we all need to move on. Please excuse me as I'm going to check on your Pa and go rest awhile. I'm feeling tired."

"Can I help you, Mother," asked Amos.

"No," she told him. "I'm fine."

"Mother Whiteaker," called Elizabeth.

She didn't look at Elizabeth. She just kept walking and said, "It's alright, dear, don't worry."

Tears welled up in Elizabeth's eyes. She knew that this could not be undone. All the relief that she felt just an hour before was gone. She was sad and anxious now.

Jeb walked out of the room without a word. Lucy sat in silence and disbelief.

Amos said, "I best be getting back to work," and followed behind Jeb.

It was awkward for Lucy, the only one left in the room with Jeremiah and Elizabeth.

She said, "I best be going, too. Amos will be expectin' some dinner soon."

As she started to leave, she turned and said, "Jeremiah, I know you had your reasons. It'll be all right."

Jeremiah managed a half-hearted smile and said, "Thank you, Lucy, I appreciate that."

Jeremiah and Elizabeth were alone. Elizabeth began to sob. Jeremiah tried to comfort her.

"There's no need for cryin'. Your Pa is all right and you don't have to worry anymore," Jeremiah told her as he held her tightly in his arms.

"Oh, Jeremiah," she said, "What about the farm? This is your home, your family's home. You have put it in danger all because of me."

"Remember, you told me that your Pa will keep his word," Jeremiah reminded her, "This war will be over before you know it and the farm will be clear again."

"Jeremiah," she said, "how can I stay here without you?"

"What do you mean? This is your home, too," Jeremiah told her.

"I can't be here. Every time your brothers or your mother look at me it will just remind us all of what is at stake," Elizabeth told him. "It might be best for me to go back down to our house by the pond and stay there."

"Don't be hasty, Elizabeth," Jeremiah told her. "Mother won't hold this against you, and she really needs your help. Just think about it some more before you make up your mind."

"All right, Jeremiah, I'll think about it," she promised.

"It's all going to work out, Elizabeth. You'll see," he said as he kissed her on the forehead.

Elizabeth wished she could be sure. She was so torn. She was grateful that her Pa was safe, but now she was worried about Jeremiah.

Chapter 26

Crossing the Line

A few weeks went by and it was quiet. Richard kept his word. He stayed close to home and didn't take in any visitors. Elizabeth was grateful. Jeremiah was relieved, and things settled down some at the Whiteaker farm.

Still, trouble was brewing. It wasn't Richard this time. It was Robert and James. There was nothing that Richard could do about it. There was nothing anyone could do.

One Sunday morning, the two Caldwell brothers crossed a line that they couldn't cross back from. They had been out all night, drinking and causing mischief. Petey confronted them, first thing, when they got home that morning.

"Where you been?" Petey asked his brothers.

"That's none of your business, Little Brother?" Robert told him not taking Petey seriously.

"It is to my business," Petey told him firmly, "With William and Sterling gone off to war and Nathaniel and Jackson moved on, somebody's gotta keep things goin' around here. You two ain't no help and I'm getting mighty tired of it."

James perceived Petey as being disrespectful and it incited him. "I ought a whip you, boy?" James told him.

"You go ahead and try," Petey dared him.

"Knock it off, James," Robert told him, "Leave the kid alone."

He turned to Petey and asked him, "Where's Pa?"

"In the library where he stays most of the time. He ain't been the same since the Marshall came and arrested him and neither of you pay him any mind," Petey explained. "He don't talk. He don't hardly eat. He doesn't take care of business around here. Sometimes he don't even go to bed. He just sleeps in his chair. I think he's scared. He's afraid we're gonna lose everything and he can't do anything about it. He needs our help, and I can't take care of everything around here on my own."

James, always looking for someone to blame said, "It's those Whiteakers," he said. "They've caused enough trouble and I'm getting mighty tired of it. We should've taken care of Jeb and that loud mouthed hired man when we had the chance." James was still holding a grudge against Jeb and Newt for what happened that night at the Whiteaker farm.

"If you recall," Robert said, "it was because of Elizabeth that we didn't."

James scowled, "Elizabeth had no business marrying into a family of Yankee lovers. If you ask me, she ain't a Caldwell anymore. She made her choice."

"What are you sayin'?" Petey asked him.

"I'm sayin' Pa don't owe nothin' to those Whiteakers," he sneared.

"But, what about their farm? What about Elizabeth? Pa promised," Petey said.

"A promise to a Yankee don't mean nothing. Look what it's doin' to Pa. He has no reason for going on. They stripped him of his pride. He has to choose between a daughter that betrayed the whole family and fighting for a cause that he believes in." James grew angrier with every word.

"Robert, it's time to put an end to all of this," James told him.

"I think yer right," Robert agreed.

"What are you going to do?" Petey asked his brothers.

"Never you mind," James told him, "It ain't yer business."

"It is my business," Petey told him, "And, you and Robert ain't leavin' me out no more. I'm old enough to do my part in taking care of this family."

"Well, now's yer chance," James sneered. It was bad judgment on James' part to involve Petey. If it weren't for all the liquor, he probably wouldn't have suggested it, but instead he egged Petey on.

Robert interrupted, "Pa ain't gonna like us letting Petey in on any trouble, James."

"Petey's right, Robert," James snapped back. "He ain't a kid no more. It's time for him to choose his own side and fight for the cause."

"If you really think you're ready to ride with us, Petey, mount up," James told him.

Petey was already wearing his holster. James threw him a rifle to put in the side of his saddle. Petey mounted his horse, and the three men rode away.

Petey didn't know where they were going. He knew they were looking for trouble, but he had no idea what they were capable of. Petey had spent his whole life bullied by

James and Robert. He had always longed for their acceptance. Now at seventeen, he wanted their respect. He wanted them to finally treat him like a man.

The three men rode for a while and stopped at the little country church. The church house was full. They could tell by the number of wagons, carriages, and horses outside. One carriage looked familiar and the markings on the horses hooked up to it confirmed that it came from the Whiteaker farm. James was looking for Jeb Whiteaker.

"What are we doing here?" Petey asked him.

"It's time those Whiteakers get taught a lesson," James told him.

"What do you mean?" Petey asked him, "What kind of a lesson?"

James snapped at him, "You wanted to come with us. You wanted to be a man. Jeb Whiteaker and his hired men have been runnin' their mouths all over town. They been talkin' about Pa and slanderin' the Caldwell name.

"It ain't right to cause trouble at the church house," Petey told him.

"We ain't gonna cause trouble here," James told him.

"You're gonna wait here with the horses, while Robert and I go in and get Jeb and that loudmouth hired man of his," James continued, "We'll be teaching them a lesson someplace else."

James jumped off his horse and threw Petey a scarf. "Put this on," James demanded.

"Check those wagons and horses and gather any firearms that they left in 'em." James told Robert.

Robert hesitated.

"Robert, let's go," James commanded. "Put the guns over in those bushes where they won't see 'em."

Robert did as he was told. The two men put on their scarves, drew their guns, and flung open the church doors while Petey waited outside. No one in the church building was armed except for Robert and James. There were gasps when the two men entered the building.

"What is the meaning of this?" the preacher demanded. "This is the Lord's Day."

James and Robert ignored him. They hurried to one of the middle pews where Jeb was sitting. James pointed the pistol at him without a word and dragged him out of the pew.

Some of the women, including Lucy and Lila screamed, some of them cried. One lady fainted. Rose moved Dorie between her and Nathaniel, sitting in the pew. She grabbed a hold of his arm and put her other arm around Dorie. She was obviously frightened.

"Who are you? What do you want?" yelled Jeb struggling with James as he forced him toward the door.

Newt, the hired man, was sitting behind Jeb. He started towards Robert, but Robert pointed his gun and motioned him toward the door, too. Newt followed. James backed his way to the door using Jeb, with a pistol aimed at his head for a shield.

The ruffians tried to conceal their identity, but there was something familiar about them to more than one person in the church that day. Elizabeth wouldn't let herself believe it. It was too painful to think that her brothers would do something like this.

After they were outside, James threw Robert some rope.

"Tie up their hands," he told Robert. Petey unsure about what was happening, quickly untied two horses that were hitched to a post. He pulled them around so that the two prisoners could mount them, and the five men hastily rode away.

There was another Caldwell in the church building that morning. Like Elizabeth, he recognized the men behind the scarves. However, he wouldn't deny it. Robert and James couldn't hide from him. He was The first man set to go after the kidnappers.

He immediately went to his wagon to get his rifle, but it was gone. He quickly started to organize the rest of the men.

"A few of you take the south side of the church house and the rest of you take the north side. Look for our guns," Nathaniel told them. "They couldn't take them with them on horseback, so they gotta be here somewhere. I'm goin' after them. Anybody else here want to ride with me?"

The congregation that day mostly consisted of women, children, and the aged men. All the other men were fighting in the war except for Amos Whiteaker.

"I'm goin'," he told Nathaniel.

Nathaniel nodded. He turned to Rose and said, "Don't worry. I'll come back as soon as I can, and I'll have Jeb and Newt with me." Then, he picked Dorie up with one arm and hugged them both tightly.

She smiled and said, "Be careful, Nathaniel. We'll be waitin'."

She tried to hide it, but she was afraid. She was afraid for Nathaniel, and she was afraid for both her brothers, Jeb and Amos.

"We'll be praying the Lord's protection for you both, Amos," Rose told him. "Be careful and bring our brothers back home to Ma and Pa."

Amos nodded. Then, he hugged Lucy and said, "Don't you worry. Go on home now and wait 'til I get back."

He turned to Elizabeth and said, "Will you make sure that she gets home safely?

Elizabeth nodded.

"Also, send a message to Jeremiah and tell him what happened," he instructed.

"Of course," Elizabeth said, "I will."

Just then, two of the young boys came out from the bushes hollering, "We found 'em. We found the guns."

Nathaniel and Amos retrieved their rifles. One of the old timers handed Nathaniel his holster and said, "You may be needed this." Nathaniel took the holster and said, "Thank you. I'm beholdin' to you."

The old timer nodded and said, "Good luck."

Then, Nathanial asked him, "Would you make sure that my wife and little girl get home all right?"

"Don't you worry. We'll see to them," the old timer assured him. Then, Amos and Nathaniel made haste and rode away in the same direction as the bandits.

The bandits rode until they were deep enough in the woods and far enough away from the church that they thought no one would find them. Then, they stopped. Petey was still unsure about the purpose of the kidnapping.

"Get off your horses." James told Jeb and Newt.

Neither of the men moved.

"He told you to get down," Robert said as he pushed Newt off his horse.

Jeb complied as Newt was picking himself up off the ground.

"Who are you and what do you want with us?" Jeb asked his captives.

James laughed and said, "You hear that?" as he looked at Robert. "He wants to know what we want?"

"I heard him," replied Robert in a cool tone of voice.

"It's pretty simple. We decided that it's time for the two of you to get what's comin' to ya'," James explained.

"What do you mean? We ain't done nothin'," Newt told him.

"We think ya' have" James said. Then, he hit him in the face with the back of his hand.

"Who are you?" Jeb demanded.

James froze for a moment and looked Jeb in the eyes. Then, he slowly reached for his scarf and pulled it off his face just long enough for Jeb to see who he was.

Jeb scoffed at him, "I should have known it was you. Only the likes of you would come into a church on Sunday morning and attack unarmed men," Jeb told him.

James hit Jeb across the face with his pistol and he fell to his knees.

"James, what are you doin'?" Petey yelled.

"You hush your mouth," James yelled back.

"You're cowards," Jeb told him as spit at James' feet.

James hit him again. Petey was frightened. He thought he was going with his brothers to defend the family honor and fight for the cause. Kidnapping and assaulting a neighbor was no cause. This wasn't right. He didn't know what to do, so he just stood there and looked on.

"You Whiteakers have caused my family enough grief," James told them.

"You cause yourself your own grief," Newt snapped back at him.

"You better be quiet, Old Man, or you'll get this pistol across your face, too," James threatened.

James continued, "You've been slanderin' the Caldwell name all over the county. Our sister turned her back on her own family for your brother," he said as he looked at Jeb. "Now our Pa ain't even livin'. He sits in a room all day, not talkin', not eatin', not fightin' for the cause that he believes in. It's all because of a promise that he made to your family. You Whiteakers have done enough harm. Now it's time to end it," James threatened.

"What are you gonna do, James?" Petey said with a quiver in his voice.

"Petey, he told you to hush," snapped Robert.

Jeb, surprised that it was Petey behind the last scarf, said to him, "Petey, what are you doin'? You don't want to be part of this."

"Be quiet," yelled James.

Jeb kept talking, "Get on your horse and get out of here, Pete. Get out of here before it gets worse."

"Shut up, I said," yelled James as he shoved Jeb.

Jeb, his face bleeding, from the blows he took from the pistol stood tall and looked his attacker in the eyes.

Meanwhile, Amos and Nathaniel had almost caught up to them. Amos was an excellent hunter and tracker. The effects of all the liquor from the night before made James and Robert careless, so they weren't too hard to track.

Because they were close, they were following quietly on foot, leading their horses behind them. They heard a gunshot. It sounded like it was only a few yards away. They hurried in the direction of the gun fire in time to see Newt lying on the ground. They were just minutes too late. Now James was pointing his gun at Jeb.

Amos yelled, "No," as James pulled the trigger. Robert on horseback turned to the sound of Amos' voice and fired his gun. Amos who already had his rifle raised fired back and Robert fell forward, obviously wounded, but able to still ride away. James quickly mounted his horse and yelled to Petey, "Let's go. Now, boy, ride!" Petey obeyed and the three men rode away as quickly as they could.

Nathaniel and Amos ran to Jeb and Newt both lying on the ground. There was nothing that they could do for Newt, but Jeb was still alive.

"I'm sorry, Jeb," Amos said tearfully as he picked Jeb's head up off the ground. "I'm sorry that I didn't get here faster."

"It's all right. You're here now," Jeb told him. "Don't you worry. Jeremiah will take care of them. He'll fix everything."

"He can't fix you, Jeb," Amos told him crying.

"Things like this don't make sense, do they? But I got to believe there's a reason," Jeb told him as he looked up to the sky. He looked at his brother one last time and closed his eyes. Those were Jeb's last words.

Nathaniel, shaking his arm said, "Jeb, Jeb, who did this? Who did this to you?"

Amos sobbing said, "Nathaniel, stop. It's no use, he's gone."

Nathaniel noticed a reflection on the ground, something shiny. He reached down and picked up a knife that one of the murderers had left behind. Nathaniel had seen the knife before.

"Why did this happen, Nathaniel?" Amos asked him. "Who would do something like this?"

This was the final straw. Now, Nathaniel had proof.

"Take care of your brother and Newt," Nathaniel told him.

"What are you gonna do?" Amos asked him.

"I'm going after them," Nathaniel told him.

"Alone?" Amos asked.

"Don't worry about it," he told Amos. "I know where I'm goin'," he said and rode away.

Chapter 27

A Repentant Heart

It wasn't long before Nathaniel caught up with the Caldwell brothers. The three men were unaware that they were being followed. Robert, badly hurt, rode slouched over, barely holding on, while Petey was leading his horse for him by the reigns.

They rode home to Caldwell Plantation just as Nathaniel knew they would. When they got to the house, Petey ran to the front door calling, "Pa, Pa, Robert's hurt." In a few moments Uncle Richard came out of the house. James had helped Robert down from his horse and was trying to bring him inside.

Nathaniel finally had proof. He had James' knife and personally was a witness to the identity of the bushwackers. He knew what he had to do. He rode towards town.

Meanwhile, at the plantation, James and Petey carried Robert to his room and laid him on the bed. Richard called for Obadiah.

"Obadiah, go get Doc Watson. Hurry." Richard demanded.

Mary and Sarah started tending to Robert's wound. Joanna quietly watched from the doorway. Richard sat next to his son on the other side of the bed.

"It hurts, Pa. It hurts real bad," Robert told him.

"I know. Don't talk. I sent Obie for the doctor. He'll be here soon, and he'll take care of you," he assured him. Robert closed his eyes and lost consciousness.

Richard turned to James and asked, "Who did this?"

James calmly answered, "Amos Whiteaker shot him."

"Amos!" Richard replied in disbelief.

Petey, overwhelmed by guilt started to cry. "He killed 'em, Pa," he said. "He shot 'em. Shot 'em dead."

"Shut your mouth, Boy," James snarled.

Sarah and Mary made eye contact with each other, but, said nothing. They continued tending to their brother who was in and out of consciousness.

"What's he talkin' about, James?" his father asked him sternly.

James was silent.

"Tell him, James," Petey prodded, "Tell Pa what you did."

Richard got up from Robert's bedside, approached James with a pointed finger and said "James, I will not ask you again. What have you done?"

"I did what I should have done a long time ago," James retorted. "You can't go on like this, Pa. You've been like a prisoner in your own home because you made a promise to a bunch of Yankees."

"I made a promise to your sister, not to any Yankees," his father told him.

"My sister? As far as I am concerned, she betrayed you and the rest of the family when she married a Yankee. She ain't my sister," James snapped.

Richard raised his hand and struck James across the face.

"How dare you!" he said.

James, with his hand on his cheek, broke down.

Tearfully, he said, "It's true, Pa, whether you think so or not. When Ma died, we quit bein' a family. We're just people livin' in the same house.

James composed himself and continued, "Me and Robert took up a cause. We decided to fight for our home, our land, and our way of life, and I can't say that I'm sorry about it."

"What.....have.......you....... done?" Richard asked angrily.

Petey blurted out, "Pa, he killed Jeb Whiteaker."

At first, Richard didn't speak. He looked at Petey and then at James and with a low, soft voice said, "I don't understand."

James still said nothing.

"He killed Newt, too," Petey continued, "Him and Robert went right into the church house and grabbed them both and shot 'em down in the woods."

"You were there?" Richard asked Petey.

"Yes, Pa, but I didn't know what they were gonna do. I didn't know," Petey explained with tears running down his face.

Richard turned to James with a piercing glare and said, "What were you thinking, involving your brother in something like this?" Richard didn't expect an answer. He started pacing the floor, trying to decide what he should have them do.

Then, he asked, "Who else knows what happened?"

"Amos and Nathaniel followed us from the church. They didn't see our faces, though. We all wore scarves," James told him.

"You fool," Richard sneered, "Do you think for one minute that Nathaniel wouldn't know you just because you were wearing a scarf over your face?"

He took a deep breath.

"You two can't be here when the doctor gets here," Richard told them. "James, take Petey, and go to one of the dugouts. You need to go quickly. I will meet you as soon as I can and bring supplies. You need to hide until I find out who knows about this and how much trouble you're in."

James said nothing. Petey still emotional said, "I'm sorry, Pa. I'm so sorry. I just didn't want to be treated like a kid anymore."

Richard pulled Petey's head to his, their forehead's touching. Richard was fighting back tears when he said, "This isn't your fault, Son. This is my fault. Now go. You need to go now."

Petey and James did as their Pa said and hid in one of the dugouts. Dugouts were temporary shelters carved out in the side of small hills by early settlers. Families would live in the dugouts until their permanent homes were built. When a family abandoned a dugout, it was mostly left in tack. They were ideal for emergency shelter, or, in this case, as a temporary hiding place.

Soon after Petey and James went to hide at the dugout, the doctor arrived at the plantation. He examined Robert's wound and asked for someone to assist him. Richard called for Obie and Cassie who came immediately.

Robert was still in and out of consciousness. He had lost a lot of blood and was in a lot of pain. His screams resonated throughout the house as the doctor tried to remove the bullet.

Richard paced the hallway. Mary and Sarah, in the parlor were beside themselves. Joanna, frightened, disappeared to the barn where she always found comfort with her animals. A good amount of time passed before the door to Robert's room finally opened. The doctor had a grave look on his face.

"The bullet is too deep," the doctor told him. "I can't get to it. I'm sorry."

"What are you sayin'?" Richard asked him hesitantly.

"There is nothing I can do," the doctor explained, "I've given him something to help with the pain."

Richard went immediately to Robert's bedside. He sat down next to his son and placed his hand on his arm.

"I'm sorry, Pa," Robert struggled to get out the words.

"Shhh," Richard told him, "Don't try to talk. You need to rest, so you can get better."

"It's alright, Pa," Robert said. "You don't have to pretend. I know I'm gonna die."

"Don't talk like that," Richard scolded him.

"Please, listen," Robert pleaded, "I got some things that I need to say."

Richard looked into his son's eyes and listened intently.

"I'm sorry that I didn't say no to James. I should have so many times. I didn't like the things we done, but we seemed to always make up a reason why we was right," Robert told him.

"None of that matters now, Robert," Richard said trying to quiet him.

"It does matter, Pa," Robert told him. "I haven't done anything good in my life. Instead, I did a whole lotta wrong to a whole lotta people." Robert started to cough. Richard reached for a glass of water on the side table and helped him take a drink.

"Do you remember hearing Ma pray, Pa?" Robert asked.

Tears welled up in Richard's eyes. "Yes, Son, I remember," he answered.

"She prayed for each of us by name every day in the parlor," Robert said. "She used to tell us that the only thing that mattered to her was that we would all be with her in heaven one day."

"Yes, she told me that, too," Richard told him.

"Pa, do you believe in God?" Robert asked him.

"I'm not sure," his father told him.

"Ma did. She used to say that the Lord would forgive anyone who asked Him to if they really meant it," Robert began to sob as he said, "Oh Pa, I've done so many bad things. Do you think that I can be forgiven for all that I done?"

"Yes, I think you can," Richard tried to reassure him.

"Ma told us that we needed to repent and believe. She said that the Lord would forgive a broken heart." Robert explained.

"I'm not sure I know what that means," his father told him, "But I know that she believed it."

"She told us that when we turn away from our old ways and turn to Jesus, God gives us a new, clean heart. It never made any sense to me until now. Oh, Pa, do you think it's too late?" Robert pleaded, "I want to be saved. I need to be saved."

Richard didn't know what to say. Tears fell down his face as he listened.

"Oh God," Robert cried out, desperately, staring up at the ceiling, "Please forgive me. I know I don't deserve it, but I am so sorry for what I've done. Help me, Lord. I believe what you say in your Bible. I believe it God. Give me a new heart. Please save me."

Richard spoke softly, patting his son on the arm, "It's not good for you to get all worked up. Try to be still."

Robert settled down and spoke no more. He seemed no longer troubled.

"He's peaceful," Richard thought to himself. Then, something that his dear wife used to say to him when he was worried came to his mind. She told him that if he would learn to trust the Lord, the Lord would give him the peace that passes all understanding."

Richard wondered if Robert had received the peace of God. Even in his unbelief, he knew that something important had happened to Robert. It gave him hope. Robert quietly passed into eternity with his father sitting by his side. There was no fear or any sign of guilt in his last moments.

Chapter 28

Nathaniel's Choice

So many thoughts raced through Nathaniel's mind on his way to town. Memories of things better left alone came to him like a flood. He thought about the day that he lost his Pa and Ma. He thought about the first day that he came to Caldwell Plantation and the slaves who lived there. He thought about Aunt Jane. He thought about the war and the day that he was wounded. He thought about the trips that he made on the Underground Railroad. He thought about the night that his friend, Sam, was shot down right before his eyes.

"There was nothing that I could do about any of that," Nathaniel thought to himself, "but I can do something about this. James and Robert have to be stopped. They have to pay for what they've done."

When Nathaniel got to town, he went straight to the Provost Marshall's office. The Marshall wasn't there, so he went looking for him. He thought he would start at the General Store.

"Howdy, Nathaniel," said the clerk. "What can I get for you today?"

"Actually, I was just lookin' for the Marshall. You wouldn't happen to know where I can find him, would you?" Nathaniel asked.

"I saw him ride out a few hours ago." the clerk told him. "Two men from the Whiteaker farm paid him a visit and he left right after that. Word has it that some men busted into the church service and took Jeb Whiteaker and his hired man out at gunpoint."

"Do they know who done it?" Nathaniel asked him.

"No," the clerk answered. "Some folks say that both Jeb and the hired man are dead. I guess the Marshall went to go find out what happened."

"Thank you for your help," Nathaniel told the clerk. Then, he went back to the Marshall's office to wait.

Meanwhile, at the Whiteaker Farm, the family was devastated. When Jeremiah got the bad news, he left camp right away to be with his family.

Elizabeth was waiting on the porch for Jeremiah to get there.

"Oh, Jeremiah," she said as she ran to him. "I'm so sorry."

"Are you alright?" he asked her as he hugged her tightly.

"Yes," she told him, "I was just so scared."

As they walked together up to the house, Jeremiah started asking her about the events of the day. They were almost to the door when the Provost Marshall arrived.

"Hello, Marshall," said Jeremiah.

"Captain," the Marshall said with a nod. "I heard there was some trouble at the church house this morning."

"Yes," Jeremiah told him. "My brother, Amos, was there. He will tell you about it."

When Jeremiah walked into the parlor, he saw his mother sitting in her chair across the room. He started to go to her, but Amos intercepted him. He threw his arms around his brother and started to sob.

"They killed him, Jeremiah," he said, "They came right into the church and took him out into the woods and killed him. It don't make sense. It just don't make any sense at all."

Amos took a step back and pulled himself together.

"I'm sorry," he said. "It's my fault. I was too late. I didn't get there in time to stop it."

"Amos Whiteaker, don't you be blamin' yourself," Mrs. Whiteaker cut in. "This is not your fault. You tried. You did more than anyone else and all that anybody could do. You were brave, boy. Do you hear me? You were brave and I am proud that you are my son."

The Marshall spoke up and said, "I need to ask you all about what happened? Could anyone identify the gunman?"

"No, they were wearing scarves the whole time. They were still wearing scarves when Nathaniel and me caught up to them." Amos told him.

"Nathaniel Caldwell?" the Marshall asked.

"Yes," answered Amos.

"So, they came into the church. They took Jeb and Newt. Then, you rode out after them?" the Marshall asked.

"Yeah," Amos told him. "It didn't take long for us to catch 'em. I don't think they thought anyone would follow. When we caught up to them, Newt was already on the ground."

Amos was choked up as he spoke.

"If we would have been one minute sooner, we might have saved Jeb," he said.

He composed himself again and continued, "Just as we got a good view of them, I saw one of the men pointing his gun at Jeb. I yelled for him to stop just as he fired. Then, one of the other men drew his gun and shot at us."

"Did you fire back?" asked the Marshall.

"Yeah. I'm sure I hit him by the way he rode off. After that," Amos said, "I brought my brother and Newt home."

"What about Nathaniel?" the Marshall continued his questioning.

"Nathaniel went after them," Amos told him.

"I'm much obliged to you for your help," the Marshall told them, "And I'm mighty sorry for your loss. I'll be goin' now, but I promise to do everything I can to find the men who did this."

The Marshall returned to town to find Nathaniel waiting for him at his office.

"Evenin'," said the Marshall as he hung his hat on a hook.

"Evenin'", said Nathaniel.

"You are just the man that I was hopin' to see," said the Marshall. "Have you been waitin' long?"

"Just all afternoon," Nathaniel told him.

"You must have somethin' mighty important to talk to me about if you've been waitin' all afternoon," he said.

"I need to talk to you about what happened out at the church this morning," Nathaniel explained.

"I just came from the Whiteaker farm. Amos told me what he knew about it. He also told me that you set out after the bushwackers by yourself," the Marshall told him.

"That's true," Nathaniel told him. "I followed 'em."

"That was kind of risky, wasn't it? There was three of them and only one of you," the Marshall said.

"Well, one of them was hurt pretty bad. They didn't know I was trailin' 'em. Anyhow, I knew where they were goin'," Nathaniel replied.

"How did you know that?" the Marshall asked him.

"I knew where they were going because I knew who they were. I knew their horses. I knew their voices. I knew where they would go. One of them dropped this." Nathaniel told him as he showed him the knife. "It belongs to my cousin. The men that you are looking for are James, Robert, and Pete Caldwell. I followed them to Caldwell Plantation and saw James and Petey carry Robert into the house."

This was exactly what the Marshall had been waiting for. For months, he suspected the Caldwells of bushwacking. Now, he had a witness.

"Will you sign a statement as to what you saw?" the Marshall asked him.

"Yes," Nathaniel told him.

Nathaniel made an official statement identifying James, Robert, and Pete Caldwell as the bushwackers at the church and James Caldwell as the one who murdered Jeb Whiteaker. When they were finished, the Marshall shook Nathaniel's hand and said, "I want to thank you, Nathaniel. This must have been hard for you, but you did the right thing."

"It's too bad that not everyone will see it that way," said Nathaniel as he said good-bye and went on his way.

On the long ride back to his farm, Nathaniel thought about what he had done. His decision to turn in his cousins would affect a lot of people, a lot of families. Some people would be glad, others might never forgive him. This would cost him. He took a stand that could leave him standing alone.

Chapter 29

The Reckoning

The Marshall didn't waste any time. As soon as Nathaniel signed the statement, the Marshall took two deputies and paid a visit to Caldwell Plantation. Cassie answered the knock on the door.

"Can I help you?" she asked them.

"We need to speak to Richard Caldwell," the Marshall told him.

"Mr. Caldwell ain't seein' nobody. His son passed this mornin' and we is all grievin'," Cassie explained.

"I'm sorry for his loss, but we're here on official business. Mr. Caldwell doesn't have a choice but to see us," the Marshall told her.

Cassie stared at him for a moment and then, said, "All right. I'll go and fetch him."

Richard joined the men at the door almost immediately.

"Good evenin', Mr. Caldwell," the Marshall said.

"What do you want?" Richard asked him even though he already knew the answer.

"I heard that your son passed today," the Marshall said.

"That's right," Richard told him.

"I also heard it was from a gunshot wound," the Marshall told him.

"Get to the point, Marshall," Richard snapped.

"Your sons, James and Pete, are wanted for the murder of Jeb Whiteaker and Newton Clark. Have you seen 'em?" the Marshall asked.

"No, I haven't." Richard lied.

"Do you know where they are?" the Marshall continued his questioning.

"No, I do not." Richard lied again.

"Are you aware, Sir, that aiding them in any way is in direct violation of the agreement that you signed with the State of Missouri?" the Marshall asked.

"I said, I haven't seen them." Richard was adamant.

"Did you know that your son, Robert, was also involved?" the Marshall asked.

"Robert was in no shape to talk when he got here. I brought him inside and tended to him. I sent my man servant after the doctor and didn't ask questions." Richard told him.

Richard didn't know that Nathaniel had identified his sons. He had no idea that Nathaniel had followed them back to the plantation. He didn't know that Nathaniel had found James' knife or that he had made a statement to the Marshall.

"Richard Caldwell, I am here to inform you that you are under arrest," the Marshall said.

"For what?" Richard argued, "helping my dying son."

"You made a promise to not aid the Confederacy or bushwackers in any way. Your son went to the church this morning, kidnapped two men, and killed them. Therefore, you aided a bushwacker," the Marshall told him.

"You have no proof of that. Furthermore, even if it were true, how could I know that? Would you deny me the right to care for my dying son?" Richard asked him.

"I have proof, Mr. Caldwell," the Marshall told him. "We have an eyewitness that saw Robert get shot. The witness followed Robert, James, and Pete right here to your house after they escaped. The witness also turned in evidence that links your son, James, to the scene of the murders. Now, I need you to come with me," the Marshall told him.

Richard had no more arguments.

"May I speak to my children before I go?" he asked.

"You have five minutes," the Marshall replied.

Richard went to the door and called for his daughters. "Mary, Sarah, Joanna, I must speak to you now."

The girls came immediately and saw the Marshall standing on the porch.

"What is it, Pa?" Mary asked.

"I have to go with the Marshall," he told her. "I need you to take care of things until this is all straightened out," Richard told him.

"Pa, no," cried Sarah, "Don't go. We need you." She threw her arms around her father.

"Sarah, stop it," Mary scolded, pulling her away. "You need to be strong for Pa."

Richard interrupted her, "Come and see me tomorrow. I'll tell you what I need you to do".

Richard calmy and quietly went with the Marshall back to the jail. Mary did as she was told. She called for Obie and went to the library to get her father's pistol out of the drawer. Sarah was following behind her.

"Mary, what are you doing?" Sarah asked her, alarmed.

"You heard Pa," she told her, "He said he needs us to take care of things."

"I heard him," Sarah told her, "But he didn't say anything about a pistol."

"He meant Petey and James, you ninny," Mary said exasperated. "Pa told them that he would find them and bring them what they needed while they was hidin' out."

"Obie," Mary called again, impatiently.

"Yes, Miss Mary," he said.

"Gather some blankets and water and hitch up the wagon. Tell Cassie to gather some food for James and Petey," Mary commanded. "You and me are gonna go find them."

"Are you sure, Miss Mary?" Obie asked her, "You could get yerself in a mighty big bunch a trouble if you get caught."

"Do as your told, Obie," scolded Mary. "I'm gonna help my brothers anyway that I can."

"Sarah, you stay here in case anyone else comes nosin' around. I'll be back soon," Mary told her.

Sarah nodded and said, "Please be careful," as Obie and Mary left.

They started with the closest dugout and searched until they finally found James and Petey.

"Mary, what are you doin' here?" Petey asked surprised to see her.

"The Marshall came and got Pa," Mary told him.

"What do you mean? Pa didn't do anything," Petey exclaimed.

"They arrested him for helping Robert. The Marshall said that Robert was a bushwacker and that Pa broke his promise by helping him," Mary explained.

Petey said, "Mary, is Robert.............?"

"Yes, Petey," Mary told him. "Robert is dead." Petey started to cry.

James was angry when he said, "Pa was helping his son."

"I know, but they didn't see it that way," Mary told him. "We brought you some food and supplies. You"re gonna have to get out of here. They're gonna be lookin' for you."

"We'll stay here a couple of days and then we'll head south," James told her.

Mary hugged Petey, "Good-bye, Petey," she said, "You take care of yourself."

James nodded to her. Then, she said, "Obie, let's go."

The next morning the Marshall paid a visit to Jeremiah. He told him that he had some bad news for him. Jeremiah didn't want to hear any more bad news.

"What is it, Marshall?" he asked.

"I'm sorry to have to tell you," the Marshall said, "but, I have Richard Caldwell in custody."

Jeremiah hesitated for a moment. Then, he asked, "What for?"

"For helping the bushwackers that killed your brother and your hired man," the Marshall blurted out.

Jeremiah felt like someone had knocked the wind out of him. He stood frozen trying to make sense of what the Marshall had just told him.

"There must be some mistake. Richard Caldwell is loyal to the Confederacy, but he wouldn't help someone who killed my brother." Jeremiah told him.

"He would if it was his son," the Marshall said.

Jeremiah sat down in his chair. He was stunned. "I don't understand," he told the Marshall.

"I have a witness who saw James Caldwell shoot your brother. The witness followed James, Pete, and Robert Caldwell back to the plantation. There, Richard Caldwell aided Robert who had been shot during their getaway. Robert died from his wounds yesterday and James and Pete Caldwell left on the run.

Jeremiah didn't know what to say. How would he tell this to Elizabeth? How would his family take it? So many thoughts were running through his mind.

"There is another problem, Captain," the Marshall told him. "Mr. Caldwell signed an agreement. He made a promise not to help any bushwackers or rebels and you signed an agreement to be responsible if he did."

"What are you sayin'?" Jeremiah asked anxiously.

"He broke the agreement, Captain," the Marshall told him.

"How, Marshall?" Jeremiah asked him. "He was helping his son. This wasn't about him tryin' to help bushwackers."

"Son or not, Robert was a bushwacker. Mr. Caldwell broke his word and you posted bond to ensure that he wouldn't," the Marshall told him.

"Are you trying to say that your goin' to take my farm because Richard Caldwell tried to save his son's life?" Jeremiah was angry.

"That's not my decision. The judge is coming to town in three weeks. There will be a hearing and a trial. He'll decide what should happen. In the meantime, Richard Caldwell will be held at the jail and me and my deputies will be looking for James and Pete Caldwell. They're wanted dead or alive."

"Is there anything else, Marshall?" Jeremiah asked him.

"No," the Marshall told him.

"Then, if you'll excuse me. I have work to do." Jeremiah told him.

"Thank you for your time, Captain Whiteaker," the Marshall said.

After the Marshall left, Jeremiah sat at the desk in his tent in disbelief. "This cannot be happening. Jeb and Robert are dead. James and Petey are wanted dead or alive. Richard is in jail and they want to take my farm. Elizabeth will never get over this," he said to himself. He cried out in an audible voice, "Oh Lord, show us mercy."

Chapter 30

Sad Good-byes

In the days that followed, two families mourned a deep loss. Jeb was laid to rest on the family farm. His family, neighbors, and friends gathered to pay their respects. The preacher spoke a comforting message and the family found peace in knowing that Jeb was safe in the arms of his Saviour.

The scene at Robert's final resting place was a sharp contrast. At Caldwell Plantation, the only family left there were Robert's sisters. Because most folks feared Robert and James, there were no neighbors or friends to come and pay their respects. There was no preacher, no message. However, Obadiah, being a godly man, recited some verses that he had memorized from Scripture. Mary, Sarah, Joanna, and Cassie listened as Obadiah ended with a prayer, each tearful and grief stricken over the loss of their brother and the events of the week.

Truly, it was tragic. Pride and the evil that lies in the recesses of men's hearts had started a chain of events that would leave a void in many people's lives. Yet, a miracle had taken place that no one knew about except for Richard Caldwell. In Robert's final moments, he experienced the miracle of regeneration. God forgave him. He reached down and saved Robert from the sin that had controlled his life for so long. He was ushered into eternal life and was also safe in the arms of his Saviour.

For Jeb and Robert, guilt, sorrow, and pain were no more. However, there was still a wake of troubles for the Caldwells and the Whiteakers to face. Jeremiah decided to wait until after Jeb's funeral to tell Elizabeth and the rest of the family about Richard's arrest. Sarah, Mary, and Joanna were preoccupied with all the things that their Pa had left undone before he was arrested. The girls were beside themselves when they got to the jail.

"Oh, Pa," Sarah said reaching for his hand through the cell bars.

Pa whispered, "Did you take supplies to your brothers?"

Mary, also with a whisper, replied, "Yes, I took care of it."

"Good," her Pa said relieved. "I want you to go back and tell them to get to St. Louis, to the Gordon's. James knows where they are. They've helped me run supplies and they run the mail. The Gordon's will help them get connections and anything they need to go further south."

"Alright, I'll go as soon as I get back," Mary told him.

"Did you have a service for Robert?" Pa asked his daughters.

"Yes," Sarah told him. "Obie read from the Scripture and helped us take care of everything."

Joanna looked at her Pa with tears in her eyes and so much pain on her face when she said, "We put him out by Mama. We thought she would want that."

"Yes, Joanna. Thank you," her father told her holding back his emotions.

Richard cleared his throat and composed himself. Then, he said, "Now, there's something else that I have tell you. It ain't gonna be easy, but I can't take care of anything as long as I'm in here. I am going to have to count on you."

"What is it, Pa?" Sarah answered with a quiver in her voice.

"First, I want to tell you that the things a person owns don't matter," he told them. "I've spent my whole life trying to get more and more things, to build more and more, to buy more and more."

"What are you sayin', Pa?" Mary asked.

"I'm sayin' that losin' Robert showed me what matters. I'd give it all away right now to have him and your mother back," he told them.

"Oh, Pa," Sarah said as she broke down and cried.

"Hush now, Sarah," Pa told her. "You have to be strong. You have to be strong like your Ma was."

Sarah composed herself for the moment.

"The banker is going to be coming out to the plantation one day soon," Pa told his daughters. "I've spent a lot of money helping to finance the Confederacy in this war. I knew that we had to win or life as we knew it would be over. What I didn't realize was that life as we knew it in Missoura' was already over," Pa explained.

"I don't understand," Mary told him nervously.

"I'm just going to say it. I borrowed money against the plantation to help the cause," he told them.

"What does that mean, Pa?" Sarah asked him.

"It means with me in jail, William, Sterling, and Jackson gone, and the Marshall looking for James and Petey, I can't pay the bank back. They're gonna' call in the note and take the plantation," Pa told them.

"Pa, please, no," Sarah cried, "We can't lose our home, too."

"Listen to me, Sarah," Pa tried to comfort her, "It's just a house."

"But, Pa, it's our home. We were born there. We grew up there," Sarah told him.

"Everything, Pa?" Mary asked him in quiet disbelief, "Are they takin' everything?"

"No," said Pa, "The furnishings belonged to your Ma."

"What good will the furnishings do us with no place to put them?" Sarah asked beside herself. "Where are we goin' to live?"

"I didn't borrow against the old cabin and some of the acreage around it. We'll keep a milk cow, the chickens, a few of the horses, the carriage, and a wagon. The bank should give us some time, but I need you to start moving as soon as you can."

"Oh, Pa, this is just too much," Sarah said.

"I'm sorry, Sarah," Pa told her.

"What about the hired men and the slaves, Pa?" Mary asked.

"We're gonna keep the overseers on until everything is taken care of," Pa told her. "Then, I want you to pay them what I owe them and an extra week's pay. Tell them that we won't be needin' 'em anymore."

"As for the slaves," Pa continued, "We're gonna need 'em to help us get settled. You girls can't do it all by yourselves," Pa replied. "Once everything is settled, we're gonna set 'em free. We can't take care of them anymore."

Sarah gasped. Mary took a deep breath. Joanna still stood silent.

"What about Cassie and Obie?" Mary asked him.

"Them, too," Pa replied. "I'm giving them a choice. They can stay with us if they want to."

The girls couldn't believe what they were hearing.

"Now, you go on home," their Pa told them. "You gotta a lot to think about and a lot to do."

"Yes, Pa," Sarah said. Mary nodded and Joanna left still without a word.

The girls did as their Pa told them to and started preparations for leaving their beautiful plantation home.

Chapter 31

Bad News

A few days after the bushwackers stormed into the church service, Lucy paid a visit to her brother and sister at the O'Connor farm. She wanted to tell Ella, Tom, and Anne what had happened to Jeb before they heard about it in town. Lucy recounted the events of that day for them.

With tears in her eyes, Ella said, "Oh, Lucy, we're so sorry for your family. What can we do?"

"There's nothin' anyone can do," Lucy told her. "It's just gonna take time for the Lord to heal the broken hearts. I know He is able, and I have faith that He will."

Lucy hesitated for a moment, and then she said, "I don't know how to tell you this."

"There's more," gasped Anne.

"Yes," Lucy told them. "Amos shot one of them, while they were escaping, and Nathaniel followed after them. Rumor in town is that he followed the three men to Caldwell Plantation."

"I don't understand," replied Ella.

"Ella," Lucy told her, "It was James, Robert, and Petey. Amos shot Robert."

"No," Ella denied it. "There must be some mistake."

Lucy shook her head. "I don't think so," she told her. "Is Robert all right?" Anne asked.

"He died a few hours after they got him home," said Lucy.

Ella felt her knees growing weak. She slowly sat down and tried to concentrate on what she was hearing. She had so many questions, but she didn't know where to begin.

Lucy told them about James and Petey being on the run. She told them about Richard Caldwell getting arrested for helping bushwackers, even though he was only helping his son. She told them about Jeremiah putting up the farm as bond and that the Whiteaker's could lose his part because of the latest chain of events.

"Oh, Lucy. It's just too much," Ella told her. Then she turned to Tom, "Tom, the girls, they're all alone. I have to go see them and make sure that they're O.K.," Ella said.

"Don't be hasty. They would have come and found you if they needed you. Let's take some time to think about all of this. Let's pray and see what the Lord wants us to do." Tom told her.

"I know you're right. It's just that I'm beside myself. I feel like I need to do somethin'," she said. Then, she turned to Lucy and asked, "How are Mr. and Mrs. Whiteaker and the rest of the family?"

"They thought it best not to tell Pa Whiteaker, " Lucy replied. "Mother Whiteaker is trying to be brave for the family, but Amos is taking it hard. He blames himself because he was too late. Jeremiah is torn between his family and his wife. He hurts for Elizabeth, but he's mourning with the rest of us over his brother."

No one knew what to say. They desperately wanted it all to be a mistake, but it wasn't. It was all true.

Lucy interrupted the silence and said, "I best be getting' back. I wish I could stay, but Amos needs me. I just wanted you all to hear this from me."

Ella got up and squeezed her sister tightly. "I love you," she said.

"I know. I love you, too," Lucy told her. She said good-bye to Tom and Anne and left them to ponder all that they had just heard.

"Tom, this ain't right," Ella told him. "Isn't there somethin' that we can do?"

"I don't know," Tom told her. "I need some time to think about it."

Ella, weary from the flood of emotions, went to her room to lie down. Tom and Anne sat silently together by the fireplace. Tom agreed with Ella that they needed to do something, but what? There in the quiet he silently prayed and asked the Lord for wisdom. He opened his Bible, hoping to find an answer. He came upon a verse in the book of Matthew that said, "Love thy neighbor as thyself." That's what he had to do, love the Whiteakers as himself.

"Anne," he said, "I can't stand by and let the Whiteakers lose their farm because Jeremiah was trying to keep a noose off Richard Caldwell's neck."

"I feel bad about this, too, but unless you have some money tucked away that I don't know about, I don't think we can help him," Anne told him.

"You know if I had the money, I would give it to him," he told her. Anne nodded her head.

"Jeremiah's in this mess because he vouched for Richard Caldwell," Tom told her. "We could vouch for Jeremiah."

"What do you mean?" she asked him.

"We can petition the court. I could write a letter and vouch for the fact that Jeremiah and his whole family has been loyal to the Union. I could tell them about how he joined up right away when the war started and how he got promoted to Captain. I could say that he has been faithful to his duty and suggest that since Richard didn't do any harm, Jeremiah shouldn't lose his farm."

"That's all true," Anne told him. I just don't know if they'd listen to you. You're not in the army. They don't know you. You're a farmer from Missoura'. Why would it matter to them?"

"It wouldn't from one farmer from Missoura', Anne," he told her, "but what if we ask everyone in town to sign it. Maybe the judge won't decide against the whole town," Tom told her.

Anne agreed and Tom sat down by a small table to start writing his petition. He quietly prayed, "Lord, if it be your will, bless this. Help the Whiteakers keep all of their land."

Chapter 32

The Escape

At the dugout, James was starting to get nervous. He didn't want to wait anymore.

"Petey, we need to get outta here before somebody finds us," James said. "If we get caught, they'll put us both in jail with Pa."

"I didn't do nothin' and I surely didn't know what you was gonna do," Petey defended himself.

"Do you think anybody is gonna believe that? We're in a lotta trouble, boy," James told him. "Pack up. We're gettin' outta here."

James and Petey packed up what they could carry and started to ride. They didn't have a plan except to put as many miles between them and the Provost Marshall as they could. James decided that they should go south. He thought that the further south they got, the safer they would be.

Even though Obie and Mary went straight to the dugout with the message from their Pa, they were too late. The brothers would not receive it. They would not find refuge in St. Louis like their father had hoped they would.

They rode until nightfall. Then, they stopped to sleep a while.

"You take the first watch," James said, "Wake me up in a few hours."

Petey didn't mind. He couldn't sleep anyway. The only thing he could do was think about everything that had happened. His mind raced. How he wished that he would have never ridden off with James and Robert that day.

Petey sat, he thought, he watched, while the Provost Marshall and his deputies were combing the countryside looking for him and his brother. He woke James after a few hours just like he asked. Then, he leaned up against a tree and fell asleep himself for a little while.

While Petey slept, James had time to think, too. He knew he needed a plan, but he had no destination. It seemed logical that the deeper south they got, the safer they would be, far from union soldiers and union sympathizers. So, south they went.

"Wake up," he said, "We need to get movin'."

Petey got up, pulled himself together and mounted his horse. The two men started riding again. News traveled fast about what had happened at the church that day. The Marshall had put the word out that James and Pete Caldwell were wanted by the law and that there was a reward.

As the two men rode, they were unaware that they had been spotted in the woods. Old Man Carter and his grandson were out hunting that morning. They were hunting for rabbits and squirrels but found two wanted men instead.

Old Man Carter didn't know the Caldwells well. He lived in the next county, but he occasionally had business dealings with Richard Caldwell. He had met James a time or two and suspected the two men that he saw in the woods that day were the same two men wanted by the Law.

He and his grandson stayed hidden. When James and Pete were out of sight, he went straight to the local sheriff and told him what he saw. It would take time for the information to get back to the Provost Marshall. The sheriff, not knowing the Marshall was already leading a posse in his direction, immediately sent word to him. Then, he and a deputy went after the wanted men on their own.

James and Petey didn't know that the anyone was on their trail. They didn't know about the reward or how many people were looking for them. They came across a farm where they stopped and asked if they could water their horses.

The farmer greeted them kindly, "Can I help you boys?" he asked them.

"We'd be obliged If we could get some water for our horses," James told him.

"Right over there," the farmer told him as he pointed to the horse trough. "You're welcome to fill your canteens, too," he said as he pointed in the other direction at the pump by the house.

"Thank you, that's mighty kind of you," James told him. Petey was nervous and didn't speak.

"Where you from?" the farmer asked them.

"We ain't from around these parts," James lied.

"It ain't safe roamin' around with this war goin' on, not to mention all the bushwacking," the farmer told them.

"You got that right," James told him. "We was thinkin' maybe we'd join up."

The farmer nodded and the conversation ended. The horses were watered, and the two men were ready for the next leg of their journey.

"Good luck to ya'. You boys be careful," the farmer told them.

"Thank you," James said. Then, he and Petey rode off.

Later that day, the Marshall and his deputies made it to the county line. They decided to stop at the nearest town to see if anyone there might know something. Their first stop was the sheriff's office. There was no one there, but there was a boy sitting on a step close by eating an apple.

The Marshall looked at him and said, "Howdy."

'Howdy," the boy replied.

"You wouldn't happen to know where I might find the sheriff, would you?" the Marshall asked the boy.

"No, he left a while ago," the boy told him.

"What do we do now?" one of the deputies asked the Marshall.

"We don't have time to wait. They already have a head start," the Marshall told him. "Let's ask around and see if anybody's seen 'em. Maybe he'll be back before we leave."

The boy noticed the Marshall's star on his chest and asked, "Are you a sheriff, too, Mister?"

"No," he told him. "I'm a Provost Marshall."

"I never heard of that," the boy told him. Then, he asked, "Are you looking for those men?"

The boy had the Marshall's attention. "What men?" he asked the boy.

"The men that Billy Carter saw out in the woods," the boy told him.

"What are you talkin' about?" the Marshall prodded.

"I saw my friend, Billy, a while ago when he came to town with his Grandpaw. They came to see the sheriff to tell him about two men they saw in the woods when they was out huntin' today," the boy explained.

"Did they see the sheriff?" he asked him.

"Billy didn't. He waited out here with me, but his Grandpaw did," said the boy.

"Is that when the sheriff left?" the Marshall asked him.

"Yeah," said the boy.

"Did you see which way they went?" the Marshall continued his questions.

"No," he told him.

"Did Billy tell you where they saw the men?" the Marshall prodded some more.

"Yeah, out at his Grandpaw's place. It's that way," the boy pointed south, "Not too far outside of town on the other side of the two hills."

"South and over two hills?" the Marshall clarified.

"Yes, Sir," answered the boy.

"Thank you." said the Marshall as he reached into his pocket and pulled out a shiny coin. He handed it to the boy and said, "This is for you. You've been a big help."

The boy's face lit up as he said, "Thanks, Mister." Then, he ran off with his shiny coin in hand.

The Marshall and his deputies rode south. It wasn't long before they saw the two hills.

"What are we gonna do now?" a deputy asked.

"We're goin' south," the Marshall told him.

The sheriff and his deputy were a few hours ahead of the Marshall. They came upon the farm where James and Petey had stopped earlier.

"Howdy," said the sheriff.

"Can I help you?" said the farmer, a little surprised to get a visit from a sheriff.

"I'm hopin' so," the sheriff answered, "We're looking for two young men, somewhere's between about eighteen and twenty-five. One is tall with light hair. The other one is smaller and a little darker," the sheriff continued. "Have you seen anybody like that?"

"Yes, sir," the farmer said, "Two men came through this morning and asked if they could water their horses. They weren't here long. They got what they needed and left."

"How long ago?" the sheriff asked.

"About four or five hours ago," the farmer told him.

"They didn't happen to tell you where they was goin', did they," the sheriff asked him.

"No," he replied. "They just said that they was thinkin' about joinin' up."

"Which way did they go?" the deputy interrupted.

"They headed south," the farmer told him.

"Thank you for your help," the sheriff said, and he and the deputy hurried on their way.

Chapter 33

A Letter

While James and Petey were on the run, their sisters were trying to pick up the pieces from the mess that they had left behind. Sarah made a visit to the post office and sent a letter to St. Louis via the underground mail route. It was to William and Sterling telling them what had happened at home.

The girls did as their Pa asked them to. They started packing up and moving down to the little cabin. The little cabin really wasn't so little. Maybe compared to the plantation house, but their Pa never did anything in a small way. It had always been the biggest and best for Richard Caldwell and his family. The cabin would make a good home for them. It would just take some time getting used to it.

As the girls worked, Sarah cried. "You need to stop this, Sarah," Joanna told her.

"I can't," Sarah told her, "I don't want to live here."

Mary scolded her, "You hush and be grateful. We need to be thankful that we have a roof over our head and food to eat. There's nothin' wrong with this place. Once we finish getting our own things in here, it will feel just like home."

Sarah didn't say anymore but tears continued rolling down her cheeks.

At the O'Connor farm, Ella was contemplating her own letter. Jackson needed to know what had happened, too. Jeb had been their friend since they were children. And even though Jackson was always getting after James and Robert, he still loved him. He loved his Uncle Richard and the girls, too.

"This will break his heart," she thought to herself, "but his family needs him. I need him."

Ella remembered the day at the post office when she ran into Sarah. Sarah told her about the mail line that she was using it to sneak letters to the Confederacy. She had to try and contact Jackson before it was too late.

Ella sat down at her desk and wrote Jackson a note. It said, "Dearest Jackson: If you can find a way, please come home. The family needs you. Uncle Richard, Petey, and James are in trouble. Come if you can and please be careful. I love you. Ella

Tom and Anne were in the kitchen. Ella told them that she had someplace that she needed to go.

"I have to see someone," Ella told them.

"You know it ain't safe to be travelin' by yourself right now, El, and I can't leave Anne here alone," Tom told her.

"I know, Tom, but it's important," Ella told him. "I'm not goin' far. I'm only goin' to Caldwell Plantation."

"You sure that's a good idea?" Tom asked her.

"Yes, I need to see Sarah," Ella told him.

"If you have to go, you should go now, so that you can be back before dark," Tom told her.

"I was plannin' on it. Take good care of Anne and I'll be back before supper," said Ella.

Ella's short journey to Caldwell Plantation was uneventful. She was thankful for that. She knocked on the door. Cassie answered.

"Hello, Miss Ella," Cassie said to her. "We wasn't expectin' you today."

"I know, Cassie, but I need to see Sarah. Is she here?" Ella asked her.

"No," Cassie told her, "But, she'll be back in a little while. She's down at the cabin."

"The cabin? Mr. and Mrs. Caldwell's old place?' Ella asked.

"Yes, Miss Ella. We's movin' the family down their just as soon as we can. They've already started," Cassie explained.

"Whatever for?" Ella asked her.

"The banker's takin' the house, Miss Ella. Master Caldwell borrowed money against it to give to the cause and now he's in jail so he can't pay it back. This whole family is just fallin' apart," she said.

Ella gave her an understanding look.

"You can wait in Miss Jane's parlor until Miss Sarah gets back. I expect her anytime," Cassie told her as she tearfully walked away.

"Thank you," said Ella.

Ella stood in the foyer for a moment. It would always be the ballroom to her. There were so many good memories here. She closed her eyes. She could almost hear the music and the laughter. "Will this be the last time that

I see this room the way it was back then?" she thought to herself.

She stepped into the parlor, walked over to the fireplace, and ran her hand over the mantle. She turned to look out the beautiful glass doors that led to the porch, remembering the night of her first party. She and Jackson snuck through the parlor and out those doors to sit on the edge of the porch. She remembered Jackson searching for the words to tell her how he felt for the very first time. How she wished she could have those days back.

Ella's thoughts were interrupted by a voice in the other room. It was Sarah.

As Sarah came into the parlor, she said, "Ella, it was good of you to come."

They hugged each other and Ella said, "Cassie told me what happened, Sarah. I'm so sorry. What can I do?"

"There's nothin' anyone can do," Sarah told her and got right to the point. "Why are you here, Ella?"

"I've been worried, worried about all of you. I had to do somethin'. The only thing I could think of was to get word to Jackson and try to get him home."

"I sent word to William and Sterling a few days ago," she said, "but I didn't think of Jackson. You're right, he'll know what to do."

"I have a letter, but I need your help in getting it to him," Ella told her as she took the letter out of her purse. "Can you find, Jackson? Can you get him this letter?"

"I don't know. I just send the letters to St. Louis. Some friends of my Pa have contacts with the Confederacy. They get the letters where they're supposed to go." Sarah explained.

"We need to try, Sarah," Ella told her.

"It's dangerous. If we get caught, they'll say that we were sendin' information to the enemy. Are you sure that you are willing to take that chance?" Sarah asked her.

"We have to," Ella told her.

"Give it to me," Sarah said, taking the letter from her hand. "Mr. Johnston will get suspicious if you mail a letter to my friends in St. Louis. He already asks me all kinds of questions about who I'm writing to when I go to the post office."

"Be careful, Sarah," she told her.

Sarah nodded.

"I'll go first thing in the mornin'," she told her.

Ella hugged her and left. She made it safely home all the while wondering if she had done the right thing. She said a prayer that the letter would reach Jackson and that the Lord would bring him home safely.

Chapter 34

A Call for Help

J ackson and George knew nothing about what had been happening back home. After a long journey, they finally met up with Jackson's regiment not too far from Sedalia. Jackson introduced George to some of the men. He had already told him about a few of them, particularly Anderson and Bradshaw who had been with him at Wilson's Creek. Others were new, all of them there for a cause, maybe not THE cause, but for a cause. George settled in and was a soldier now.

Their regiment had orders to go south toward Springfield. They were almost there when they stopped and made camp. They were told to get ready for a group of Confederate soldiers who were coming back from a skirmish. They were to feed them, give them a place to rest, and tend to any wounded.

It wasn't too long after they made camp that the soldiers arrived. Jackson was hauling water up from the nearby creek when he heard someone call his name. He turned toward the sound of the voice and saw his cousin, Sterling Caldwell.

"Sterling," he called as he set the water buckets down and hurried to greet him.

"It's really good to see you, Jackson," Sterling told him shaking his hand.

"Are you alright," Jackson asked him. "We heard that you all had a run in with the Yankees down by Springfield."

"Yeah, we did, but I'm alright," Sterling told him. You should've been there. We sent 'em runnin' right back where they came from."

Jackson was looking around as he asked, "Where's William?"

"He went back home," Sterling told him.

"Why? Is something wrong?" Jackson asked him.

Sterling motioned Jackson to follow him with a nod of his head. When Sterling was confident that no one was listening, he told Jackson what had happened.

"Nothin's right," Sterling explained. "We got a letter from Sarah a while ago. Robert and James got caught bushwacking and Pa got arrested for helpin' them. I don't know everything that happened, but James and Petey are on the run, and Robert got shot."

"Shot?' Jackson exclaimed.

"He's dead, Jackson," Sterling told him.

Jackson had no words. He tried to hold back his emotions.

"What about Ella?" Jackson asked him.

"As far as I know, she's fine," Sterling reassured him, "but things aren't good at the plantation. William left to see if he could do somethin'. I didn't go back because we didn't leave on good terms. Pa wouldn't listen to nothin' and I knew that James and Robert were up to no good. That's why we joined up. When we left, I didn't plan on goin' back," Sterling explained.

"Who's takin' care of things?" Jackson asked him.

"I don't know," Sterling told him, "But, there's somethin' else. Sarah said that James killed Jeb."

"Are you sure? Why? There must be a mistake!" exclaimed Jackson.

Sterling nodded his head and stared at the ground,

Jackson couldn't talk about it anymore. He needed to think. He said, "Let's find you somethin' to eat and a place to get some rest, Sterling. You've earned it."

Jackson was unaware that Ella had also sent a letter, a letter he would never receive. Mr. Johnston had grown suspicious of Sarah and was keeping track of her mail. When she sent Ella's letter, he didn't mail it. He decided to turn it in to the Provost Marshall. Since the Marshall and his deputies were on the hunt for James and Petey, Captain Whiteaker was in charge until he got back.

Mr. Johnston went to see Captain Whiteaker with Ella's letter. When he got to the camp, he requested to see the captain and was escorted to the captain's tent by one of the guards.

Jeremiah, obviously surprised to see the Postmaster, said, "Hello, Mr. Johnston. What can I do for you?"

"I was told in town that you were in charge until the Provost Marshall got back," he said.

"That's right. Are you here on official business?" Jeremiah asked him.

"Yes," Mr. Johnston told him. "You see, Sarah Caldwell has been sending letters to St. Louis for quite a while now. Sometimes she'll send two or three letters without waiting for a reply."

"Have you ever asked her about the letters or who she's mailin' them to?' Jeremiah asked him.

"Yes, Sir, I have," he told him. "She acted put out by my asking and told me that who she mails letters to was none of my business. I think she could tell that I wasn't gonna give up on it, so she told me she was writing her beau."

"And you don't believe her?" he replied.

"No," said Mr. Johnston. "I never heard anyone talk about Miss Sarah having a beau. And, if you ask me, the letters she gets from St. Louis don't look like a man wrote 'em. Furthermore, if she does have a beau, how come he's never come to see her, and why doesn't she go to see him?" Mr. Johnston asked.

"You have a point," Jeremiah told him.

"I brought you her latest letter," Mr. Johnston said as he pulled Ella's letter out of his pocket.

The two men shook hands and Mr. Johnston left the letter in the captain's custody. Jeremiah sat down at his desk and opened the letter. It was a letter to the confederacy just as Mr. Johnston suspected, but it wasn't a letter from Sarah. It was from Ella Caldwell. Jeremiah suspected that she was sending letters for other people besides her and Ella. He wanted to find out who, so he decided to watch and wait. He wrote a message to Mr. Johnston instructing him to allow Sarah to continue mailing her letters. Mr. Johnston was to collect them and give them to the captain.

Chapter 35

A Petition and Freedom

R ichard was right about the banker. A few days after the girls got settled into the cabin, the banker came to break the bad news. He said that he was sorry to have it to do it, but he was calling in the loan. He gave them five days to pay the money, or he was taking the house and most of the property.

After he left, Mary walked up to the plantation house. She didn't know why. She just wanted to be there. She was wondering aimlessly around the rooms, thinking, remembering, when she heard a rider coming in. She looked out from an upstairs window and saw a confederate soldier. He looked dirty and ragged, like he had been riding a long time.

"Another one," Mary thought to herself. She was resentful. After all, if her Pa hadn't insisted on helping the confederacy, she wouldn't be losing her home in the first place.

Resentment turned to fear when she remembered that she was there all alone. She had no idea who the soldier was or how desperate he was. She froze, hoping that he would take what he wanted, the little that was left, and go away. She heard the front door open. Then, she heard footsteps as he wandered from room to room.

She listened intently to the sound of footsteps on the stairs. She reached for a bedwarmer that was leaning against the fireplace and stood behind the bedroom door. She held it up, ready to strike whoever walked through that door. The door already parted, started to slowly move. Her heart raced and she was overcome with fear as she bolted from behind the door. The soldier moved out of her striking range quickly and took hold of her by both of her hands. She dropped her makeshift weapon as she screamed and try to free herself.

A familiar voice said, "Mary. Mary, it's me. It's alright. It's me."

Mary got a hold of herself and looked on a familiar face. She started to sob. The soldier held her tightly and said, "It's alright. I'm here now." William had come home.

She told William about everything that happened and about the visit from the banker. She told him their Pa's instructions. Everything had changed since he left, and he would have no time to get used to it. He had to accept it and do what he could to take care of his family.

"I'm sorry, Mary," he told her. "I tried to get here sooner, but I ran into some Yankees. I came up on a skirmish and couldn't turn my back. We were outnumbered, so I stayed to fight."

"You're here now. That's what matters," Mary told him.

While Mary helped William get settled in at the cabin, Tom had started gathering signatures for his petition. Anne was awaiting the arrival of the new addition to their family. Jeremiah was gathering evidence against the women who had been sending information to their confederate relatives. As for Jackson, he was on his way home, too. Soon after he heard the news from Sterling, Jackson started for home.

At the O"Connor farm it was a bright morning. The sunshine streamed through the kitchen window as Ella was making breakfast. Anne was sitting at the table snapping green beans for the afternoon meal when Tom came downstairs.

"Good mornin'," he said as he kissed Anne on the cheek.

"Good morning, Tom. How did you sleep?" Ella asked him.

"Just fine," he said as he poured a cup of coffee. "I was thinkin' if it was alright with you two, I would go out today and get the rest of the signatures for my petition."

"I think that would be fine," Anne told him. Ella gave him a nod of approval as she flipped a flapjack in the pan.

"After I have a bite to eat, I'll head on out. I promise to be back before nightfall," he told him.

Tom ate his breakfast, and he was off. Most folks were happy to sign the petition, even those who were Confederate sympathizers. They respected Jeremiah for standing up for his family even though they were on different sides of the war.

Jeremiah had heard about the petition. He was grateful and appreciated Tom's efforts. However, he didn't have much hope that it would carry any weight with the judge.

The judge was due into town in less than two weeks. Jeremiah was anxious for all this to be over, but he dreaded it at the same time. He was still collecting Sarah's letters from Mr. Johnston. He would wait one more week before he decided what to do about it.

William and Mary woke up early that same morning, too. William sent her to town to tell her Pa that he was home. He had to be careful. It wasn't safe for a confederate soldier with the Union Army camped just a few miles down the road.

Richard was glad to see his daughter and relieved that they had gotten settled into the cabin. He could tell that she had something important to tell him, but he waited for the right moment to ask her. They could hear the jailer talking to someone else in the next room. He probably wouldn't be paying any attention to Richard and Mary.

Richard whispered and said, "What is it, Mary?"

"It's William, Pa," she whispered back. "He's home."

Richard was surprised and grateful at the same time. "How did he know?" her Pa asked her.

"Sarah sent a letter to the Gordon's for him. He came as soon as he found out," Mary explained.

"And Sterling?" he asked.

Mary shook her head. "No, Pa. He stayed behind," she told him. "William wants to know what you want us to do."

"Pay the overseers like I told you and tell them we don't need them anymore," Pa told her. "As for the slaves, there is a slave refugee camp outside of St. Louis. I want William and Obie to take the slaves there and set them free. Take one of the wagons and load it with enough food to feed them for three days. They can take with them whatever else they can carry," he told her.

Mary agreed.

"Did Obadiah bring you?" he asked her. She nodded. "Send him in here. I need to talk to him, too. Then, you go on home and tell William what I told you."

"Goodbye, Pa. Don't worry. We'll take care of everything," Mary reassured her father.

Obie was waiting for Mary by the carriage.

"Obie, Master Caldwell wants to speak to you. The jailer will tell you where to find him," she told him.

Obie was surprised but did as Mary told him to do.

"Can I help you, boy?" asked the jailer.

"I's here to see Master Caldwell, Sir. He asked to see me," he told the jailer.

The jailer stared Obie down as he reached for the keys and opened the cell block door.

"You got five minutes," he told Obie.

"Yes, Sir," Obie replied. He found his master at the end of the row in the last cell.

"Miss Mary said you wanted to see me, Sir," Obie told him.

"Yes, Obadiah," Richard said, "I have somethin' important to tell you. Times are changin'. I think you know that."

"Yes, Sir, I know'd it," Obie told him.

"Because of how everything is changing, I can't keep slaves anymore. I won't be able to take care of them," Richard told him.

Obie asked him anxiously, "Are you gonna sell us off, Master Caldwell?", afraid of the answer.

Richard looked Obie in the eye and said, "Obadiah, you have been loyal to me all of these years and so has your Mamie. I trust you. That's why I am askin' you to do something important for me."

Obie nodded.

"I need you to help Master William take the slaves to St. Louis. I am setting you all free," he told him.

Could this really be true? Free! Did he say free? Obadiah had been waiting for this his entire life.

"I don't understand. You settin' us free?" he asked his master to repeat it.

"You heard me. I don't have a choice. I can't take care of all of you anymore," he told him.

"Why's we goin' to St. Louis? What will we do when we get there?" Obie asked him.

"There's a camp there for slaves. The Union Army set it all up. They will give you all a place to stay and enough food to eat until the war is over. Then, they will help everyone start over someplace else. You'll be free." Master Caldwell explained.

Obie was speechless, trying to process what he had just been told.

"There's somethin' else," he continued, "You and Cassie can stay if you want to, not as slaves, but as paid servants. You would be free. You'd have a place to stay and get paid for your work, but only if you want to. It's your decision."

"When will we be leavin'?" Obie asked.

"Right away," Master Caldwell told him. "Now, you go on."

"Yes, Sir," Obie told him as he turned to walk away.

His Master called out to him one last time, "Obadiah."

Obie turned back. The two men looked each other in the eyes then Master Caldwell said, "Good-bye."

Obadiah nodded and said, "Good-bye, Sir." Neither knowing for sure if this would be the last time that they would see each other.

Obie and Mary went back to the plantation and gave William his father's instructions. He paid the overseers and sent them on their way. The slaves were given one day to get ready for the trip. William gave them the choice to leave on their own or go with him and Obie to St. Louis.

Going on their own was dangerous. They could be mistaken for runaways. Worse yet, they could encounter bushwackers. Obie persuaded them that going with William was the safest option.

Cassie decided to stay with the Caldwells, if only for a while. She loved them. She had taken care of each of the children and watched them grow up. One day she would go, but right now they needed her, and she couldn't leave them. She was free to choose for herself. She chose love.

William and Obie did as they were asked. They loaded the wagon with enough food to feed everyone on the trip. Then. they moved on to St. Louis where every man, woman, and child from Caldwell Plantation would finally be free.

Chapter 36

The Women and the War

W hile William and Obie were on their way to St. Louis with the slaves, the bank took over Caldwell Plantation. The banker. being a pro-union man, offered the Union Army use of the house for the duration of the war. Caldwell Plantation was near the camp and would be suitable for officer's quarters and conducting union business.

Jeremiah was opposed to it. He had a history in that house. It had been his wife's home. His superiors disregarded his objection and accepted the bankers offer anyway. Caldwell Plantation became Union Officer's Quarters and Headquarters. Jeremiah would never have imagined this, Yankee's in Richard Caldwell's Plantation.

Jeremiah had continued to monitor the mail with the help of Mr. Johnston. They confiscated letters from four other local women besides Sarah and Ella. He decided he had enough evidence. It was time to end the underground mail line.

Sharing information with the enemy was a crime. It was Jeremiah's duty to enforce the law, but he didn't like the idea of arresting women. The jail in town was no place for them. Yet, he couldn't allow them to continue what they were doing. He had to find another solution.

Jeremiah's solution was Caldwell Plantation. It would be used to house women prisoners instead of officers. They would be kept there comfortably under continuous watch, while the library would be used as an office for conducting official business.

Jeremiah ordered that the four women who were using Sarah's mail line be arrested. Jeremiah would deal with Sarah himself. It was the least that he could do out of respect for his wife.

He rode to the log cabin that the Caldwell's now called home. It was so different from the majestic plantation house that his wife had grown up in. There was one big room on the main floor that had a large hearth to heat it. It was big enough for a large group of people to gather in and feel comfortable. There was a kitchen off one side of the main room and a bedroom off the other side. There was no proper dining room, but a long wood table stood in one side of the main room just outside the kitchen. It was large enough to seat almost two dozen with a chair on each end and two long benches on each side the length of the table.

The cabin had two lofts. One loft was accessed by a ladder for the boys. The other one had a narrow staircase leading up to it for the girls.

As Jeremiah approached the cabin, he was overcome by sadness for Mary, Joanna, and Sarah. Caldwell Plantation had so much activity once, so much life. He knocked on the big, wood door. Joanna answered. She didn't say anything. She waited for him to speak.

"Hello, Joanna," he said.

"Hello," she replied. She didn't invite him in or even ask him what he wanted. She just stood there.

"I've come to see Sarah," he said, "Is she here?"

"Wait here," Joanna told him. "I'll get her."

It was a strange encounter. Joanna acted as if she didn't even know Jeremiah. Shortly after, Sarah appeared at the front door. Joanna stood quietly behind her.

"Jeremiah, what are you doin' here? Is Elizabeth with you?" she asked him.

"No, I'm sorry she's not. I'm here to see you, Sarah," he told her.

"Me? Alright, won't you come in?" she asked him.

"I'm here on official business," Jeremiah explained.

"If you're here about James and Petey," she said, "I don't know where they are."

"No, this is about you," he told her. "I have in my possession some letters."

Her heart started to race. He was holding some of the letters that were supposed to go to the Gordon's in St. Louis. She could see that they had been opened.

"What do you know about these letters, Sarah?" he asked her, showing her the letters.

Sarah looked at the letters relieved that they weren't hers. "How should I know? They aren't my letters," she told him.

"I'm aware of that. I know who they belong to, but it was you that was mailing them," Jeremiah told her.

"So, I dropped some mail off at the post office for my friends. There's no law against that," she replied sharply.

"There is, if the mail is going to confederate soldiers and you are the contact person," he told her.

Sarah was quiet. Then she said, "What are you goin' to do?"

"I have to arrest you," he told her.

Her knees were weak, and she felt faint. Joanna showed no emotion. She just listened.

"Jeremiah, you can't be serious. You're going to throw me in a jail cell like a common criminal?" she asked him.

"You know better," he told her, "Now let's go."

"I have to go with Jeremiah, Joanna," she told her sister. "Please tell Mary."

Joanna nodded and Jeremiah took Sarah away.

The other women were already at the plantation when Sarah got there. Sarah was shocked and angry that the Yankees had taken over her family home.

"Does Elizabeth know about this?" she asked him filled with anger. "How could you, Jeremiah?"

Jeremiah didn't answer her. He instructed one of the guards to help her get settled and inform her of what would be expected.

Each "prisoner" was given a cot, a blanket, and a wash basin. They could move freely about the house, except for her Pa's library. They could cook and do other household chores and go outside for some air. However, they would always be under the watchful eyes of a guard.

She chose her old room even though it didn't look like or feel like her room anymore. It was plain with all her things gone. Not to mention, she was sharing it with another lady instead of one of her sisters.

After Jeremiah delivered Sarah into custody, his next stop was the O'Connor farm. Ella's situation was different. Jeremiah didn't believe that Ella had been sending messages to the Confederacy. He suspected that it was her first letter, a cry for help to her husband after everything that had happened. No one knew that the intercepted letter belonged to her. As far as Sarah knew, Ella's letter had made it to St. Louis. Mr. Johnston thought the letter was Sarah's. Jeremiah could look the other way and no one would ever know, but it was his duty to confront her about it.

At the farm, Anne answered the door with a warm greeting. He asked to see Ella and Anne invited him in. Ella joined him shortly. She was alone. As she was wiping her hands on her apron she said, "Hello, Jeremiah. What brings you out here?"

"I think it's best if I get right to the point," he told her. "I'm here on official business, Ella."

"What kind of official business?" she asked.

He pulled her letter out of his jacket and handed it to her. She took the letter and slowly moved toward a chair, silently sitting down.

Then, she said, "Where did you get this?"

"That doesn't matter," he told her. "What matters is that you wrote a letter to a confederate soldier about two bushwackers and asked him for help."

Ella calmly said, "I didn't know what else to do. Jackson had to know. He's my husband. This is not about the North and the South for us, Jeremiah."

At least now she wouldn't be wondering about Jackson. He didn't get the letter, so he wouldn't be coming home.

"What are you going to do?" she asked him.

"I arrested Sarah and the other women who were sending letters earlier today," he told her.

"This can't be happening," she thought to herself, but she refused to let him see her crumble. She wasn't sorry for what she did. She didn't believe it was wrong.

"Can I tell, Anne, that I have to go, so she and Tom won't worry?" she asked him.

"That won't be necessary," he said. "Is this the only letter that you sent?"

"Of course, it is," she told him.

"Do you promise not to send anymore letters to the confederacy?" he asked her.

"Yes," she replied.

"Then, I am placing you under house arrest, Ella, here on your farm," he told her. "You are not to have any contact with the Caldwells or any other confederate sympathizers. I will be checking on you regularly. Do you understand?"

"Yes," she told him.

"No one knows that I intercepted your letter except for you and me. I want to keep it that way. This is between the two of us. Don't go to town. Stay here and stay out of trouble. Do you understand?" he said.

Ella nodded.

Jeremiah turned for the door.

"Jeremiah," she said to him as he was leaving, "Thank you. You are a good man."

"Not really," he told her. "I'm just a man caught in the middle of my duty and my family and friends. I'm just tryin' my best to do what is right." He tipped his hat to her and left.

Ella told no one about her conversation with Jeremiah. She would do as he asked and stay at the farm. She would have to find ways to keep herself busy. She needed something to take her mind off everything that happened. She needed a distraction. The Lord provided just that. Soon after Jeremiah's visit to Ella, Tom and Anne's baby arrived. They welcomed Caroline Della Shaw into the world, named for both of her grandmothers.

"How's my wife, Doc? How's Anne?" Tom asked after he was given the good news.

"She's resting right now. This took a lot out of her," the doctor told him. "It's going to take a while for her to recover. She needs lots of rest and a lot of help until she is well again. I'll be back tomorrow and check on her."

Tom went to be with his wife and new baby. Ella went and sat by the fire. Her thoughts were of Jackson. Since he didn't get her letter, there was no hope of seeing him any time soon. She wondered where he was and what he was doing. Little did she know he was on his way home to her.

Chapter 37

Captured

It had been almost a week since the Marshall and his deputies had gone out in pursuit of James and Petey. A reward was being offered, but so far there were no leads. Most people thought they were long gone and that they would never see the Caldwell brothers again.

The posse was getting closer to the Arkansas border. This made their pursuit even more dangerous. Both the Union and Confederate armies as well as bands of bushwackers had been active in that area. The Marshall was considering turning back.

"How long are we gonna chase 'em, Marshall?' one of the deputies asked him.

"We'll go as far as the next town. If we still come up with nothin', we'll turn back," the Marshall told him.

The sky was getting dark. Storm clouds were rolling in. James and Petey, still unaware of anyone following them decided to find shelter until the storm passed.

"Keep your eyes open for a dugout or cave," said James, "We need to find a place to wait out that storm brewin' over there."

They were riding through a wooded area when the rain started to come down. The rain made the wooded terrain slippery. James' horse lost its footing, slipping down an embankment and falling into a large hole in the ground.

"Are you alright, James?" Petey called down to him.

"I think so," James told him as he tried to get his horse to stand up.

"Hold on. I'll be right there," Petey said as he descended down the embankment.

"I think he broke his leg when he fell," James told him. "He ain't gonna move."

"If we have to ride double, it's going to slow us way down," Petey told him.

They had no choice. The two men continued in the storm, riding double on Petey's horse. There was no time to waste waiting for the storm to pass with only one horse to get them where they wanted to go.

The Marshall and his deputies continued their pursuit. They came across two riders who were also wearing badges. The Marshall asked them where they were going.

"We're after some bushwackers who came through our town a few days back," the Sheriff told him.

"You wouldn't happen to be looking for the two men that Old Mr. Carter and his grandson saw while they were out hunting, are you?" the Marshall asked him.

"As a matter of fact, we are," said the Sheriff, "You're lookin' for 'em, too?"

"Yeah, we been ridin' almost a week," the Marshall told him. "I'm the Provost Marshall up north of here."

"If you could use two more men, we'd like to join you," the sheriff told him.

The Marshall accepted their offer, and the sheriff and his deputy joined their posse. They continued to ride south on James' and Petey's trail. They crossed a large clearing with woods on the other side. They were looking for tracks left behind from the storm.

"You two go that way," the Marshall pointed to his deputies. "Sheriff, you and your deputy go along that tree line and see if you see anything."

The sheriff nodded and he and his deputy rode along the tree line as instructed. At first, they didn't see anything. Then, the deputy noticed James' horse. They hurried to meet up with the Marshall to bring him to the ravine where the horse fell.

"Do you think it belongs to one of them?" the deputy asked the Marshall.

"I think it's a good possibility," the Marshall told him. "If they've only got one horse, we should be able to catch up to 'em pretty quick."

They rode a little further and finally found some tracks. The posse stayed on the trail. James and Petey were almost to the Arkansas border.

"Do you hear that, James?" asked Petey as they rode. James listened.

"It sounds like water," James told him. "We better stop and water this horse or we'll both be walkin'."

James took the horse by the reigns and led him to the stream close by. The posse was right behind them.

"We've gotta be close," the Marshall told the sheriff. "If we find them, I want to take them back alive."

The Marshall had no idea how close they really were. He heard rushing water and directed his men to water their horses, too. Petey was cooling off along the stream. James said he'd be back in a minute and disappeared behind some rocks. Suddenly, a voice behind Petey's head said, "Don't move." It was the sheriff.

"Who are you?" the sheriff asked him.

"Who wants to know?" Petey replied.

"Don't get smart. We've rode a lot of miles lookin' for you. Where's your brother?" the sheriff asked him.

"I don't know what you're talkin' about, Mister. I ain't go no brother," Petey told him.

"Then, who you travelin' with?" the sheriff continued to question him.

"Nobody. I'm by myself. I was on my way to join up." Petey told him.

"Is that so?" said the Sheriff.

"Yes, sir," said Petey.

"What if I tell you that I think you're one of the Caldwell brothers and that you're runnin' from the law?" said the sheriff.

Another voice from behind the sheriff said, "I'd say that I think you're right."

The sheriff froze.

"Now, don't you move," said James and as he moved around to face the sheriff. "Petey get the rope off the saddle."

Petey did as James asked him, too.

"Now tie him up," he told him.

Petey moved toward the sheriff to tie up his hands while James pointed his gun at him. As soon as Petey got close enough, the sheriff tried to get the jump on him. James reacted and fired his gun. The sheriff fell to the ground.

"Let's go. NOW!" said James as he mounted the horse.

Petey stood over the sheriff. "James, look what you've done," he said. "You killed a sheriff."

"Let's go," said James, hearing riders coming towards them. There was no time to waste. He turned his horse and rode away as fast as the horse could carry him, leaving Petey behind.

Petey ran after him yelling, "James. Wait, James. Please don't leave me. Come back."

It was too late. Petey was caught, abandoned by his brother.

"Put your hands up," said a man holding a gun.

Another man was shouting, "Watch him. You two come with me," as they quickly rode after James.

Petey put his hands in the air. The man handcuffed him and pushed him to the ground. Then, they waited.

Meanwhile, the Marshall and two deputies were in fast pursuit of James. James pushed and pushed and pushed until his mount would be pushed no more. The horse reared up. James held on, but the defiant horse gave his pursuers just enough time to catch him.

"Hold it right there," said the Marshall pointing his gun at James.

James didn't move. He was caught. The deputy took the horse by the reigns and told James to dismount. He did what he was told, and the deputy cuffed him. The Marshall pointed in the direction where the others were waiting and told James to start walking. The sheriff's deputy was waiting patiently with Petey. He was glad to see the rest of the posse with James in custody.

"Looks like you got your man, Marshall," said the deputy. The Marshall nodded.

The sheriff's deputy gave the sheriff's horse to the Marshall.

"I'm sorry about the sheriff," said the Marshall to the deputy.

"Thank you," said the deputy, "He was a good man."

Petey and James mounted up without a word. Petey couldn't even look at James. He was broken and betrayed. Neither spoke as they rode. Petey was sad, remorseful, full of regret. James showed no emotion, no remorse.

Petey wondered why he ever wanted to be like James or Robert. He regretted that, too. There was no turning back. He had to face the consequences. He was determined that he would face it like a man, and he would face it on his own.

When the Marshall and his posse got back to town, they caused quite a stir. Most everyone knew the Caldwell brothers, so word traveled fast that they had been caught. The Marshall was greeted at the jail by the jailer, who told him that the judge was already in town. He tied up his horse and went straight to the hotel to find him. The jailer followed the deputies and the prisoners inside.

Inside the jail, Richard was filled with despair when he saw that his sons had been caught.

"Pa!" Petey shouted.

"Quiet, no talkin'," said the jailer.

The prisoners were placed in separate cells and were not allowed to converse. They were under continuous watch while they would await their trial.

At the hotel, the Marshall stopped at the front desk and asked Mr. Randall to see the judge. He went upstairs and knocked on the judge's door. Soon, Mr. Randall reappeared with the judge behind him.

The judge extended his hand to the Marshall and said, "Congratulations, Marshall. Mr. Randall told me that you caught both bushwackers and brought them in alive."

"That's right," said the Marshall, "We got lucky. I came to ask about the trial. I think we should do it as soon as possible."

"I agree," said the judge, "Let's go over to the courthouse where we can talk in private."

The Marshall followed the judge to the courthouse. The jailer had given him all the information about all three cases. He had a sworn statement from Nathaniel Caldwell and Amos Whiteaker also as a witness. James and Pete Caldwell were being charged with bushwacking and murder. Richard Caldwell was being charged with aiding bushwackers. The judge also had a petition on behalf of Captain Jeremiah Whiteaker, regarding his posting bond on behalf of Richard Caldwell.

The Marshall didn't know about the petition. That happened while he was chasing James and Petey.

"It looks as if these cases are all related," stated the judge.

"That's correct," said the Marshall, "And, unfortunately, we will be adding one more charge against James Caldwell. He killed a sheriff while he was on the run."

The judge shook his head. "It all seems very straight forward," he said, "I think that the day after tomorrow will give me enough time to be ready. Please post a public notice outside the courthouse and the jail."

The Marshall thanked the judge, excused himself, and did as the judge asked him to.

Chapter 38

The Trial

News about the trial and those who were involved traveled around the county like wildfire. It seemed that everyone had an opinion about what they thought the outcome should be. If James and Petey were convicted, the punishment would be death by hanging. If Richard were to be convicted, he would face the same and Jeremiah would lose his farm. No matter what the verdict in each case, it would affect many people, many families, this generation to the next.

At Caldwell Plantation, Mary and Sarah were beside themselves. They feared for their brothers, and they feared for their father. Joanna showed no emotion, still closed and withdrawn. William had come back from St. Louis with an empty wagon and a heavy heart after he heard the news that James and Petey had been caught. He and Obie safely delivered the slaves to the refugee camp where Obie had a decision to make. He wouldn't leave his Mamie behind, so he came back, too. Only this time, he came back a free man.

At the Whiteaker farm, the tone was emotional. Mrs. Whiteaker was strong, but still overwhelmed with grief. Elizabeth was fearful. She was afraid for her brothers and her father. She was also afraid for her husband and his family, too. The guilt from what her father and brothers had done to the Whiteakers was weighing her down, taking a toll on her relationship with them all.

Jeremiah was doing his best not to buckle under the burden of what he had done. He was only trying to protect his wife, but it had been in vain. With the arrest of her father and brothers, her fears had now been realized. Only this time, he couldn't help her.

Amos was angry. The only thing on his mind was revenge. He wanted the Caldwell Brother's to pay for what they had done to his brother.

Lucy feared for her husband. She was afraid that Amos' anger was planting a root of bitterness deep in his heart. She prayed for God to replace it with the spirit of forgiveness instead. She didn't want the actions that took his brother's life to ruin his.

As for the other Caldwells, Jackson and Ella both longed to ease the pain of each of their friends and loved ones, but it was out of their hands. They were helpless. They knew that they had to trust the Lord and believe Him at His Word.

Then, there was Nathaniel. For the first time since his Ma and Pa died, he was able to start letting go. He had let go of his parents. He was letting go of the Caldwells, the slaves, the south, the north, and everything in between. He knew, for the first time, that he had done everything that he possibly could about all of it. It wasn't his cross to bear. He needed to give it to the One that had the power to control it.

The morning of the trial, there was standing room only at the courthouse. People were even crowded outside the front doors. Others were looking in the open windows that lined each side of the building.

Seated inside was Mary who was there against William's wishes. He stayed behind, fearful of being arrested himself. Joanna also stayed behind. Obie was there of his own free will. Elizabeth would sit beside her husband and Amos and Nathaniel would be witnesses. Tom was there to support Lucy and the rest of the Whiteakers, while Ella, still under house arrest, would stay home with Anne and the baby. Sarah, also under house arrest at Caldwell Plantation waited nervously to hear word about what would become of her brothers and her father.

The judge entered the courtroom, sat down, picked up his gavel and brought the courtroom to order. The room went completely quiet with the sound of his hammer.

"This court will now come to order," said the judge. "Bring in the accused," he instructed one of the deputies.

The prisoners had entered the building through the back door and were waiting in a small room behind the courtroom. The deputy disappeared for a moment and returned with Richard, James, and Pete Caldwell in his custody. The three men sat across from the jury, handcuffed, facing the judge. James was instructed to stand behind a small podium positioned next to a small table where the town's only lawyer was seated.

The young lawyer, Henry Culpepper, had arrived in town about six months before from Boston. He was fresh out of law school, looking to make a name for himself and eager to win a case. The lawyer on the other side was a union army colonel named Matthew Thornton. He was seasoned with a commanding presence and no tolerance for confederate sympathizers.

The judge turned to the Marshall and asked him to read the complaint against the defendants.

"Yes, Your Honor," replied the Marshall, "The United States vs. James Caldwell for bushwacking and three counts of murder. The United States vs. Pete Caldwell for bushwacking and conspiring to commit murder. The State of Missouri vs. Richard Caldwell for treason: aiding bushwackers and confederate soldiers."

"James Caldwell, how do you plead?' asked the judge.

"Not guilty," replied James.

"Pete Caldwell, how do you plead?" asked the judge.

"Not guilty," replied Petey.

"Richard Caldwell, how do you plead?" asked the judge.

"Not guilty," replied Richard.

"Colonel Thornton, your opening statement," he instructed the Colonel.

"Thank you, Your Honor," said the Colonel. "During these proceedings, we will prove that on the fourth day of this month James and Robert Caldwell, both armed, entered the Hope Creek Country Church. Pete Caldwell waited outside preparing for their getaway. James and Robert kidnapped Jeb Whiteaker and Newton Clark and fled from the church on horseback. Later, both Jeb and Newton were shot and killed by the accused. We will also prove that one, James Caldwell, shot and killed a local sheriff while to trying to make his getaway."

The Colonel sat down.

"Mr. Culpepper, your opening statement?" asked the Judge.

"Thank you, Your Honor," said Mr. Culpepper. "It is true that two men entered the Hope Creek Church on the fourth day of this month while another man waited outside. It is also true that two of the men kidnapped Jeb Whiteaker and Newton Clark and took them to a place where they both were shot and killed. However, the men that entered the church were wearing scarves and could not be identified." Mr. Culpepper paused. Then, he said, "That will be all, Your Honor."

The Colonel called his first witness. Amos Whiteaker approached the bench. He stopped in front of the Marshall who asked him to take an oath to tell the truth. He then took a seat to the left of the judge, facing the crowd, both lawyers, James, Petey, and Richard. His eyes were fixed on James and Petey, the two men that he held responsible for the murder of his brother.

"Mr. Whiteaker, on the fourth day of this month, you were at the Hope Creek Church for the morning service. Is that correct?" the Colonel asked Amos.

"Yes," replied Amos, "I was there with my wife, my brother, Jeb, and our hired man, Newt."

"Can you describe the events of that morning to the court?" he asked Amos.

"Yes," said Amos. "The service had just started when the doors flew open. Two armed men came in. One of them snatched Jeb out of the pew. Newt tried to help Jeb and the other man grabbed him, too. They told everyone not to move and kept their guns pointed at Jeb and Newt."

"Did you know the assailants?" asked the Colonel.

"No, they had scarves over their faces," replied Amos.

"What happened next?" the Colonel continued.

"They took Jeb and Newt with them, and they all rode off. Once they were gone, everyone started to scramble to their horses and wagons and such. All the guns were gone, so Nathaniel told the younger boys to go lookin' for them. They found 'em in the bushes beside the church house," Amos told him. "Then, me and Nathaniel went after them."

"Did you catch them?" asked the Colonel.

"Yes," replied Amos. "It didn't take us long."

"What did you see?" the Colonel continued his questioning.

Amos hesitated for a moment, trying to hide his emotions. Then, he said, "Newt was already on the ground. We got there just in time to see one of them shoot Jeb down. I hollered and one of the other men aimed his gun in my direction."

"Did he fire at you?" interrupted the Colonel.

"No, I got a shot off before he could," replied Amos. "I was sure that I hit him because when he rode off, he was hunched over."

"What happened next?" asked the Colonel.

"I ran to Jeb," Amos said, choking up. "He died in my arms. Then, I brought him and Newt home."

"No further questions, Your Honor," said the Colonel.

"Mr. Culpepper, do you have any questions for this witness?" asked the Judge.

"Only one," replied Mr. Culpepper as he walked toward the witness stand. "Mr. Whiteaker at any time during this terrible ordeal were you able to identify the assailants?"

"No," said Amos.

"Thank you, Your Honor. That will be all," said Mr. Culpepper.

"Mr. Whiteaker, you may step down," instructed the Judge. "Colonel Thornton, please call the next witness."

"Thank you, Your Honor," said the Colonel. "I'd like to call Nathaniel Whiteaker to the stand."

Nathaniel approached the Marshall in front of the witness stand and made his oath. He seated himself and waited. His Uncle Richard seemed surprised, wondering how Nathaniel fit into the web that he and his sons had weaved.

Nathaniel didn't look at his uncle or his cousins. He looked out in the crowd at so many familiar faces. He saw Tom and the Randalls. He saw the Whiteakers and his cousin, Mary. And he saw Obadiah standing in the back of the room. The two men locked eyes. Then, Obadiah gave Nathaniel a nod. The affirmation from his friend gave Nathaniel enough courage to do what he had to do even though it would change everything.

The Colonel approached Nathaniel and said, "Sir, could you state your name for us one more time?"

"Nathaniel Caldwell," he answered.

"You have the same last name as the accused," said the Colonel.

"Yes," said Nathaniel, "Richard Caldwell is my uncle. He raised my brother and me from the time we was kids. Petey and James are my cousins," Nathaniel said.

"So, you would say that you know these men well?" asked the Colonel.

"Yes," said Nathaniel.

"Would you tell the court where you were and what happened on the fourth day of this month?" asked the Colonel.

"I took my wife and daughter to church," he answered. "We were sitting in the service. The preaching had just started when James and Robert barged into the church and took Jeb and Newt out by gunpoint," Nathaniel said calmly.

There were gasps and buzzes of comments coming from all over in the courtroom. The Judge's gavel came down to bring order in the court, while Mr. Culpepper called out, "Objection, Your Honor."

"Order in the court," said the Judge.

"Your Honor, I object. It is clear from, Mr. Whiteaker's testimony that the men who came into the church were wearing scarves. No one, including Mr. Whiteaker, could identify them beyond a shadow of a doubt," explained Mr. Culpepper.

"Sustained," said the Judge.

The Colonel continued, "Mr. Caldwell can you tell the court what happened next?"

Nathaniel repeated Amos' account of what happened.

"What did you do after Jeb Whiteaker was shot and the assailants rode away?" asked the Colonel.

"I rode after them," said Nathaniel.

"Did they know that you were following them?" questioned the Colonel.

"No, I stayed way back. I knew where they was goin', so I wasn't worried about losin' 'em," said Nathaniel.

"How did you know, Mr. Caldwell?" the Colonel asked him.

"I recognized their voices, their horses, and I found a knife on the ground that I'd seen before.," said Nathaniel.

The Marshall held up the knife.

"Have you seen this knife before," the Colonel asked Nathaniel.

"Yes," replied Nathaniel.

"Where?" he continued his questioning.

"It's the knife that I found on the ground where Jeb and Newt were shot. It belongs to my cousin, James. James Caldwell," said Nathaniel.

More gasps and rumbling filled the room.

"Order," said the Judge.

"I recognized the horses, I recognized the voices, and I recognized the knife. That's how I knew to go to Caldwell Plantation."

"Did you actually see the accused at Caldwell Plantation?" he asked him.

"Yes, they got there right before I did. I heard Petey calling for his Pa and saw James helping Robert into the house," Nathaniel told him.

"Was Robert hurt?" he asked.

"Yes," said Nathaniel, "Amos had shot him."

"Mr. Caldwell," the Colonel addressed him, "Let's be clear. Can you identify the three men that stormed into the church house, kidnapped two men, and shot them?"

"Yes," said Nathaniel, "It was James, Robert, and Petey Caldwell."

Again, the courtroom rumbled.

"Order, order in the court," the Judge said as he pounded his gavel.

"No more questions, Your Honor," said the Colonel.

"Mr. Culpepper, do you have any questions for this witness?" asked the Judge.

"Yes, Your Honor," replied the lawyer.

"Mr. Caldwell," he asked, "you grew up and lived with the accused at Caldwell Plantation. Is that correct?"

"Yes," replied Nathaniel.

"Were you happy there?" Mr. Culpepper asked him.

"I was taken care of," said Nathaniel.

"I asked if you were happy," the lawyer kept prodding. "What was your relationship with the family like?"

"Aunt Jane was kind and caring and I was close to some of the children," Nathaniel told him.

"What about James, Robert, Petey, and your uncle?" asked the lawyer.

"Objection, Your Honor," said the Colonel.

"Overruled," said the Judge, "Answer the question, Mr. Caldwell."

"I didn't get along too well with James and Robert," he admitted.

"What about your uncle and Pete?" he asked him.

"Petey's just a kid," Nathaniel told him. "He never bothered me none."

"And, your Uncle," the lawyer insisted.

"I didn't appreciate the way he did business, making money off the hard work of people that don't have a say," Nathaniel told him.

"Caldwell Plantation is a slave plantation. Is that true?" Mr. Culpepper asked.

"Yes," he told him.

"How do you feel about slavery?" asked Mr. Culpepper.

"Objection," chimed in the Colonel.

"Overruled," said the judge.

"I don't think anybody has the right to own another human being," said Nathaniel.

"Including your uncle?" asked Mr. Culpepper.

"That's right," Nathaniel said as a matter of fact.

"Did you know that James, Robert, Richard, and Pete Caldwell were confederate sympathizers?" he asked.

"Yes," replied Nathaniel.

"But you stayed with them anyway?" he asked him.

"I only planned on staying a little while after my Aunt Jane passed. I felt like I owed it to her to help the family get back on their feet," was Nathaniel's response.

"I see," said Mr. Culpepper. "Your views about slavery must have put quite a strain on your relationship with your uncle and your cousins." He didn't wait for a reply. He started raising his voice, seemingly agitated. "Mr. Caldwell," he said, "Isn't it true that you resent your uncle and cousins so much for owning slaves and being confederate sympathizers, that you made all this up?"

"Objection, Your Honor," shouted the Colonel.

Mr. Culpepper kept talking over him and the noise from the crowd in the courtroom. "Isn't it true that you rode alone, so that you could make up this story about following James, Robert, and Pete Caldwell to their plantation home? Isn't it true that you lied about it all, so that they would be punished for their political views about slavery and the war? Mr. Caldwell, you made all of this up just to get even!"

"No," shouted Nathaniel as he came up off his chair.

"Order," called the Judge as he pounded his gavel. "Order I said."

"I followed all three of them to the plantation, and I saw them take Robert inside. I ain't lyin' about anything, but you're right. They should pay. They've been doin' wrong for a long time and gettin' away with it," Nathaniel shouted.

"That will be all Your Honor," said Mr. Culpepper.

"Mr. Caldwell," said the Judge, "you are dismissed." Then, he turned his attention to the Marshall.

"Your Honor," said the Marshall, "the court calls the defendant, James Caldwell."

After James took his oath the Colonel said, "Colonel Thornton, you may begin your questioning," directed the Judge.

"Mr. Caldwell, where were you on the 4th day of this month?" he asked.

"Me, Robert, and Pete started out that mornin' for St. Louis. Pa sent us to market on some business," he told the Colonel.

"Did anyone see you there?" asked the Colonel.

"No, we didn't make it. We got ambushed by some bushwackers and had to put up a fight. We got separated from Robert. Petey and me didn't know that he got hurt. The bushwackers were after us so we kept ridin' trying to lose them. When the Marshall and his deputies caught up to us, we thought they were the bushwackers. The next thing we knew we were being brought back here accused of murder," he explained. "We didn't kill nobody. The bushwackers attacked us. We didn't bushwack nobody."

Petey stood next to his brother with his head spinning. James was lying. He knew that James would expect him to lie, too.

"So, you deny storming into the church that morning, kidnapping Jeb Whiteaker and Newt Clark, and killing them in cold blood," said the Colonel raising his voice.

"Yes...I....do," James was adamant.

"Do you also deny killing the sheriff who was pursuing you?" asked the Colonel.

"I didn't know he was a sheriff. I thought he was one of the bushwackers that was chasin' us," James explained.

"No further questions," said the Colonel.

"Mr. Culpepper, would you like to cross examine the defendant?" said the Judge.

"No, Your Honor," said Mr. Culpepper.

The Judge turned again to the Marshall. "The court calls Pete Caldwell," he said.

Petey's heart was pounding. He felt sick to his stomach. He closed his eyes tightly, wishing that he could just disappear. The Colonel began his questioning.

"Mr. Caldwell, where were you on the 4th day of this month?" he asked.

"I was with James and Robert, just like James said," he answered.

"Where exactly was that?" the Colonel continued.

Petey, obviously nervous, repeated the account that James gave in his testimony.

"So," said the Colonel, "you also deny any involvement in the events that happened at the church house that morning?"

Petey hesitated for a moment. He looked around the room at all the people he knew that had been affected by what his brothers had done. He could feel James' cold stare.

"Answer the question, Mr. Caldwell," demanded the Judge.

"I don't know anything about it," Petey blurted out.

"Mr. Culpepper, any questions," asked the Judge.

"None Your Honor," said Mr. Culpepper.

"Then, we'll hear your closing statements," said the Judge.

The Colonel stood and faced the jury as he spoke.

"Gentlemen," he said, "these are troubling times. Men are engaging in lawlessness all over this great State and along the Kansas border. This so called bushwacking is like a disease, a disease that is ravaging our communities. It must be stopped. The only way to stop its spread is to hold those who engage in it accountable for their actions."

He pointed to Nathaniel and Amos, as he said, "You have heard the sworn testimony of these two men, men who are upstanding citizens in this community. You have heard the eyewitness account of Nathaniel Whiteaker who positively identified, James, Robert, and Pete Caldwell as the bushwackers who murdered Jeb Whiteaker and Newton Clark. Justice must be served. I implore you to grant the victims of his heinous crime the justice that they deserve." The Colonel returned to his chair.

Mr. Culpepper stood up and approached the jury.

"Gentlemen," he said, "I think that we are all in agreement that what happened at the church was a sin against God and His people. We also can agree that what happened in that meadow a few miles away was a horrific crime. Yes, justice must be served. However, convicting anyone without proof beyond a shadow of a doubt is not justice." He paused and took a deep breathe.

Then, he continued, "The men who invaded the church, and kidnapped Jeb Whiteaker and Newton Clark on that fateful day were wearing scarves. The only person who identified the assailants was Nathaniel Whiteaker. Mr. Whiteaker admitted in this court room that his relationship with his cousins was strained. I propose to you that Nathaniel Whiteaker saw an opportunity to get revenge on his cousins and made up the story about following the bushwackers to Caldwell Plantation. It was all part of a plan to pay them back for any wrong that he felt that they had done to him or the slaves on the plantation. Nathaniel Caldwell is not a credible witness. Therefore, you cannot convict these men based on his testimony."

There was a buzz in the courtroom as Mr. Culpepper returned to his seat. Then, the judge, instructed the jury.

"Gentlemen," he said, "we will resume at 1:00pm to hear your verdict. We will also hear the case against Richard Caldwell. Court adjourned."

The Judge pounded his gavel on the table and left the room. The Marshall took James, Pete, and Richard back to their cells and the crowd dispersed. The proceedings resumed promptly at 1:00pm when the jury entered, and the Marshall escorted the defendants back into the courtroom.

"Have you reached a verdict?" asked the Judge to the jury.

The jury foreman stood up and said, "Yes, Your Honor, we have. In the case of the United States vs. James Caldwell for bushwacking," said the foreman, "we find the defendant..........GUILTY!"

James showed no emotion, but the crowd roared as the Judge struck his gavel on the table.

"In the case of the United States vs. James Caldwell for murder one," continued the foreman, "we find the defendant...........GUILTY!"

More roaring, accompanied by cheers from some and sobs from others, as James stood frozen like a statue. He made eye contact with no one, staring coldly at the wall. Richard looked at the floor, unable to offer any help to his sons. Petey tried to stay composed while he awaited his own verdict. Again, the Judge struck his gavel to the table. "Order," he said, "Order in the court."

"In the case of the United States vs. James Caldwell for murder two and three," said the foreman, "we find the defendant................GUILTY!"

The crowd quieted once again as the Judge instructed the foreman to continue. Petey waited.

"In the case of the United States vs. Pete Caldwell for bushwacking," said the foreman, "we find the defendant..........GUILTY!"

The sound of that word took the breath right of him. Panic set in. He put his hand on his hip and the other on his head. He turned from one side to the other, looking into the crowd, trying to comprehend what was happening.

"In the case of the United States vs. Pete Caldwell for conspiring to commit murder," said the foreman, "we find the defendant..........GUILTY!

The reaction of the crowd for this verdict was different, at first only murmurings, then, sobs from Elizabeth and Mary crying out.

"NO! This isn't right," she said as she stood up trying to appeal to the crowd, but no one could help Petey even if they wanted to.

The Judge brought the courtroom back to order again as he prepared to pass down the sentence.

"James Caldwell," he said, "You have been found guilty of bushwacking and murder. Do you have any final words before you are sentenced?"

"No, I got nothin' to say," said James.

"Pete Caldwell," said the Judge, "You have been found guilty of buswacking and murder. Do you have any final words before you are sentenced?

"I didn't do nothin'. James tell 'em. I didn't know what you was goin' to do. James tell 'em, please. Pa, you tell 'em. I didn't know Pa. I didn't know," Petey said frantically.

"Mr. Caldwell," said the Judge, "Get a hold of yourself."

Petey put both of his hands over his face and tried pull himself together.

"James Caldwell," said the Judge, "I sentence you to death by hanging in accordance with the punishment for the crimes of bushwacking and murder. You have five days to make peace with those whom you have offended and with Almighty God."

Richard laid his head in his arms on the table. James showed no emotion. He was unwavering.

"Pete Caldwell," said the Judge, "I sentence you to death by hanging in accordance with the punishment for the crimes of bushwacking and conspiracy to commit murder. You also have five days."

Then, Richard blurted out, "No, he's just a boy. You can't do this. Take me. Please, take me instead." It was all too much.

"Mr. Caldwell," scolded the Judge, "That's enough."

Petey was sobbing uncontrollably, as were his sisters Elizabeth and Mary. The deputy removed both James and Petey from the courtroom and took them back to their cells. James and Petey's fate had been decided. It was now time for the Colonel to present his case against Richard Caldwell.

"The State of Missouri vs. Richard Caldwell," called the Marshall.

Richard was barely able to pull himself together enough to take his oath. Then, the Judge nodded to the Colonel to begin his questioning.

"Mr. Caldwell," said the Colonel holding up a piece of paper, "I have here a copy of an affidavit that you signed promising to cease and desist from any kind of rebel activity. Do you recognize this?"

Richard looked at the paper and answered, "Yes."

"Mr. Caldwell, please tell the court, what is your relationship to Robert Caldwell," instructed the Colonel.

"Robert was my son," replied Richard soberly.

"On the fourth day of this month, did you take Robert into your home and provide him with medical care?"

"Yes," replied Richard.

"Why did he need medical care?" asked the Colonel.

Richard was dazed. He couldn't concentrate.

'Mr. Caldwell, answer the question," the Judge told him.

"He had been shot," Richard said quietly.

"How?" asked the Colonel.

"I didn't ask. He needed help, so I called for the doctor and did what I could," replied Richard.

"Sir, do you realize that you are openly admitting to aiding a bushwacker?" asked the Colonel raising his voice.

"Objection, Your Honor," said Mr. Culpepper. "It is not a crime to give medical attention to someone in need, especially your own son."

"Overruled," said the Judge.

The Colonel continued, "Your Honor, I'd like to admit into evidence the sworn statement from Nathaniel Caldwell given to the Provost Marshall. I'd like to remind the court that he gave this same testimony earlier today in the cases of the United States vs. James and Pete Caldwell."

He handed the statement to the Judge and continued, "It states, 'I, Nathaniel Caldwell, swear that on this day, I witnessed James Caldwell and Richard Caldwell help Robert Caldwell into Richard Caldwell's home.'"

Richard felt like he was in a fog. The man who was always resolute, the who never showed emotion was crumbling in front of everyone who knew him.

The Colonel addressed Richard again, "Mr. Caldwell, did James and Pete Caldwell, convicted murderer and a bushwacker, bring a wounded Robert Caldwell to your home?"

"James, Petey?" he asked quietly, "No."

"Why Sir, would Nathaniel Caldwell make up a story like that?" asked the Colonel.

"I don't know," said Richard.

"If James and Pete didn't bring Robert to your home, how did he get there?" asked the Colonel.

"I don't know. I walked past the window of my study..... no.......I mean yes, my study and saw him slouched over on his horse. I ran out to help him," Richard seemingly confused answered the question.

The Colonel had no further questions and Mr. Culpepper chose not to cross examine the defendant. It was time for the closing arguments.

The Colonel approached the jury and said, "Gentlemen of the Jury, Richard Caldwell has admitted to providing medical assistance to Robert Caldwell for a gunshot wound. Previous testimony placed Robert Caldwell at the scene of the murders of James and Robert Caldwell. Amos Whiteaker testified that he shot Robert at the scene. Nathaniel Caldwell testified that he followed Robert, James, and Pete Caldwell to Caldwell plantation from the scene of the murders. It is clear. Richard Caldwell aided a murderer and bushwacker by providing him with medical assistance. He is guilty of violating his agreement with the State of Missouri." The Colonel took his seat.

Mr. Culpepper, "Your closing statement, please."

"Gentlemen of the Jury," said Mr. Culpepper, "It is true that Mr. Caldwell helped his son after he had been shot. However, according to his testimony, he had no knowledge as to how his son was injured. HIS SON, Gentlemen! Ask yourself what you would do if you found your own son wounded. Would you stop and ask about the circumstances? I THINK NOT! You, as did Richard Caldwell, would urgently tend to him to save his life. Richard Caldwell aided his SON, which is not a crime. I dare say that anyone in this room would have done the same thing. Richard Caldwell is NOT guilty."

Mr. Culpepper took his seat, while the Judge dismissed the jury to deliberate. He called for a recess and then, everybody waited.

Chapter 39

The Verdict

While they waited, some of the spectators con-
gregated, discussing the outcome of the day's
proceedings. Others, like Nathaniel, sat quietly alone.
Jeremiah sat with Elizabeth and Mary, trying to comfort
them, while Amos, Lucy, and Mrs. Whiteaker returned to
the Whiteaker farm exhausted and emotionally drained.

In less than an hour, the jury returned with their verdict.
Richard faced them to hear their decision. The foreman
stood and said, "We, the jury, find the defendant, Richard
Caldwell, "GUILTY" of aiding bushwackers and rebels."

The same buzz filled the room. A feeling of dread swept
over Jeremiah. He knew that this meant he would lose his
part of the family farm. He squeezed Elizabeth's hand.
She didn't move. She made no sound. Her father had
just been found guilty of treason. Mary sobbed. Nathaniel
showed no emotion. Neither did Richard. He looked tired
and beaten. Nothing mattered to him anymore, including
the verdict.

The Judge brought the court to order and said, "Richard
Caldwell, you have been found guilty of the charge brought
against you. The penalty for such a crime is death by
hanging. However," the Judge paused, "considering the

special circumstances of that day I do not believe that your actions were politically motivated. I believe any father would have done what you did. Therefore, I am sentencing you to one year in federal prison."

The people in the courtroom were shocked. Elizabeth and Mary were relieved. Richard and Nathaniel both still showed no emotion. Richard's life was spared, but he was a broken man. His gaze was empty, as he was escorted back to his cell.

"In the last matter of the day," said the Judge, "We have the State of Missouri vs. Jeremiah Whiteaker. Mr. Whiteaker would you please rise?" Jeremiah stood and faced the Judge. "I have a copy of the agreement that you made with the State of Missouri on behalf of Richard Caldwell. Your property was the guarantee that he would cease and desist from aiding rebels and bushwackers. Under normal circumstances, I would seize your property for the State of Missouri."

"However," he said holding a piece of paper. "I also have a petition. The good citizens of this county have vouched for you. They say that you have been a good friend and neighbor to all and that you have been loyal to the Union by conviction and with your deeds, serving as a captain in the Union Army. The petition asks that you not be punished because of your family relations."

"Because this petition was signed by just about everyone in the county," continued the Judge, "I am going to trust the good people who have vouched for your character. I am going to allow you to keep your farm and release you from any responsibility for the actions of

Richard Caldwell. "This court is adjourned," he said as he brought his gavel down for the last time.

The mix of emotions was overwhelming. Jeremiah and Elizabeth were grateful. yet grief stricken. Tom, too, was grateful that his petition would help save the Whiteaker farm, but he, too, was grieved over the verdicts. He wanted justice to be served, but he couldn't erase the history that he shared with the Caldwell family. It was a history that he would always remember fondly, despite what happened during the war.

Obadiah was also grateful. He was grateful for his freedom. He had been waiting for it his whole life. But freedom didn't change what he felt for the Caldwells. He had lived in their home and been a part of their lives since he was a child. He loved them, especially Nathaniel. He was broken over what would soon happen to James and Pete, but just as broken over what the family that he cared about had become.

The ride back to the Caldwell home was a long one for both Obie and Mary. William met them outside, anxious to hear what had happened. He was relieved about his Pa but broken up about his brothers. Joanna, sitting on the porch with one of her cats on her lap, listened silently. She didn't look up as she stroked her cat's back, but tears streamed down her face. Mary immediately went up to the plantation house to tell Sarah, who was still under house arrest. Both sisters broke down weeping in a firm embrace, trying to console one another.

At the O'Connor farm, Tom broke the news to Anne and Ella as gently as he could. They were both heartbroken over Petey. Ella knew that Jackson would try to stop this if he could, but he never got her letter. He was off fighting somewhere for a cause that he really didn't believe in out of loyalty to a family and a community that was falling apart right before her eyes.

At the Whiteaker farm, there was relief. The family had been given justice for Jeb and Newt, even though the verdict couldn't bring them back. Yet, the tone down at the house by the pond, where Jeremiah and Elizabeth lived, was different. The judge's decision to let them keep the farm was appreciated, but somehow seemed like a such a small thing compared to the other events of the day.

There would be more loss for Jeremiah and Elizabeth, especially Elizabeth. She would lose two brothers because they had committed a terrible crime against her husband's family. She was caught in the center of a tangled web.

It was a web that had affected their whole community, a tangled web of many spiders. It was spun by men who had different political beliefs who raised their families to think the same. It was spun out of a desire for wealth and prosperity even at the expense of men and women in bondage. It was spun by prejudice, by fear, and by war. It was spun from the pain of loss and rejection. It was a complicated web that had caught many people. Many feared that they would never be free of it.

Chapter 40

The Call, The Purpose, The Plan

At the jail, the prisoners were still under continuous watch. The day before the hanging, the preacher came to see them. One by one, he gave each of the men the Gospel and told them that they could be forgiven despite anything that they had done in this life. He explained that eternal life was not based on their works, but on the merit of the finished work of Jesus Christ at the Cross of Calvary. He told them that Jesus paid the penalty for the sins of all who would believe on His name. He told them that they could be washed clean and become a new creation.

James wanted no part of what the preacher told him. He was angry, bitter, and full of hate. He blamed God for everything that had happened to him and his family. He could not understand that it was because man had sinned that sickness, disease, greed, murder, corruption, war, and everything like it, had come into the world. He refused to take responsibility for his actions and accept that he must reap the consequences of his actions.

Richard, a completely broken man, could not forgive himself. He knew that what his wife had told him and what this preacher was telling him was the Truth. He saw it manifested in the life of his faithful wife and he witnessed the miracle of regeneration in Robert's heart before he died. Yet, he could not accept forgiveness for himself because he knew how undeserving he was. He could not comprehend that there was no one deserving of God's gift of eternal life. He couldn't understand that God saves even the chief, the worst, of sinners. He returned to his cell still a broken man.

Petey begged the preacher for help. He told him over and over that he didn't want to die, but the help that the preacher had to offer was not what Petey was asking for. The only help that he could offer this young man was the Truth of the Gospel. He could only point him to Calvary and show him God's offer of eternal life. The Lord opened Petey's eyes to eternity and he repented of his sins and put his faith and trust in Jesus Christ. Petey became a new man just like his brother only a few weeks before. God gave him peace. It was a peace that passed all under-standing, just like the Bible said.

Meanwhile, no one knew that Jackson was on his way home. He didn't know there had already been a trial or that the verdicts had been reached. He knew that his family and his community was in trouble and that he had to do whatever he could to help them. He rode as fast and as long, as he and his horse could, stopping to rest only when they had to.

The fateful morning was here. Ella felt helpless. She needed Jackson to be there, but her letter didn't get to him.

"His heart will be shattered when he finds out what has happened. He won't be able to live with himself because he wasn't here to try and stop it,' she thought to herself.

She couldn't just sit by while all of this was happening. She took down her shawl hanging by the door and stepped out onto the porch. Tom was already outside, hitching up the wagon to go to town. Ella climbed in.

"Do you really think that this is a good idea, Ella?" he asked her.

"No," she replied, "but, I'm goin' anyway."

Tom had no idea that she had made Jeremiah a promise to not leave the farm. She didn't want to break her promise, but she felt compelled to go. Neither Tom nor Ella spoke on their way to town.

Mrs. Randall, with a heavy heart made James and Petey their final meal. She used her finest recipe and her best ingredients. It was a small thing, but she had nothing else to offer them.

The Randalls were strong Unionists. They hated what had happened at the church house and to Jeb and Newt. However, that didn't change the fact that they had known James and Petey as children and they had compassion on them.

After the men finished their meal, the preacher said a final prayer, and the Marshall and the deputy led them to the center of town. The townsmen had worked for two days, building the platform where James and Petey would meet their fate.

Many of the townspeople had already started to gather near the temporary gallows. Jackson had ridden all night and was almost there. He intended to bypass town as it wouldn't be safe for him there, but he passed by two men who were on their way out.

"Howdy," said one of the men.

"Howdy," replied Jackson.

"If you're goin' to watch the hangin', you better hurry. They're 'bout ready to start," he told Jackson.

"Hangin'. What hangin'?" Jackson asked.

"The two men who busted in the church and killed those farmers a few weeks ago, they're hangin' 'em today," said the man.

This is what Jackson had feared. Without any thought to himself, he rode quickly into town. Ella and Tom rode in from the north, as Jackson was riding in from the south. Tom and Ella got their first. Tom helped Ella out of the wagon, and they started pushing their way through the group of people that had assembled.

James and Pete had been led to the platform. Both resisted, but to no avail. They were standing next to each other with hoods over their heads as the hangman put a noose around each of their necks. Jackson, coming in over some high ground could see Petey and James standing on the platform. He panicked when he realized that he was almost too late. Impulsively, he called out Petey's name and started to ride urgently towards the crowd. Then, he called again, "Petey," he yelled.

Petey blindfolded couldn't see who was calling him, but he recognized the voice.

"Jackson," Petey yelled back. "Jackson, is that you? Help me, Jackson, help me!"

Jackson's interruption caused confusion in the crowd. Ella also recognized Jackson's voice and tried to fight her way toward him. The Marshall, unsure of what was happening and not wanting an interruption, instructed the hangman to drop the floor. The hangman obeyed and started to cut the rope. The floor dropped before Jackson could get to the platform. He pulled his rifle from his saddle bag to shoot down the rope holding Petey. As he aimed his rifle at the hangman's rope, the Marshall pulled his pistol and aimed it at Jackson. He fired at Jackson as Jackson shot the rope. The Marshall's bullet knocked Jackson off his horse. He laid on the ground.

Ella screamed his name as she kept pushing through the crowd. When she finally got to him, she fell to the ground next to him, lifting his head, holding him in her arms. "Oh Jackson," she said. He turned his head and looked up at the platform. He was too late.

"Someone go and fetch the doctor," demanded Tom.

Jackson tried to talk.

"Shhh, be still, ya' here," Ella told him with a reassuring smile.

"I was too late. I should have been here," he said as he started to cough.

"Where's the doctor?" Ella pleaded, "Somebody, please, he needs a doctor."

"Somebody, give me a hand," Tom demanded as he lifted Jackson off the ground.

Two men from the crowd helped him carry Jackson to the doctor's office. They laid him on a table and the doctor immediately went to work to remove the bullet. Ella waited. She prayed and asked God to be merciful to them one more time.

Her Lord was always faithful, giving her the faith that she needed to get through every situation. "God has proved Himself over and over," she told herself. "He will give me strength." Then, she waited some more.

While Ella waited, the events of the past months came over her like a fog. Nothing would ever be the same in their little community again. Nathaniel had packed up his family and whatever he could put into his wagon and went North. He finally could move on. He gave his farm to Obadiah with the promise of the deed. As soon as it was legal in Missouri for a freed slave to be a landowner, Obadiah's dreams would come true.

Caldwell Plantation would only be a shell of what it was in its splendor. The Yankees would occupy it until the end of the war, when the women being held there would be set free. Richard would serve his time and go back to the log cabin a broken man. Mary, Joanna, and Sarah would care for their father the rest of his days, but he would never get over the incredible loss that he had suffered. William would stay and try to get the family back on their feet, but Sterling would never return. He would start a new life on his own far from Caldwell Plantation.

The Whiteaker's would have closure, but, without Jeb, there would always be a void in their family. Jeremiah and Elizabeth would eventually heal and move on with their lives. They would have a family and live out their days on the Whiteaker farm. The farm would stay in the family for generations.

Tom and Anne would work the O'Connor farm and prosper there with their own growing family. George would come home safely from the war and work a farm of his own.

Ella's thoughts were interrupted by the doctor, "You can see him now. It's good news. He's gonna be alright."

Ella hurried to Jackson's side and stroked his hair. He opened his eyes and saw her face.

"I was too late, El," he told her. "I tried, but I was too late."

"This wasn't your fault," Ella told him, "There was nothin' that you or anyone else could do. Bad things happened and too many folks got caught up in it that shouldn't have."

"James and Robert set out on a crooked path along time ago," Jackson told her, "but, Petey wasn't like them."

"I know," Ella told him, "Some things just don't make sense. Petey and James, folks hurtin' one another, and this awful war, none of it makes sense."

"It don't make sense to us," Jackson told her, "but God has a plan for all of it."

He continued, "One night while I was gone, I was readin' my Bible and the Lord gave me a verse, Ecclesiastes 7:13. It said, 'Consider the work of God: for who can make that straight, which he hath made crooked?' Even the crooked path, Ella, is for His purpose."

"It seems like some people are just stuck," she told him. "They won't turn to the straightway no matter how many times you warn 'em or how many times they hear the Truth."

"It's because of our hearts," Jackson explained. "When our heart changes, our path changes, too. Only the Lord can make a crooked path straight. Everyone is hopin' for this war to end. They're hopin' for peace, but the end of the war won't bring peace that lasts. The peace that lasts is only found on the straight path.

He was resolved about what he was telling her.

"I'm not going back to the war," he said. "I'm goin' home with you where we will start a family and make a life. We're gonna take the straight path together."

With tears in her eyes, she said nothing. She laid her head on her husband's chest and closed her eyes as she said a quiet prayer, "Thank you, Lord, for watching over us. Thank you that crooked paths can be made straight in You."

Lightning Source UK Ltd.
Milton Keynes UK
UKHW011821260822
407881UK00001B/134